BURIED CODE

J. P. FARRELL

Buried Code, Published May, 2020

Editorial and proofreading services: Kathleen A. Tracy, Karen Grennan
Interior layout and cover design: Howard Johnson
Photo Credits: *Dark sky above the green corn field* stock photo; istockphoto.
com; Stock photo ID:982414848

 **SDP Publishing**

Published by SDP Publishing, an imprint of SDP Publishing Solutions, LLC.

SDP Publishing
Permissions Department
PO Box 26, East Bridgewater, MA 02333
or email your request to info@SDPPublishing.com.

ISBN-13 (print): 978-1-7343317-0-7
ISBN-13 (ebook): 978-1-7343317-1-4
Library of Congress Control Number: 2020907020

PROLOGUE

The game had begun.

On a perfect summer afternoon in the small town of Green River, Indiana, a group of young boys carrying shovels tromped through the cornstalks. Pretending to be pirate hunters, they had separated into teams and were looking for buried treasure. The team with the most treasure won.

As the setting orange sun shone over the cornfield, the game was nearing its completion, and the red team led by nine-year-old Cole Adams were on their final treasure trove hunt. Their shovels dug deep into the loose soil, clearing out an area three feet wide, six feet long, and four feet deep. Cole's older brother Ted showed up with his friends in tow.

"Hey, Cole, you find your treasure?" he said sarcastically, then laughed. The other older kids joined in.

"Don't you have something better to do, Ted?"

"Yeah, we do. But Dad sent me out here to get your ass back for supper. And he's not too happy," he taunted.

"Shut up!"

Cole plowed his shovel hard into the dirt in frustration, and the shovel clanged, the sound of metal against metal.

"What the heck?" he muttered and speared the shovel in another spot. It clanged again. "There's something here."

With cries of *Treasure*! Cole and his friends started furiously digging, the older kids watching with keen interest as the boys unearthed what looked like some kind of silver object. They eagerly scraped away the dirt surrounding it, revealing a porthole-sized window. Cole dropped to his knees and cleared the remaining sediment off to get a closer look. He cupped his hands and peered into the porthole. Out of the blackness a distorted face suddenly pressed against the glass, and Cole jumped back as if on fire, his heart almost pounding through his chest.

Screaming at the younger kids to get out of the hole, Ted and his friends grabbed the panicked kids' hands to pull them up.

Cole was the last one out, and he stood on the mound of dirt and stared at the porthole, equal parts terrified and mesmerized. The face looked to be almost disintegrating, something you'd see in a zombie horror film. Ted yanked him away, and they joined the others racing back to the farmhouse.

Seven Years Later

As the sun began its descent, a dry desert wind whipped dust and sand in circular patterns in Area 51, a remote, highly-classified detachment of Edwards Air Force Base located within the Nevada Test and Training range 150 miles north of the Las Vegas Strip.

A tall, lean, bearded man in a white overcoat pressed his thumb against the biometric scanner, opening the entrance that led to a highly secure underground lab. He sat down in front of a computer and began entering a series of passwords. He hit a few more keys, and the screen filled with files. The man snapped in a flash drive, and with another keystroke hundreds of files began downloading onto it. When the download was finished, he pulled out the flash drive and dropped it into his side pocket.

He plugged in another flash drive, which uploaded a malicious software program. After the surveillance cameras and computers crashed, he removed the flash drive and slapped a puck-sized device on the side of the desk. He pushed a button and activated the device, the numbers on the counter lighting up like a Christmas tree. The man reached under the desk, pulled out a nine-millimeter handgun, then calmly stood and began firing at his colleagues who scrambled for cover. But he methodically tracked them down, killing one after another.

A loud alarm sounded, and blue lights attached to the walls flashed. Security responded and raced to the room. The man calmly reloaded the gun, pushed open the lab door, and waited in the hallway. He shot the first two guards to arrive, killing them instantly, then pivoted to his left and gunned down two more. Another pair of guards came around the corner from the right, firing their weapons. A bullet pierced the man's shoulder, causing him to stagger and fall to the floor. On his way down he was still able to shoot the two approaching security guards, who both fell.

He struggled to his feet, hid the gun in his pocket, and leaned against the wall. When the next wave of security arrived off the elevator, he played victim.

"The shooter's back there," he gasped, pointing toward the lab. "Hurry."

Holding his bleeding shoulder, the man got in the elevator and rode it to the top level, exiting into the desert air. As he headed towards a secluded area of the base, he saw security teams arrive in Jeeps and run into the facility.

The man pushed out a pre-cut opening in the chain-link fence and squeezed through. When he was fifty yards away from the base, a flash of light lit the area followed immediately by a loud explosion that rocked the ground. As sirens echoed off the surrounding mountains, a plume of smoke rose over the base.

The man walked toward the motorcycle waiting for him. Except for the hole in his shoulder, the plan had gone off perfectly.

A few weeks later on a Sunday morning in a posh San Francisco hotel, Luke Richards was enjoying a predawn breakfast with an associate. They were sipping strong black coffee when a tall, lean man with silver hair, a hardened face, and his arm in a sling, walked up to their corner table.

Luke looked up. "Are you Henry?"

"Yes. The sky is orange," he said in a monotone. "They told me you would be here."

Luke smiled. "We've been expecting you; better late than never. I'm Luke, and this is my associate, Mal. Take a seat."

Henry sat down and adjusted his sling to get comfortable. "They said you would pay me my remaining balance."

Luke leaned back. "What happened to your arm?"

"I took a bullet in the shoulder. Now, how about my money?"

Mal pulled out a thick envelope bulging with hundred-dollar bills. "I think this is what you are looking for. But first we need the flash drive."

Henry pulled the flash drive out of his pocket. "You mean this? No money, no flash drive."

"A man of principle, I like that." Luke sat forward. "What you did out there was amazing. We need to check the flash drive first. You understand."

Henry gave the flash drive to Mal, who pulled a laptop from his bag. He inserted the drive then inspected the files.

"It looks authentic, Luke."

"My money?" Henry said.

Mal handed him the envelope. Henry opened it and started to count the bills.

"It's all there," Luke said.

Henry stashed the envelope in the inside pocket of his jacket. "They said you would offer me a job."

"Do you ever smile?" Luke asked. Henry just stared at him. "Okay, then. You have a great reputation of getting things done no matter what the odds are. To tell you the truth, I didn't think you could pull this off."

Henry sat stone-faced.

"Anyway, we would like to have you come aboard as our security blanket, which means safeguarding the merchandise and working outside the box, if you know what I mean."

"I do, sir."

"This is a very long-term assignment. The rewards will be great if it all works out at the end. This is the first step of a very long process."

"That's fine with me."

"Good. You don't mind moving to Indiana, do you?"

"It doesn't matter where I live."

"Do you have any family?"

"No, sir."

"Why am I not surprised?" Luke muttered then asked. "You hungry?"

"I'm all set, sir. I'll be leaving unless you have anything further you want to say."

"Just welcome to Round Robotics. We can reach you at the same number?"

"Yes."

Mal leaned in and gave him a business card. "We'll be in touch in the next few weeks."

The man nodded, got up, and left.

They watched him walk away. "What do you think of that guy, Luke?"

"Crazy eyes, with no personality or soul. He's a psychopath."

"Can we trust him?"

Luke shrugged. "Trust. That's a funny word. People you think are loyal sometimes aren't. Then guys like him, you just give them a sense of purpose, and they become loyal as a dog. We don't have to worry about him. And we might need someone like him down the road to do some uncomfortable things."

Chapter 2

The George York Steakhouse, a popular eatery in midtown Manhattan, catered to the power brokers of the world. It was a place where big deals were made. Tonight, the restaurant was full of patrons enjoying fine dining after a long week.

Forbes Shannon's white hair and hard wrinkles reflected three failed marriages and business battle scars that had taken their toll. He was a well-respected, world-renowned hedge fund tycoon and philanthropist, whose circle of friends included many of the world's rich and powerful globalists. He sat in a booth, sipping a glass of Chateau Laffite Rothschild. The lighting was dim, and conversations echoed off the high ceilings.

The maître d' led Senator Joe Brock to Forbes's table.

"Ah, Senator, you're running late."

"I'm sorry; I should have called."

"No problem. I've been enjoying this fine glass of wine. It's good to see you. It's been a while. Let's get you a drink."

After the Senator ordered a dark beer, Forbes leaned in. "You're looking trim, Senator, but those good looks are showing some wear."

"Stress will do that to you."

"Yes, stress. Well, you won't have to worry about those college bills someday, now will you?"

"What's your point?"

"You know my point, Joe." Forbes flashed a broken grin.

"We've taken good care of you, all those business trips with beautiful women. You don't think it was just your good looks. Oh, maybe you do."

The politician gave Forbes a cool glare. "Do you think you own me?"

"We do, Senator. Once you accepted the money, the women, you became part of the team. You had your dessert before your vegetables. You knew what you were getting into."

Brock leaned in and said in a low voice, "The deal was I give you everything I know about Senator Ben Johnson, and that's it."

"That's true. But we aren't asking too much more of you."

"I don't like the sound of that," he said, annoyed. "What do you mean?"

"Look, we've paid you well, and we are going to continue to pay you."

"I don't want your money. I'm done."

"Unfortunately Senator, it doesn't work that way. I shouldn't have to spell it out. You're a smart politician. Just consider us business partners."

"That's not the deal we made, Forbes."

A waitress arrived with the beer. "You ready to order?"

"If you could come back in a few minutes," Forbes said.

When the waitress walked away, Brock said, "I have the information about Johnson on a flash drive with me."

"Perfect. Just hold on to it for the moment. I'll have someone pick it up. You understand what we requested?"

"Yeah, I do."

"Nothing can be left out. I mean nothing. What you might think is irrelevant could be very relevant."

"I know things about him that nobody else would."

Forbes smirked. "That's why we're paying you. If he liked a girl in first grade, we need that information. If he chipped his tooth sledding when he was a kid, we need to know."

"I get it. I did the best I could from what I remember."

"Let me ask you something. What makes someone like you turn on their best friend since childhood?"

Brock took a long drink of beer then sat back. "You tell me."

Forbes smiled. "A typical politician's answer. Alright. You're both highly competitive. You grew up playing sports together as kids. You went to the same schools. In high school you were both named to the all-state lacrosse team. You both got lacrosse scholarships to Rigley University. You've competed against each other your whole lives. How am I doing?"

"You're just reading from the dossier you put together on me."

Forbes frowned. "We all have dossiers on us, Senator Brock. Let me cut to the chase. You love his wife. She spurned you back in college, she went out with Senator Johnson, and the rest is history. Women do that to men. She was the one thing you couldn't beat him at, even though you were the better-looking guy with all the charm, the one all the girls fell for—except the one girl you wanted. You even married her best friend, thinking someday you would somehow end up with her. Now we come along, and you're more than willing to give us everything you know about Senator Johnson. You didn't ask many questions; you just figured we wanted to destroy him with some smear campaign, then someday you would be her comforting shoulder."

"Bravo," Brock clapped softly, sarcastically.

"Good looks and a charming personality only get you so far, Senator."

"You think you know me so well."

"We do. Your vices are women, booze, money, and making sure people think you're a great family man. Perception is a big part of your life. You go to church every Sunday. You make people feel important, but you don't give a shit. It's our job to know everything, Senator."

"And what's so great about Senator Johnson?"

"He's the opposite of you; that's why the woman he married spurned you. But he's the one with presidential charisma."

"Is that why you're interested in Senator Johnson's history?"

"Partially."

Senator Brock shook his head. "How do you know he'll run? He's never mentioned an interest in doing that."

"Maybe you'll be his vice president. Two life-long friends running together. Maybe I'm getting a little ahead of myself."

"You know, Forbes, there's something you're not telling me."

"You're right. In due time, though, you'll know the whole story. In fact, I'm going to give you a special screening when the time is right. We're talking three to five years."

"That's a long time in politics, Forbes. You know that."

"Regardless, I'm going to make you very wealthy, Senator. In a way, you're a lucky man."

He rolled his eyes. "Really?"

"As you know I'm a shrewd investor, but I like to get in early on the next great thing. The world is about to change. We are about to enter a new era where we have to think about colonizing the universe. It'll create the same fear that Christopher Columbus probably faced when he sailed off looking for a new world, especially when people thought the world was flat. This world isn't going to last forever. The old ways won't work if we are going to move forward as a civilization. We've had a big breakthrough in a technology that is going to revolutionize the world if used strategically."

"Why don't I feel good about all this?"

Forbes grinned. "You will over time. What other choice do you have?"

The waitress came by. "Are you ready to order?"

"I think so," Forbes said.

"I've lost my appetite," Brock replied, getting up from the table and placing the flash drive on the table. "I need to be going."

"You are going to miss a fine meal, Senator. This is the last time we'll talk for a long time, but we'll contact you when the time is right. And just remember; going forward don't get sloppy and keep the booze under control."

Brock smirked. "Don't worry about me, Mr. Forbes," he said and walked away.

Chapter 3

On a 1500-acre farm in Green River, Indiana, a miniature drone the size of a dragonfly floated through the morning air, taking images of the surrounding cornfield. Seventeen-year-old Cole Adams mapped out the field circumference and downloaded the data onto a laptop, muttering, "Perfect."

He played with the corn harvester's electronics and made some adjustments. He uploaded the cornfield dimensions into the harvester's computer and smiled at his accomplishment. He couldn't tell his father until he ran some more tests. Changing the onboard harvester computer was a crazy idea, but he had a knack for these things. The hard part was usually convincing his father, who was so old school.

Leaving the barn, Cole's eleven-year-old brother Scott ran up to him. Cole let him control the drone, watching its video images on the laptop as it soared in the air. Their father, Mike, walked up, wearing overalls and a straw hat.

"The fun and games are over, boys," he said sternly. "It's time to do some real work around here."

Scott pleaded for a little more free time, but his father didn't want to hear it.

"When I was your age—"

"Yeah, we get it, Dad," Cole said. "What do you want me to do?"

"Start harvesting the field, okay? Take your little brother

with you too so he can learn something. I'll be out there shortly to check on you guys. And no horsing around."

"Got it."

Cole and Scott went into the barn and hopped into the harvester. Cole started it up and maneuvered the machine out to the cornfield. He braked once he was out of his father's sight.

"What're you doing?" Scott asked.

"You'll see."

They climbed off the machine and stood on a worn dirt path in between the cornstalks. Cole opened the laptop. "Watch this."

Scott stared in amazement as the harvester began moving on its own along the cornfield perimeter, chewing up the corn and feeding it into the bucket.

"This is so cool!" Scott said. "Does Dad know about this?"

"This will be our little secret, Scotty." They fist bumped.

A half-hour passed. They sat on the side of the dirt road as the harvester mowed down the cornstalks. The dragonfly drone hovered above the harvester so Cole could watch on the laptop. It was unbelievable. This was the future—driverless machines. His experiment had worked.

"This is so cool," Scott repeated. "But if Dad finds out, I think he might be a little mad."

As he finished his thought, Mike's pickup truck drove up, the tires spewing dirt. He braked hard when he noticed his two sons on the road and the harvester moving in the distance.

He jumped out of the truck. "What the hell is going on?" he asked angrily.

Scotty looked at Cole.

"Who the hell is driving the harvester?"

"Nobody," Cole said meekly. "I'm controlling it from the laptop."

Mike's face flushed. "Shut it down—now!"

Cole pressed a few computer keys, and the harvester slowed to a stop.

"Don't you ever do something like that without checking with me," Mike said, standing over Cole. "You think you are so smart, but you don't know what could be out there—a sinkhole, a person, God knows what. I don't want to lose my farm, okay? You know how much one of those machines cost. I'm the one who'd have to pay for it; you'll just go on with your life. You finish the field the old-fashioned way; you got that? And don't you ever do anything to my farm without checking with me first, you understand?"

"Yes, sir."

"Scotty, get in the truck. Cole, you and I will continue this conversation after dinner."

Cole's family gathered for dinner at exactly six in the evening. Ted was away at college, leaving Cole to look after his three younger siblings: Scott and their two sisters: fourteen-year-old Mary, and Maureen, the eight-year-old baby of the family, who was the most like Cole.

For as long as Cole could remember, they'd all had assigned seating, with his father of course at the head of the table. Even the two dogs knew their place. There was no deviation under Mike's rules. He believed in routines, promptness, discipline, treating people with respect, and hard work—traits he had hammered into his children. Whether it would be on the farm or in the city, they were going to live productive lives.

Cole's mom, who sat at the other end of the table, was basically the good cop, the voice of reason, especially when her husband lost his cool. His paternal grandfather also lived with them. He would watch the family dynamics, smile at the conflicts that developed from time to time, making a few sarcastic jokes at his son's expense. The Adamses were a close-knit family, but not without their moments.

Cole ate in silence, listening to the dinner conversation, glancing over at his father from time to time. Mike acted like nothing had happened today, but Cole knew his father hadn't forgotten. Cole got up from the table, washed off his plate, put it in the dishwasher, then went out to the porch. The sun was setting, its orange hue lighting the horizon.

Cole sat in a chair, looking up at the sky. It wasn't long before his father stepped out and settled into a chair opposite Cole.

"You did a good job today out the field," he said.

"Thanks."

"I know you meant well today."

Cole just nodded.

"You know, since your brother went off to college, I've probably been harder on you without realizing it. Teddy just did what he was told. He didn't shake the apple tree like you do. I want you to be creative and think outside the box, but as long as you're on my farm, I want you to check with me when you decide to defy the laws of physics, okay?"

Cole was surprised at the light-handed treatment, which made him feel a little guilty about not telling his father first. "I get it, Dad."

"You know, I'm harder on you than everybody else because you have a lot of potential. But don't let that get to your head. Potential only means you haven't done anything yet. The teachers tell me they wish they had twenty-five of you. Hell, I don't know too many people whose kid has a chance to get into Stanford. You're smart and hard-working, Cole, but being smart is not all what it's cracked up to be if you don't understand the consequences of your actions. There's a lot of smart people out there who don't think things through, and it causes irreparable damage. It's like doctors; they always focus on the cancer, but they don't look at the quality of life down the road. They treat everybody the same. Maybe someone doesn't need the chemo. You know what I'm saying?"

"Dad, I know what you're getting at. Just being smart doesn't make you smart. You need some common sense."

"That's exactly what I'm getting at. Think it through."

"I'm sorry about today. I should have told you, but I thought you would have said no."

"I probably would have at first, but we could have worked it out where I felt comfortable. Just think it through next time." He got up and patted him on the shoulder, smiling gently. "Remember, in life it's all about learning from your mistakes."

"Thanks, Dad."

A young girl walked up to the porch. "Hello, Mr. Adams," she said, her sweet voice echoing off the porch.

"Hello, Paige. You getting ready for your senior year?"

"I'm ready. I can't wait."

"Hey, Dad; can I take the new truck?"

"I guess so. Paige, keep an eye on him."

"I sure will, Mr. Adams."

Cole felt as big as life driving his father's new Ford F150 around town with Paige Turner. She was the ultimate tomboy of the group with blue eyes, black hair, and cute freckles on her nose, along with a sassy attitude. She was the girl who wore a baseball cap with her ponytail sticking out through the back of the cap. Cole had hung out with her as long as he could remember. She was just one of the guys. And when it came to sports, she was a star in field hockey and softball.

Cole's head swiveled as he drove through the center of town, waving at people he knew. It was one of those typical small-town Main Streets, lined with red brick buildings, including a barbershop, diner, drug store, local bank, ice cream parlor, and hardware store. Cole rolled the pickup to a stop in front of the local burger joint and went inside with Paige.

Their partners in crime were waiting for them in a booth. Josh Finnigan was the wise guy of the bunch, the talkative, funny young man with the red hair and freckled face who made everyone laugh. Sitting next to Josh was Rick Long, a quiet, down-to-earth country boy with dark hair, broad shoulders, and a penchant for wearing cowboy boots. They had all been childhood friends since kindergarten.

"What a surprise, finding you guys here, feeding your faces—like always," Cole said as he and Paige slid into the booth.

"Got to eat," Rick said.

Josh tossed a French fry at Paige, grinning.

"What do you want to do tonight?" Cole asked. "I got my father's new F150 pickup."

"We could cruise around, get some beers and go down to the lake," Josh suggested.

"I was thinking a movie or something," Paige said. "I have field hockey practice in the morning."

"Maybe we should do that," Rick agreed.

"Of course. Whatever Paige says, we always end up doing it," Josh said through a mouth full of food.

Cole grinned. "She's a woman. What's that old saying? Happy wife, happy life."

Paige looked at Cole with a gentle smile.

"Cole, we aren't married," Josh said. "I'm never getting married. I'm going to date as many hot ladies as I can. And don't forget the pact we made years ago that we'd all go to Pale State."

"I'll be there my field hockey scholarship," Paige said.

"And where else would I go?" Rick asked.

"You're going there too, right?" Josh said to Cole.

Cole hesitated. "I don't know. My father is hoping I get into Stanford with a full ride."

"Oh, right. You're too smart for Pale State," Josh said.

"It's a great school," Cole said. "It's got a good science program—"

"You don't have to make an excuse. There's no comparison between Stanford and Pale. But California? You'd be miserable. You'd miss all these cornfields anyway."

"You're right, Josh," Cole agreed.

"Remember when we were kids, and we were digging for the buried treasure?" Rick asked. "That strange face."

"That's something you never forget," Paige said. "And remember how we all had to be tested for radiation? The whole thing still gives me shivers thinking about it."

Josh made scary ghost sounds.

"It definitely wasn't something from this world, no matter what hogwash story the government claimed," Cole said.

"Like it was really some military plane that crashed." Rick rolled his eyes. "Yeah, right."

Josh pushed his empty plate away. "Remember how they closed off Cole's dad's farm so nobody could get close to see. I bet they took that ship to Area 51."

"And where the hell is Area 51?" Rick asked.

"It's in Nevada. Cole isn't the only one who's into science," Josh said, defensive seeing Paige and Rick's surprised expressions. "I would love to get a tour of that place. I'll bet that's where they take all the UFOs."

Chapter
4

As the first light of dawn crept through the trees, the rooster sounded off on schedule. Cole got up, went into the bathroom, and splashed water on his face. He looked in the mirror, swiveling his head and grinning at his perceived good looks.

He dressed in jeans, flannel shirt, and pulled on a sweatshirt for good measure. He went to the kitchen where his grandfather sat at the table in the shadows, quietly sipping coffee.

"What are you doing up this early, Grandpa?" Cole asked, making himself a bowl of cereal.

"Old habits are hard to die. I like the quietness of the early morning. A man can play with his thoughts without interruption. A better question is, where are you going?"

Cole sat down across from him. "Fishing. You taught me the tricks of the trade."

"Yes, I did," he said with a smile. "It was fun taking you out when you were a little kid. You've grown up so fast. I can remember the first fish you caught; you were so excited. Your father wanted to grill it, but you let it go. Not surprising since you usually took the opposite view of your father on everything."

"Dad's pretty smart."

"Yeah. I was probably too tough on him as a kid. His brothers went to the city; he took the farm. Now he's tough on you, but he knows you have a real future in the world. Your father did too, but he decided to stay and help me out."

"I don't think he has any regrets, Grandpa."

He nodded. "He married a good woman. He has great kids, and he sure found a way to make the farm very profitable, something I had trouble doing. Then again the last I checked, the Earth wasn't making any more land. Well, anyway, good luck fishing."

Cole attached the trailer holding the motorboat to a small tractor and drove a mile to the lake. He backed up the tractor to the water's edge then got out and slid the boat into the lake. Cole grabbed his fishing rod and jumped in. He found a good spot about twenty yards from shore and dropped anchor as the early morning sun was slowly burning off the surface mist.

Over the next hour he caught a couple of good-sized bass but threw them back in. He liked the thrill of catching fish, but it was never about eating them. There was something about being out on the lake, the connection with nature, the eagles soaring above, the mist that would hover above the lake, watching fish jump out of the water to catch bugs, and seeing a family of deer grazing along the shore.

He started raising the anchor, which was oddly heavy. Using all his strength, he kept pulling. As the anchor broke the surface, so did the body entangled in it. Cole jumped back, his heart pounding. Taking deep breaths, he calmed himself until shock and fear turned to curiosity. He leaned forward to get a better look at the corpse, which looked fresh without any noticeable decomposition. It was a man between twenty-five and thirty. Cole wondered how long the body had been there and if anybody was looking for him. He looked around; the lake was deserted and quiet. He started the outboard motor and slowly returned to shore.

Cole hopped out of the boat and grabbed the body's arm to pull it out of the water. He stopped when he noticed there was a strange hole in the man's wrist. He looked more closely then stared in disbelief. The hole exposed electrical circuitry. Cole was jolted by the realization it wasn't a human body; it was something out of a science fiction movie—or from another world. The memories of that summer day when he was nine roared in his head.

He rolled the body into the boat, got the boat onto the trailer, then jumped in the truck and sped home. He drove to an old shed that his father never used and dumped the body inside. This time he was going to do his own detective work to find out what he'd found. He half wondered if he could figure out how to restart it.

When Cole parked in front of his house, their two-year-old German Shepard, Buddy, was on the front porch and greeted him with a friendly bark. Cole patted the dog's head then went inside.

"How was the fishing?" his grandfather asked.

"It was great, caught a few bass."

The old man angled his head. "You okay? You look a little pale."

"Everything's fine," he said, knowing it was anything but.

Chapter 5

The bell rang at three o'clock sharp in Green River High School, and students rushed outside into the brisk, early spring air. Cole got in his father's F150 and drove slowly through the school parking lot. He noticed Paige talking to Zach Edwards, the star quarterback—the guy the girls couldn't take their eyes off of.

Cole felt an unusual pang. He stopped the truck and watched Paige from afar. Every time she smiled or laughed, he felt betrayal. Those smiles and laughs had always been for him. Even though they'd been friends since they were little kids, he suddenly felt a rush of emotions, including jealousy, and realized he had romantic feelings for Paige. Watching the good-looking quarterback charming her was killing him.

He put the truck in drive and pulled up next to Paige and Zach. Cole rolled down the window.

"Hey, Paige; you need a ride home?"

Paige hesitated.

"I got to go," Zach said. "I'll see you tomorrow."

She jogged over to the truck with a bounce in her step and a wide smile. On the way home, Cole could tell Paige was thinking about Zach, causing him to brood. Paige noticed.

"It's not like you to be this quiet," she said.

"I'm tired," he lied. "I didn't get much sleep last night worrying about what college I'm going to get into. My father is really counting on me getting into Stanford, but sometimes I just want to go to Pale with you guys. I would only be two hours from home."

"Zach Edwards got a full boot to Pale for football."

"Great," he muttered sarcastically.

"What?"

"I said good for him," he lied again. "Hey, I want to show you something back at my house."

She smiled. "I like surprises."

He parked in front of the farmhouse, and his mom stepped onto the porch with a wide smile.

"Hello, Mrs. Adams," Paige said.

"Hi, Paige. Hey, Cole, you got something in the mail today." She walked down the porch stairs to hand him a letter. "It's from Stanford."

"Oh boy." He stood staring at the letter. "I guess I should open it."

"I'll leave you to it; let me know how it goes," his mom said, heading back into the house. She paused at the door. "Don't worry about your father. I know he's counting on you getting into Stanford, but he'll be fine if you don't."

Cole held out the letter to Paige. "I want you to open it."

"Me?"

"Yeah. Let's do it on the porch."

They sat down opposite each other, and Paige slowly opened the envelope. She took out the letter and read it, her face unreadable. Then she gave a whoop.

"You're in!" she shouted. She came over and hugged him. "Congratulations, Cole."

He should have been ecstatic, but he wasn't and had to fake his emotions. "Let me see the letter." He read it smiling but inside felt miserable.

"You're going to Stanford—and with a full scholarship," Paige said with pride. "That is like the hardest school to get in. Your father's going to be really proud."

"Yeah. It's awesome."

She looked at him with beautiful blue eyes, and all he wanted to do was kiss her.

"So what did you want to show me?"

He put the letter back in the envelope, folded it, and stuck it in his back pocket. "Yeah, follow me." As they walked, Cole told her, "I cleaned up the shed and made it into a lab. I even hooked up lights to a battery, so I can work in there at night."

"Because that's what smart Stanford guys can do."

He smiled. "Anyway, I thought I should show my lab partner my creation."

She smiled back at him. "As long as I don't have to do any lab experiments."

When they reached the shed, Cole took off the padlock he had installed and pushed open the door, letting Paige go in first. She looked around, impressed. Cole booted up his laptop then started typing. In the corner the "drowned man" he had pulled from the lake lit up.

Startled, Paige jumped back and pressed her hand against her chest. "You almost scared me to death."

"It's harmless."

"What the heck is that?"

"I pulled it from the lake a few months ago. At first I thought it was a dead body. But after a while I realized it was something from our past—what we discovered as kids."

"What do you mean?"

"It's got to be the same kind of thing we saw that day. Some kind of artificial intelligence automaton that some-how ended up in the lake. I spent weeks drying it out then used one of those heart defibrillators to jumpstart its sys-tem. There's a control unit in its head, but I don't under-stand it. Yet."

"This is unbelievable."

"Just wait. I was able to download memory files that weren't corroded onto my laptop. Look."

On the computer screen was a video of four of the robotic AIs walking in a field.

"They look so human," Paige said, awestruck. "How long ago were they here?"

"I don't know, but look in the background."

Clearly visible was a large, black funnel cloud that turned into a roiling tornado, which made a direct hit on where the AI men were, flinging their spaceship around like a toy plane. The screen went dark.

"They never knew what hit them," Cole said. My guess is, this is one of the AIs that was out in the field, and it got flung into the lake. The spaceship ended up buried in our field with another AI man inside. Who knows what happened to the others? Now watch this."

He typed in another command, and the six-foot android came to life. "Hello, Cole. Who do you have here?"

"Robby, this is Paige."

"Hello, Paige."

"Paige, this is Robby."

Her jaw dropped. "It's alive?"

Cole shrugged. "It can reason. It might be smarter than us. You can ask it questions, and it will try to answer, but some of its files are damaged. Watch. Robby, where are you from?"

"We are from the Triad solar system, 440 light-years away. Our job is to explore the universe, collect samples, and do scientific studies for human ecosystems."

"Who created you?" Cole asked.

"I don't know; I can't recover those files."

"I'm convinced they were created in the likeness of their creators," Cole told Paige.

"Meaning, there are other humans in the universe like us?"

"Kind of like us but a lot more advanced because this technology is light years ahead of anything on this planet. But from what we dug up in that cornfield, our government now has this technology—if I could crack the code, obviously they could too. I can only imagine what the government is doing with this technology."

"That's a scary thought," Paige said. "I can't believe you figured all this out. You really are a savant."

"Well, especially compared to Zach," Cole blurted.

Paige frowned. "He plays football, so he's just a dumb jock?"

"I was just kidding. Sorry if I hit a nerve," Cole said, aware that it was his third lie of the day.

Paige knew that Cole didn't just say things, but she didn't push it. "Apology accepted. So does your dad know about this?"

"Are you crazy? I can't tell him. You're the first one I've told; you've always been my partner in crime. Remember when we put a bunch of frogs in Josh's room as kids, and he found one in his sock when he was putting it on?"

"That was your idea."

"It most certainly was not."

"Oh, yeah, that was my idea," she said, and they both laughed.

"But seriously, you can't tell anyone about this. Not even Rick and Josh. I'll tell them at some point."

"Can I ask Robby a question?"

"Sure."

Paige thought a moment. "Robby, how many languages can you speak?"

"Infinite."

"Do you know how long you've been here?"

"You mean sleep state?"

"I guess."

"Time has no meaning to me. But this planet's day is based on twenty-four hours."

"How many planets have been found that can support human life?"

"My files are damaged. I can't extract that information."

"That's too bad," Paige sighed. "How about this? Are you able to connect to others like you, like an alien internet?"

"Yes."

Cole did a double-take. "Paige, I think you're the genius. Robby, do you know if any are operational here on Earth?"

"There are three."

Paige and Cole looked at each other.

"Can you contact them?" Cole asked.

"Do you want me to?"

"No, don't," Cole ordered then quickly shut down the AI.

Paige saw the concern on his face. "What's wrong?"

"If Robby connected to any of the others, the government would be knocking down our door in no time. Remember what they did last time when we didn't know what was going on. Now, who knows what they'd do."

"I see your point," Paige said.

Cole turned off his laptop and walked to the door. "That's enough fun for today. Let me get you home."

He locked the shed door behind them, aware he had created his own Frankenstein. He should have been focused on what he was going to do with Robby, but he had a more pressing matter on his mind.

"Hey, Paige, um …"

"What?"

He took a deep breath. "Would you go to the prom with me?"

She froze, looking both shocked and pained. "Zach already asked me, and I said yes. I'm so sorry."

"Don't be sorry. No big deal," he said, the disappointment etched in his face. "We're just friends, right?"

"Hey, you know who likes you? Brit Robinson. She's a cheerleader, really cute and super nice."

"That's good to know." He forced a pained smile.

"Oh, Cole. It's just a dance."

"Sure."

The drive to Paige's house was silent—Cole focusing on the road ahead, Paige staring out the side window. He dropped her off, and as he drove away tears rolled down his cheeks.

Cole parked the pickup and walked slowly onto the porch and dropped into a chair, watching the setting sun, beating himself up for not asking her sooner. He'd assumed she'd always be there. It never occurred to him she'd consider going to the prom with someone else—especially Zach Edwards of all people. He made a face, and swiveled his head, and ranted out loud "Zach Edwards!"

"Just because he plays football?"

His mom came to the door. "It's time for supper."

He turned away, not wanting her to see his teary eyes. "I'll be right there."

She opened the porch screen and sat down next to him. "What's wrong? I can tell when something is bothering you."

"I'm fine."

"It's okay if you didn't get into Stanford."

He almost laughed. "I got in, Mom."

Her face brightened and she hugged him. "That's great news; you should be so proud of yourself."

"I am. It's great."

"It doesn't sound like it. Why are you so glum? What's going on?"

"It's nothing, Mom."

She just stared at him, waiting. Cole knew she wasn't going to leave until he talked to her.

"It's Paige. I wanted to take her to the prom, but somebody else asked her already, and she said yes."

The hurt in his eyes broke her heart. "Knowing Paige, she probably didn't want to hurt the boy's feelings."

"This isn't just any boy, Mom. This is Zach Edwards, Mr. All Everything at school. The big star quarterback with movie star looks."

"Cole, you and Paige have been kindred spirits for as long as you've known each other, which is pretty much your whole lives. But with love, sometimes it's good to hang out with others to know for sure what you are feeling is true."

"Mom, I know what I'm feeling. I know she's the one. I've always known that. When I saw her talking to Zach Edwards today, laughing and smiling, my heart sank."

"Life doesn't always go the way you want it to, Cole, but the charming guys over time lose their charm. It's the guys with the good hearts that turn out to be the real charmers. Maybe it wouldn't hurt to ask someone else to the prom."

"Paige told me about a girl who likes me. So thoughtful."

"I think you should ask someone. You'll have fun."

"How did you know Dad was the right guy?"

"We were friends since middle school. But when we were in high school, we hung around with different groups. I was in the honor classes. Your father wasn't."

"So I got my brains from you."

She laughed. "I would say so. Your father's a jock; I was in the math and science club. I had a 4.0 in school. I could have gone to a good college. But your father asked me to prom, and the rest is history. I guess you could say we've been high school sweethearts for life."

"See, that could happen to Paige."

"Well, like you and Paige, your father and I were friends first, so the relationship came easy. We laughed, we talked, we just got along. We were also both homebodies. On the important stuff, we wanted the same things."

"That's nice, Mom."

"You really don't want to go to Stanford, do you?"

He shrugged. "To be honest I like it here. The cornfields, the people."

"So you'd rather go to Pale State?"

"I don't know. I don't want to disappoint Dad; I know he's counting on me going to Stanford."

"He just wants the best for you. I think wherever you decide to go, it will be a success." She stood up. "Come on; let's go in for supper. It will all work out, Cole."

"I hope you're right."

Cole peered into the bathroom mirror. He adjusted his bow tie and straightened his black tux. He stepped out to the kitchen where Brit Robinson was waiting, wearing a beautiful, but conservative, dress and a wide smile. She had blond hair, blue eyes, and a slim figure. Most of the guys in their class would have killed to be taking Brit to prom, yet Cole couldn't erase Paige from his mind. But he put on a happy smile and posed with Brit for the photos her family were taking.

After they walked into the Green River Gardens, Brit headed to the lady's room, and Cole watched the couples file in. He spotted his buddies Josh and Rick on the patio and walked over to greet them.

"Hey, guys. Where are your dates?"

"They went to the lady's room," Rick said.

"Have you seen Paige yet?" Josh asked with a grin.

"No."

Josh and Rick look at each other and chuckled.

"What's wrong with you guys?"

"Let's just say Edwards knew what he was doing."

"What do you mean?"

Josh smirked. "You'll see."

Cole spotted Brit looking for him. "I'll see you guys inside," he said, suddenly eager to get away from his friends.

He tried to make it a fun night. Brit was cute and funny, but she wasn't who he wanted. When he saw Paige from a distance, he understood what Josh and Rick had been snickering about. In her striking red minidress and matching heels, she was definitely no tomboy tonight. Seeing her was painful, so he decided it was better to stay away. But from time to time he'd glance over at her table to see if she was having a good time, hoping she would find Zach a boring jock. What he saw said the opposite.

"Anything wrong, Cole?" Brit asked softly

"Not at all. Hey, you want to dance?"

"Sure."

They stepped on the dance floor to a full-throttle song. Cole showed off his dance moves, swiveling his hips with a gusto that made Brit laugh. He was relieved she seemed to be having fun. He snuck a peek in Paige's direction. As he twisted his hips back and forth, he would casually look over at Paige's table, hoping she would notice him, but nothing.

The music turned romantic, and they slow danced. As he maneuvered Brit around the dance floor, his eyes strayed over to Paige's table again, wishing he was the target of her affection.

When the song ended, Cole and Brit returned to their table. Cole excused himself and headed to the lobby bathroom. He bumped into his science teacher standing at the door.

"Hello, Mr. Foles."

"Hey, Cole. Having a good time?"

"Sort of."

"You took your partner in crime, right?"

"Who, Paige?"

"Yeah."

"Zach Edwards beat me to it."

"Oh. The star quarterback . . . that's a tough one."

"You can say that again."

"Have you accepted Stanford's offer yet?"

He shook his head. "Not yet."

"Well, that's the golden ticket."

"Thank you again for the recommendation letter."

"Happy to do it. You were a great student, Cole—just don't let that go to your head," he said with a smile.

"Don't worry, Mr. Foles; I'll keep that in the vault."

When Cole came out of the men's room, Paige was just about to go into the ladies' side.

"Cole, hi."

"Hi. You look really beautiful tonight."

He couldn't remember ever seeing her in a dress before. Or even dressed up. But underneath Paige the tomboy was a striking woman. He was more smitten than ever.

"Thanks. And you look handsome as ever." She reached up and straightened his bow tie. "There; perfect. You having a good time with Brit?"

"Yeah, she's a really good dancer. And a good kisser too." As soon as he said the lie, he felt stupid and wanted to take it back. "Hey, Brit is having people over after the prom. Will I see you there?"

"I doubt it. I think Zach is inviting people back to his house."

"Oh, okay. Maybe tomorrow?"

She just smiled and headed into the bathroom.

Cole watched her walk away, feeling something had been forever lost.

A few days later Cole caught up with Paige in science class. "Hey, I haven't heard from you since the prom."

"I've been kind of busy with softball."

"Okay. Would you want to catch a movie on Friday or something?"

"Sorry; I can't. Zach asked me to go to the movies with him."

Cole couldn't hide his disappointment. "So that's why I haven't heard from you."

"No, I've just been busy."

"I get it. See you around."

When he got home from school, Cole sat on the porch with Rocky. Gazing out at the cornfields always had a calming effect on him.

His grandfather came out, sat down, and took out his pipe and tobacco. "Paige troubles?" he asked gently.

Cole looked over. "Does everybody around here talk about me?"

"Well, lately, yes." He lit his pipe and leaned back. "You're the talk of the house. *Is he going to Stanford, or is he going to find true love with Paige?*"

Cole looked at his grandpa with affection. "You've always been able to make me smile. Just wish you didn't smoke that stuff."

"Would you rather me break out the whiskey, which might not be a bad idea. You got to have some vices in life, or it's pretty damn dull."

"I get that."

"When you get to my age, the good and bad memories usually revolve around those vices, sad as that might sound. I'm not living; I'm just watching life now. And sometimes it's kind of comical. I have arthritis everywhere. A bum knee. A not-so-good back. Let's not even talk about my heart. But I can still get around even at ninety-two. Point being, it's never as bad as you think. You don't want to go to Stanford? Don't go. See, I solved that problem. Easy."

"I wish it were that easy. I don't think Dad is going to understand."

"He'll get over it. You'll be a success wherever you go, so I wouldn't worry about it." He took off his cap. "Now your woman issue, that's a tough one. Paige is a good catch.

She's got a good heart. She's a sweet kid. But she's a woman. I never did understand them other than to know you can't live with them, and you can't live without them. A damn quagmire, I must say."

"When did you become so wise, Grandpa?"

"That's what happens when you've been around too long."

Cole's father drove up in his old pickup. He got out and strode over to the porch. "Hey, Cole. You've been a hard one to pin down lately."

"Your son has something to tell you," Grandpa said, putting his cap back on.

"Grandpa!"

"What's wrong?" Mike asked.

Cole took a deep breath. "I don't want to go to Stanford. I know you were counting on it, but it's just not me. I'm going to Pale State. I'm sorry, Dad."

"Pale State? You're better than that, Cole. You're getting a full scholarship to Stanford for God's sake. Who turns down Stanford?"

"Young love is a powerful force," Grandpa observed.

"What the hell does love have to do with this hogwash?"

"Paige is going to Pale State,"

"Grandpa!" Cole snapped.

"You're not going to Stanford because you want to be close to Paige? Really?"

"Calm down, Mike. If I remember, you did a lot of stupid stuff when you were courting Mary. Or did you forget? We could call her out here."

"You know, Dad, you really don't help things around here sometimes." Mike stomped into the house, slamming the door behind him.

"He's really pissed off now," Cole said, looking miserable.

"He'll get over it. He knows I'm right. You can't fight love." Grandpa puffed out a few smoke rings. "If you went to Stanford, you would always be wondering about Paige.

It would torment you for the rest of your life. Closure is always important, however things turn out."

Cole knew there was no point denying his motivations. "Thanks, Grandpa."

"One last piece of advice. Carnations are better than roses."

Cole shook his head; Grandpa was the best at throwing curveballs. "So you're a flower expert."

The old man stared at his pipe like it was a crystal ball. "I've handed out a few bunches in my time, to your grandmother. Roses are overrated; they're expensive and only last a few days. Carnations are the holy grail of flowers; they're affordable, and they last for weeks, looking just as beautiful as the day you bought them."

"I'll keep that in the vault."

"You can thank me later."

Four Years Later

Cole left the Beta Chi Gamma house and headed to class, excited to begin his senior year. The fall foliage was in full display around the Pale State campus, and there was a bite to the early morning air. He smiled, remembering how his Grandpa used to call it football weather. Even though he was starting his fourth year at Pale State and belonged to the same fraternity as his best friends Josh and Rick, the sight of the autumn leaves changing colors still made him a little homesick.

He took a seat in the advanced robotics and automation class next to Josh, who was also majoring in engineering technology. Professor Smith leaned against his desk, arms folded across his thin frame, waiting for the students to settle in. With his blue blazer and white beard, he looked more like a museum docent than renowned scientist.

When the room quieted, he said, "Welcome back to robotics. I hope you all had a productive summer break. The prime focus of this class will be your robotic projects that will be presented the final week of the semester. It will count toward 50 percent of your grade, so I suggest you start working on it now. Your project should reflect everything you've learned so far—and then some. At the presentation will be representatives from numerous industries, and some of you will get great job offers based on your presentations. So do your best. Also, you can partner up to create your project if you prefer a team approach. If you have any questions, come see me after class. Okay, today we're going to talk about algorithms you can use to help a robotic grasp and manipulate an object ..."

Ninety minutes later Cole and Josh exited the classroom, their heads full of data and calculations.

"So, we are going to be partners on the project, right?" Josh asked,

"Of course. We're a team."

"Do you have any ideas yet for the project?"

Cole smiled. "Not just an idea; I already have a project that's literally out of this world."

"What do you mean?"

"It's in the shed back home. We are definitely going to get a 4.0 in this class and plenty of job offers."

A few weeks later Cole left the noise of the frat house to spend some quiet time in the library designing a series of algorithm programs that would allow AI systems to respond to stimuli instead of reacting to a clock signal. The goal was to take human traits and adapt them to AI. He had learned a lot from Robby the robot over the years. The deeper he probed his AI friend, the more amazed he was with the alien technology.

Cole packed up his laptop and headed out of the library and back to the BCG house. Footlights illuminated the brick pavers but left the quad bathed in deepening shadows. Walking with his head down lost in thought, he bumped into someone walking toward the library.

"I'm so sorry—" He stopped mid-apology when he saw who it was.

"Paige."

She smiled. "Hey, Cole.

The sight of her still made his breath catch. "Sorry, didn't mean to hip check you off the sidewalk."

"No, I should have been paying more attention. How you've been?"

"Can't complain. Just buried in work. Everyone's piling it on the last year."

"Tell me about it."

"I haven't seen you around campus much this semester."

"Between field hockey, classes, and trying to get a nursing internship, it doesn't leave any time for fun. Or sleep for that matter."

Cole forced himself to acknowledge the elephant in the room that was the wedge between them. "So how's Zach doing. I've seen him at a couple frat parties, but he doesn't say too much to me."

"Well, that's not too surprising," she said, with an expression Cole couldn't quite decipher. "He's really busy with football. This is an important year for him. He's got a good chance of getting drafted by the NFL."

"So I hear." Actually, the only person he'd heard it from was Zach, who loved bragging about his pro prospects. "Just think; you might be one of those football wives starring in your own reality TV show."

"Slow down there, boy genius. You and that imagination of yours."

They both laughed. For some reason, her response made Cole feel lighter. Hopeful even—something he always held close to his heart.

"So, Cole, you seeing anyone?"

"Me?" He grinned. "I have so many girls who want to go out with me, I just can't make up my mind."

"Typical frat boy," she said, matching his joking tone. "Allergic to commitment."

Cole sensed the words they were both saying wasn't what they were each feeling. He also knew Zach's frat prided themselves on being hard-partying ladies' men.

"Hard to take commitment seriously when you're at a wild after-hour party," he said jokingly.

"According to Zach, everybody at his frat is in bed by twelve," she quipped.

"Well, you know what they say; what happens in the frat stays in the frat."

She rolled her eyes.

Feeling emboldened, Cole said, "I'm meeting Josh and Rick at Joe's Pub tonight for beer and pool. Why don't you join us? It'll be fun. Like old times. We won't be out too late."

"I wish I could," Paige said, sounding wistful. "But I have to study for a test. Raincheck?"

"Sure. And I'm going to hold you to it."

"Please do."

There was an awkward pause. Looking into her blue eyes, Cole wondered what would happen if he pulled her close and kissed her. Would she kiss back, or have him arrested?

"Well, I better be going. It was good seeing you."

"You too."

They said goodbye and went their separate ways. After a few steps Cole paused and turned to take one last look and saw Paige had stopped and was gazing back at him. They both shook their heads, smiled at each other, then walked away.

Cole arrived at his fraternity with a little bounce in his step. The house was an old yellow Victorian with a large porch that housed thirty Beta brothers. When he pushed his bedroom door open, he found Josh, his roommate, there with Rick and another frat brother, Matt. They were drinking and smoking a joint while leering at a laptop and laughing.

John called Cole over. "You always wondered if Mandy Gray's rack is real. Well, look for yourself."

Cole stared at the screen. "What the hell are you thinking, Josh? We could get expelled. Or arrested."

"Relax, Cole. Nobody's going to know." Josh held out a joint. "And you've got to admit it's a hell of a rack. And all real."

"Yeah, it's definitely real," Cole agreed. "But you can't use the dragonfly drone to stalk girls."

The dragonfly drone, which was no bigger than the actual insect, was fitted with a camera and designed for intelligence work. Having drunk and stoned frat boys spying on Omega sorority girls getting ready for a Friday night—what could possibly go wrong? In his head, Cole could hear his father's words: "You're not as smart as you think."

Cole deleted the video and programmed the drone to come back to Beta Chi.

"You're just no fun anymore, Cole," Josh said with mock sadness, then drowned his sorrows in some more cold beer.

Later in the evening, Cole, Josh, and Rick landed at Joe's pub. They drained a few beers and played 8-ball for hours.

After ordering yet another round of beers, Josh nudged Cole. "Look who's here—Mandy Gray. Don't you have a much better appreciation for her now?"

Cole's smile faded when he noticed Zach Edwards sitting at the end of the bar having a great time with a blonde who was not Paige. In between their laughter, Zach and the girl were all over each other, kissing and whispering to each other flirtatiously. Cole had no doubts this wasn't the first time Zach had cheated on Paige.

Josh followed Cole's gaze. "You should take a picture and text it to Paige."

"No. She has to figure it out for herself."

"I'm with Josh," Rick said. "You have to tell Paige."

"I can't. It never works out for the messenger. But I can let him know what a piece of crap he is."

Cole moved to the bar and slipped onto the stool next to the cozy couple. "How're you doing, Edwards?"

Zach turned around. "Well, look who's here," he said, slurring slightly. "The campus police have arrived."

The girl disengaged from Zach and picked up her purse. She leaned over and whispered to Zach loud enough for their section of the bar to hear. "I'll be waiting in my car. It's the black Mustang."

After she left, Cole said, "Hot date?"

"What are you going to do? Tell Paige?"

"That you're an asshole? I think she's already figured that out."

"Let me tell you something. After I get done having a good time with Brii, I'm going to see Paige—and have an even better time. And you'll be drinking suds from a tap. Another lonely night for you."

"You're pathetic, Zach. Paige deserves so much better."

Zach shoved off his stool and leaned into Cole. "I'm going places. And I'm the one with Paige." He jabbed his index finger into Cole's chest. "You're the friend-zone loser. I would love to stay and chat, but I have someplace better to be, so go play with your pool stick."

Cole flicked Zach's finger off his chest. "Karma is a bitch, Edwards. Just hope I'm around to see it."

He slid off the stool and walked back to the pool table.

"How'd it go?" Rick asked.

"I really hate that guy," Cole said, then downed the rest of his beer.

"Fuck him," Josh said. "Let's get out of here and find a party. Oh, and I sent you a few good pics."

I t was 10:00 a.m. Josh was sitting on his bed as Cole entered the room. He handed him a letter.

"What's this?"

"Read it."

Cole scanned the letter. "I can't believe this. How the hell did they find out?"

"I don't know."

"We have to see the Dean at three o'clock," Cole said, his mood in a tailspin. "We could get expelled. Four wasted years."

"I know. I'm sorry."

"Well, I hope it was all worth it."

"Look, he might just give us a warning or something."

"You know what they do to guys like us?" Cole said. "They make a damn example of us. I can just see myself trying to explain this to my dad. *We came up with this crazy idea of using my little dragonfly drone to check out the sorority. Seemed like a good idea at the time.*"

"Maybe we're overreacting."

Cole shook his head. "You know what I'm thinking right now?"

"What?"

"Zach Edwards will go to the NFL, marry Paige, and have a college degree to boot, and I'm going to be back on the farm feeding chickens."

"Calm down. We'll get past this. We always do."

The three partners in crime marched up to the dean's office at 2:55 p.m. dressed in their best suits. They all thought Matt was the rat. They sat quietly in the waiting room opposite the secretary, focused on her computer.

At 3:00 the secretary stood up. "Dean Benson is ready to see you now." She opened the dean's door and they walked in single file.

The dean gestured to three chairs that were lined up opposite his desk. "Please sit down."

As they got settled he removed his glasses and pushed his hand through wavy, gray hair. He got up from his chair, walked to the large window, and gazed out at the school grounds.

"You know, I looked up your transcripts, and they're impressive. On paper." He sat down at his desk and folded his hands. "Now, whose bright idea was this?"

Josh began to say it was his, but Rick cut him off. "It was all three of us."

"Continue."

Cole said, "I built a dragonfly drone, and we were having some beers and kind of started playing around with the drone. One thing led to another, and it ended up in the Omega sorority."

"Oh, it just happened to end up there? Sounds more like a conscious decision, right?"

They nodded their heads.

"Any photos or video?"

"It's all deleted," Cole said. "There's no record of anything."

"And you want me to take your word for it."

"Yes. I take full responsibility."

"For all your sakes that better be the truth. Not only have you damaged the reputation of yourselves and your fraternity, this is a very serious accusation. Have you ever heard of felony voyeurism?"

Their faces turned a pale white.

"Voyeurism can be a class B misdemeanor or it can be a Level 6 felony, punishable by six months to three years in prison," the dean said, staring at them intently. "You boys have put yourselves in the position of destroying your professional and personal reputations. Damn stupid. As of now nobody from the sorority has brought this to my attention, so I'm sticking my neck out for you. I'm going to give you the benefit of the doubt unless something comes up otherwise. You understand?"

"Yes," they said in unison.

"Good. Now get out of my office."

They stood up and thanked the dean.

"You got something to say Finnigan?"

"No, sir."

"I didn't think so."

Cole immersed himself in his studies, kept himself out of trouble, and autumn passed quickly. Shortly before winter break he was thrilled to hear from Paige, who asked if she could ride back to Green River with him. He of course said yes.

That Friday he pulled the F150—which was now his— in front of her townhouse, and Paige immediately ran out. He never got tired of seeing her ponytail bouncing in the wind or her smile, which never failed to give him a pang of longing. She tossed her suitcase on the back seat, then got in, giving Cole a cheery hello.

"Why you so happy?" he asked.

"I just finished all my finals, I get to relax for the next few weeks, and I get to ride home with you."

"Nice to hear riding with me makes you happy."

"Why wouldn't it?"

Buoyed by her response, Cole put the car in gear and headed for home. The drive to Green River was the most time he and Paige had spent together in years. The conversation never lagged, and they bantered like old times. Cole didn't want the drive to end; being together in the truck he could pretend Zach didn't exist. When they were almost home, he forced himself back to reality.

"I'm not complaining, but how come you didn't drive back with Zach?"

She paused. "Because we broke up."

Cole's immediate response was profound satisfaction, followed by concern for Paige. "When did that happen? Why did it happen?"

"A couple months ago. And why? He was busy with football. I was really busy with school and sports ... I didn't really have the time for a boyfriend."

"A boyfriend like him, anyway." Cole hesitated then added. "He cheated on you."

Paige sighed. "Yeah, there was that."

He glanced at her in surprise. "You knew?"

"Eventually. But if you knew, why didn't you tell me?"

"I thought about it a million times, but I didn't want to be that guy."

"What guy?"

"The guy who tries to break up a relationship to get the girl. That's not how you get the girl of your dreams, even if it means being stuck in friend-zone limbo forever."

Paige gave him a slow, sly smile. "Maybe not forever."

Cole's heart did a flip. "What's that supposed to mean?"

"What do you think it means?"

He smiled. "That you like torturing me."

Paige laughed. "What it means is that now I have the time for a boyfriend. Know anybody who might be looking for a girlfriend?"

"I think I just might."

"Well, good, because I'm available tonight."

Cole had hoped for, prayed for, the chance to be with Paige for so long, but now that it was happening, it felt surreal. And while he felt deliriously happy, he couldn't resist yanking Paige's chain, just a little.

"So, if I asked, you'd go out on a real date with me?"

"I'd love to."

"Huh. Good to know. Let me think about it."

The look of surprise on Paige's face made Cole laugh out loud. "Gotcha."

She punched his arm hard enough to make the truck swerve, then sat back against the seat. "I guess I deserved that."

"Maybe just a little," he teased, then flexed his arm. "That's some right hook you have there."

"Sorry. Years of wielding a field hockey stick." Paige reached over and gently rubbed his bicep. "Better?"

Cole put his hand over hers and linked their fingers. "Much."

Paige sighed. "I've missed you."

"Me too." Cole let go of her hand so he could turn on the blinker to exit the freeway. They were almost home. "Why didn't you tell me you had broken up with Zach back when it happened?"

Paige dropped her head against the headrest "I needed some time to myself. To concentrate on school. I really didn't have time to dwell on a boyfriend."

"I've always wondered why you went out with Zach."

"He asked me," Paige said with a self-conscious laugh. "He was easy on the eyes. And he paid attention to me. Until he didn't. The truth, I never really saw me spending my life with him."

"Then why'd you stay with him as long as you did?"

"I don't know. It just seemed easier to let it run its course."

Cole paused, not sure how to phrase his question. "So it was never really serious?"

"I'm still a virgin if that's what you're wondering."

Cole blushed. "You didn't need to tell me that."

"It's true. That's probably why Zach cheated on me." Paige looked at Cole. "Were you ever involved with anyone?"

"So many I've lost count."

Paige rolled her eyes. "Seriously."

"Seriously, there's never been anybody else. I've always known you were the only girl for me since first grade when I knocked my lunch tray over, and you picked it up."

"You're so sweet, Cole. I remember that day." She smiled with her eyes and his eyes smiled back.

"You looked at me with those beautiful blue eyes, and at that moment I knew you were the one. I thought: *I'm going to marry her someday*. I know that sounds crazy."

"It doesn't. I felt something too."

Cole turned down the road leading to the Turner family home. As long as they were baring souls …

"I've missed you so much, Paige. I thought I'd lost you."

"When I was with Zach, I thought about you all the time. I missed our friendship. I missed the person I could talk to about anything. I missed my best friend."

"So, to save the friendship, I guess we have no choice but to be a couple."

"I agree; to save the friendship we need to be a couple," she said with a wide smile.

He grinned. "So we are on the same page."

They looked at each other and started laughing.

Chapter 9

Winter break went by in a blur, filled with happy days spent with his family and Paige. With the break almost over and school starting in a couple of days, Cole invited Josh over to work on their robotics project.

When Cole had initially told Josh about finding and restoring Robby, he was understandably disbelieving. So the first time seeing Robby in the faux flesh a few days earlier had left Josh suitably shocked. Cole was still trying to wrap his head around an alien humanoid. Today he was going to introduce them.

It was cold and snowing as they tromped to the shed through barren, ice-covered trees. Cole unlocked the shed, turned on the lights, and started the generator. Josh cranked up the floor heater while Cole brought Robby out of his sleep state.

Josh sat next to Cole. "Does it walk around?"

"I think it can, but I don't want to activate its synaptic nerve. Robby has connections like nerves. It's amazing. Whoever designed him are light years ahead of us. I'm just scratching the surface. And I worry it could be playing me."

"What do you mean?"

"I think I'm controlling it, but what if it's just playing along."

"Oh, that's not worrisome," Josh said under his breath.

Cole hit some keys, and Robby's eyes opened wide, like one of the animatrons he'd seen at Disney World as a kid.

"Hello, Cole." Robby's brown eyes looked at Josh. "Who are you?"

"That's Josh. He's a friend of mine. He's going to be working with us on the robotic project I told you about. Josh, say hello to Robby."

"Hi, Robby."

"Cole has told me all about you, Josh. We are doing a presentation soon. I look forward to it."

"Okay, Robby. I'm going to put you back in sleep mode."

"Goodnight, Cole."

Josh was star struck. "This is amazing. It appears so human. Well, its personality is lacking a little bit, but no worse than half the frat guys. We are definitely going to get a frigging A."

A few months later the front rows of the Pale State auditorium were filled with anxious students ready to show off their AI creations. Sitting in the back was a contingent of business suits browsing through the program that had been passed out.

Cole and Josh were backstage waiting for the presentation to begin. Josh got up and surveyed the crowd through a crack in the curtain.

"There's a good-sized crowd out there. A lot of suits in the back." Josh sat back down. "You nervous?"

"For some reason, no."

The students cheered when Professor Smith walked to the podium.

"Hello, everyone. I'm Professor Smith. This is our tenth annual robotics showcase. I'm very excited about the ten presentations created by a very smart group of students. So without further ado, let's begin the show."

The lights dimmed, and the program began. Each presentation had the audience buzzing. There were miniature drones, walking bots, a robot that climbed using soft tendrils, 3D printed soft mesh robots, and smart micro-robots. John and Cole were the last presentation.

Robby sat in a chair in the center of the stage. The auditorium was dark except for a soft light shining on it from above. Cole was at the podium with his laptop. After Josh had handed out questions the audience could ask Robby, Cole hit the keys, and Robby awoke. A murmur rippled through the auditorium at how human-like their creation looked. If it wasn't for his mechanically generated voice, it would have been impossible to tell it wasn't human.

The presentation was going better than Cole could have hoped, until the last question when after answering, Robby ad-libbed a joke that had the audience laughing and cheering, But before Cole could grasp the significance of Robby going off-script with an answer Cole had not programmed, one of the businessmen in the back row got up and walked briskly down the aisle. By his expression he was not amused.

The man stopped in front of the stage and slow-clapped. "Bravo, that was a great ventriloquist act. It belongs in a circus. My name is Sid Martin; I'm senior vice president of Round Robotics here in Indiana. I know robotics better than anyone. These two young men are either very gifted students, or this was the biggest fraud I've ever come across in the robotics field. I happen to believe the latter."

The audience got very quiet. Josh and Cole looked at each other, unsure what to do. Before Cole could respond, Robby got up and stepped forward to the edge of the stage.

"Mr. Martin, are you calling me a fraud?"

The audience cheered, Mr. Martin turned red, Cole stood there in shock. He tried to put Robby in sleep mode but couldn't. A quick diagnostic showed Robby had connected his own synaptic system. Cole tried an override to turn him off, but that failed too. Robby walked back to the chair, and as soon as he sat down, sleep mode was available again. Cole quickly shut Robby down.

As the Professor walked out on stage, Josh asked, "I thought you said it couldn't walk."

"I guess it could," he shrugged.

What he didn't say is that Robby had played him, and now Cole had created a Frankenstein the world was not prepared for.

Cole and Josh were talking to Professor Smith backstage when Sid Martin approached them. He shook both their hands.

"Sorry for being skeptical out there, but I've never seen two students create anything quite so advanced."

"That's okay; it made for good theater," Josh joked.

"Its body language, voice inflection, and audio response were truly amazing. If you don't mind me asking, what is the control structure your using?"

Cole shook his head. "It's proprietary."

"Fair enough. I was talking to Professor Smith here because I would like to show you guys around our Round Robotics facility tomorrow."

When Josh and Cole hesitated, Professor Smith said, "I would take Mr. Martin up on his offer. Missing one day of classes is worth it."

"I guess we could then," Cole said.

"Good. Just give me your numbers, and I'll make arraignments to have you picked up around ten tomorrow."

Chapter 10

The next day, a black limo rolled to a stop in front of the Beta Chi Gamma fraternity at ten o'clock on the dot. Cole and Josh, wearing dress shirts and ties, sauntered down the sidewalk and settled into the back of the car for the half-hour drive to Greensburg, Indiana, an outer suburb of Indianapolis.

When they reached Round Robotics, the limo stopped at a heavy, electronic security gate at the entrance. The perimeter of the grounds was surrounded by a ten-foot electrified fence with barbed wire at the top.

Two large security guards wearing sunglasses ushered Cole and Josh out of the car and confiscated their phones.

"What's that all about?" Josh asked.

"It's just procedure; you're entering a high-security area where no visitor phones are allowed," the larger guard explained. "Sorry for the inconvenience. You'll get them back when you leave. Let me see your IDs."

They handed their driver's licenses to the guard, who scanned them with a handheld device. He nodded to the other guard, who made a phone call from the guard booth. A few minutes later a small electric vehicle approached from inside the compound. The gate opened.

"This car will take you from here. Ms. Walsh will greet you."

Josh and Cole got in the car. They were the only ones in it. As soon as the guards closed the doors, the vehicle departed.

Josh grinned. "An autonomous vehicle. This place is awesome."

Cole was apprehensive. "My question is, what are they hiding here that needs all this security?"

A few minutes later, the car rolled to a stop in front of a reflective glass exterior office complex. An assortment of colorful flowers lined the brick walkway.

A beautiful young woman with long legs and wearing a blue dress came out of the main lobby, heading in their direction.

Josh elbowed Cole. "Do you see what I see? Wow, that girl is hot. I hope they all look like that around here."

The doors opened, and they stepped out of the car. The woman shook their hands. "Hi, I'm Carol Walsh, Mr. Martin's secretary. Please follow me; he's waiting for you."

They walked through the main entrance into a large atrium, went past security, and got on an escalator to the mezzanine, which was lined with tall ferns. They followed Carol to the first office on the left. She rapped on the door before entering. Sid Martin was at his desk, talking on the phone. He held up a finger, indicating he'd be with them in a moment. Carol gestured for Cole and Josh to sit then left the room. They both marveled at the opulent décor. The mahogany furniture complemented the hardwood flooring. The sunlight streaming through the large window reflected off the high ceiling, illuminating the room with a warm glow.

Sid hung up and walked around the desk to shake Cole and Josh's hands. "Hey, I'm glad to see you guys. You want anything?"

They shook their heads.

He sat back down, hands folded on the desk. "So, what do you think about this place?"

"It's quite an amazing place from what I've seen so far," Cole said.

Josh added, "The driverless car was unexpected. I didn't think there were companies like this in Indiana."

"You're not the first to say that. When we were looking for a location, there was a fear originally that maybe we couldn't attract the best and the brightest settling here. But that hasn't been a problem. Not being in Silicon Valley is what makes us different. We are a creative company. The best in our field. We've attracted a crop of talent who've graduated from the top schools all over the country but love the cost of living out here. We've also found quality local talent. Plus, we have plenty of acreage to expand and do field testing without anybody stealing out secrets."

"Is that why they took our phones at the gate?" Cole asked

"Oh, I'm sorry for the inconvenience, but industrial espionage is a major problem, and we can't be too careful. There are a lot of companies who would love to steal our proprietary patents. If you decide to work for us, you'll get a locker to put your phone in. There are no phones or computer devices of any sort in the lab or out in the field." He stood. "Before I give you a tour and introduce you to some people, I have a question."

Cole and Josh listened expectantly.

"What did you think of my secretary?"

The question made Cole uncomfortable. "She seemed nice." Josh nodded in agreement.

"I know that, but what did you think of her? Josh, didn't you say you thought she was hot?"

Josh eyed him warily. "How would you know that?"

Sid smiled. "Our cars have ears."

Thinking it must be a trick question, Josh shrugged. "Hard to say."

Sid laughed. "Come on; you thought she was hot, didn't you? I'm not sexist. I'm just trying to make a point. If I meet some clients here and come out with my secretary, who do you think gets their attention? It surely isn't five-foot-six, graying, nearsighted little old me."

They both smiled but were still confused about where this was going.

"When you work here, you'll understand the way the

world looks at life. My secretary is a beautiful woman. That is, anyone coming here notices. She's perfect in every way to nearly every man's eye. To a woman, she's a damn threat. You see how that works?"

Cole shook his head. "I can't believe it."

Josh was lost. "Believe what?"

"She's an AI robotic humanoid."

Sid grinned at Josh's expression. "Pretty amazing stuff, huh? She's unique. She only does simple tasks. Men are so busy looking at her that they don't realize she's a humanoid. If you ask her any questions, she just repeats the same script. She shakes your hand then says: *I'm Carol Walsh, I'm Mr. Martin's secretary. Please follow me; he's waiting for you.* It's a pretty simple script, probably needs to be updated, but I guarantee nobody really notices."

"That is amazing," Josh said.

Sid pressed the intercom on his phone. "Carol, could you come in." He sat back in his chair. "This is the future. This model will someday be in every house. Can you imagine the growth of this company? And you guys are on the ground floor. I don't want to get ahead of myself yet, but this is an opportunity of a lifetime."

There was a quick tap-tap on the door then Carol walked in. "What do you need, Mr. Martin."

"I would like a cup of coffee with cream."

"I'll be right back."

Cole was impressed. "That was quite a show."

Two minutes later Carol came back with a hot cup of coffee. "Is there anything else I can do for you, Mr. Martin?"

"No, I'm fine, Carol. Thank you." After she left Sid said, "This humanoid lacks emotional intelligence, but we're working on that. And yes, Carol can have sex. Of course, models with that feature will cost extra," he said with a grin. "That's where the world's heading, like it or not. If Round Robotics doesn't do it, someone else will. Why don't I show you guys around and then when we're done, we can come back here and talk about your futures."

They walked down a long, glass corridor, looking down on the white-coated scientists working below. Some were focused on robotic structures, testing endurance, commands, strength, and agility. Others were working on computer programs.

"We spend a lot of time testing and retesting body structures, algorithm programs, etc.," Sid explained. "Depending on the complexity of the AI and depending what a client might request, a final product today could be upwards of hundreds of millions of dollars. A more simplified version like the secretary model you saw is substantially less."

Speechless, they just nodded, overwhelmed by the experience.

Sid pointed. "You see that man below, with the beard and gray hair? That's William McDonald, the head scientist at Round Robotics. You can learn a lot from him. Let me introduce you."

They took an elevator down to the lab floor. Just past the elevator doors was a security desk. A tall guard stood watch behind the pretty secretary.

"Please contact Mr. McDonald and tell him I have two applicants who would like to meet him."

"Of course, Mr. Martin."

Josh stared at the secretary.

Sid whispered in his ear. "She's human."

"Yeah, I knew that."

The lab door slid open, and William McDonald walked out to greet them.

"These are the two students I told you about. Cole Adams and Josh Finnigan."

"What Sid told me about your AI robotic project sounds pretty amazing. To fully figure AI out, we need to develop human-like intelligence, not just computer programs or fancy algorithms. You met Sid's secretary, Carol. That's basic AI, but we are doing a lot more here. Let me ask you something, Cole."

"Sure." Cole felt like a lab specimen the way the scientist was eyeing them.

"We do a complete background check on every employee. Whatever you've done on the internet never goes away. In today's world, you can figure out the character of a human being just through their social media activity. Sad but true, nobody's a mystery, one of the major downsides of the internet. But there isn't much out there about you, Cole. You've stayed off the foolish social media sites. That's smart. My question is, why did you turn down a full ride to Stanford?"

Cole couldn't begin to guess how Dr. McDonald knew. He stuck with the truth. "Love."

"Ah, a girl," McDonald smiled. "That's a great answer. Logically it made no sense; Pale State compared to Stanford, there's no contest. Yet it was the right decision. Did you get the girl?"

Cole just smiled.

"You see? AI would always pick Stanford. That's the dilemma."

They followed Sid through another long corridor and passed another set of doors that were off-limits.

Josh stopped. "What's in here, Mr. Martin?"

"That's a high-security area restricted to only employees with special clearance. Sorry: I can't give you a tour there."

When they got back to Sid's office, his desk phone was ringing. As he walked to answer it, he noted, "Old-fashioned, but it can't be hacked or take pictures."

Cole and Josh waited, while Sid took the brief call.

Sid hung up the phone and leaned back in his plush chair with his hands clasped behind his head. "That was Dr. Mc-Donald. He likes you guys. He has given me permission to offer you a very lucrative compensation package. This is a once in a lifetime offer. We have about a hundred employees today. In a decade we'll have ten times that, so you're getting in on the ground floor. We are the leaders in the robotics industry that nobody has heard of yet. The big boys aren't going to be able to compete with us. I probably shouldn't be telling you this, but we are negotiating a huge defense contract and plans to go public; the IPO is already in the planning stages. You'll get a bunch of stock prior to the IPO at pennies on the dollar. When we go public, you'll be very rich. So, what do you think?"

"Sounds too good to be true," Cole said carefully.

"AI is the next frontier."

"What would our salaries be?" Josh asked.

"Did I forget to tell you that? You start at $200,000. Nice, huh? Nobody else is going to offer two newly-minted college graduates that type of money, but we pay on potential. You also get four weeks of vacation, a 401(k), full health benefits, and life insurance, and I'm sure there are a few other perks I've forgotten. HR can give you the full package. To me this is an easy decision. The start date is June 15."

This is way too easy, Cole thought. Something didn't add up with this mystery company out in no man's land protected by a team of security.

All Josh heard was dollar signs, and thoughts of a brand-new car danced in his head.

"I don't need an answer this minute," Sid said. "Go home and think about it. I don't want to rush you, but we do have other candidates, so if I don't hear from you by 4:00 p.m. tomorrow. I'll assume you have decided to pursue other opportunities. But I promise this is as good an offer as it gets."

It was clear the meeting was over. They stood up to leave, and Sid walked them out of his office. He stopped by Carol's desk and picked up two envelopes.

"One last thing. If you do decide to come on board, the company requires you to sign a contract. Here's a copy for each of you. Make sure to read it. If you have any questions, my card's attached to the form. Really, don't be afraid to call."

Chapter 11

C ole had deep reservations about the company. His instincts rattled a warning that something wasn't right. The money was too easy and too much. Security was tight. Surveillance cameras were everywhere. And there was something about Dr. McDonald that he couldn't put his finger on. But in the end he felt there was no way to turn down the offer. It meant so much to his family, especially his father, to be offered so much financial security, especially with the farm's profits erratic from year to year. But he couldn't shake the feeling that there was something dark behind the curtain.

Cole and Paige came home for spring break, and he decided it was the perfect time to pop the question. They both had good jobs waiting for them after graduation, so they were financially secure. The ring was bought and put away in a secure place. He knew she was the one he wanted to spend the rest of his life with and saw no reason waiting to make it official. It was time to close the deal with the woman he loved.

It was a beautiful sixty-degree afternoon with a slight breeze. He stepped off the porch in jeans and a black sweatshirt with his dark hair slicked back. He jumped into the pickup and drove over to Paige's house. He was greeted at the door by her dad.

"Hey, Cole. Paige will out in a moment. Why don't you come in."

"That's okay. I'll just wait out on the porch."

A few minutes later, Paige stepped out on the porch wearing body-hugging jeans, a white sweater, and sneakers to match. He looked at her with a sigh.

"You look stunning."

"In this old stuff? You really are too sweet."

"I have a surprise for you."

She smiled. "I like surprises."

He pulled the bouquet of flowers from behind his back

"Oh, I love carnations and all the different colors. They're so pretty."

Thank you, Grandpa, Cole thought. He took her hand. "Ready to go?"

"Give me one second. I'm going to put these in a vase."

When they got to the truck, Paige kissed Cole on the cheek. "That was a wonderful surprise. Thank you."

"The flowers were only part of the surprise."

"There's more?"

"You'll see."

He drove back to his house. As she climbed out of the truck, Paige had no idea what they were doing. "What are you up to, Cole Adams?"

"Let's take the tractor out to the field. I want to show you something."

They pulled themselves onto the big tractor, Cole started the engine, and they rumbled toward the field.

Paige remembered a similar day when they were nine. "Do you remember when we took your father's tractor down to the lake for the first time?"

"How could I forget. We thought we were so cool, fishing off the big rock. And we brought a lunch. That day was exactly like today."

"Life was so simple back then."

"If I remember right, your father wasn't too happy."

"Yeah. I got grounded for a month, but it was worth it."

"What's that?" Paige asked, pointing. "It looks like a fancy barn."

"My father's getting into the wedding business. He had an idea about building a beautiful reception hall surrounded by cornfields and positioning it to get the most out of sunsets. He thinks he's going to make a fortune."

"And probably will; it's a good idea. Is that what you wanted to show me?"

"Sort of." Cole rolled the tractor to a stop. "Come on; let's go in. I'll show you around."

He unlocked the door and led her in. Paige looked up at the high, wood-beam ceilings, the bar made of mahogany with granite countertops, and the large windows overlooking a patio that faced west.

"This is really nice. I just love the natural light and the dark hardwood flooring. He did a good job."

Cole went behind the bar and turned on the sound system, which played songs he'd programmed in the night before. Then took out a bottle of Pinot Noir from the wine cooler and grabbed two glasses.

"Come on, let's go outside."

"What are we doing?"

"I figured we'd be the first to try out the sunset."

"Aren't you being the romantic one."

"You bet. And my dad will never know I took the best bottle of wine he had."

Paige smiled. "Okay, I'm in."

They sat in padded wooden chairs, facing the field, a small table in between. They spent the rest of the late afternoon sipping wine, talking, bantering, and enjoying each other's company. The sun was low on the horizon, painting the sky orange when "their" song came on the sound system. That was Cole's carefully planned cue.

Cole got up and stood in front of Paige.

"You want to dance?" she asked with puzzled look.

"Not yet."

Cole got down on one knee, pulled a small box out of his back pocket, and opened it to reveal a small but beautiful diamond ring.

Looking shell-shocked, Paige covered her mouth with her hands. "Oh, my God."

"Paige Turner, I love you with all my heart. Will you marry me?"

Her breath caught as the tears came. "I love you so much too. Of course I'll marry you."

He slid the ring onto her finger then they kissed as if it were their last embrace. When they finally ended their embrace, Paige held her hand up in the waning light, turning it to see the light reflect off the diamond.

Cole turned to watch the sun disappear into the horizon. "This is the happiest day of my life."

Paige cupped his face in her hands. "Mine too."

They kissed until the stars came out.

The rest of the evening was a whirlwind of telling their respective families, heartfelt congratulations, and sharing tears of joy. Driving home from Paige's that night, Cole had never felt so content. He was marrying the love of his life and soulmate. Despite his qualms about Round Robotics, he had a secure financial future, and his two best friends would be working there too. Instead of going their separate ways, his group would all be together. A life of living happily-ever-after was within reach.

If he could just shake the feeling of dread that a storm was coming.

Chapter 12

Their last party week in college before finals was upon them. Cole, Josh, and Rick sat around drinking beers in Cole's bedroom, figuring out the evening's plans.

"I can't believe it's been four years and that we graduate the end of this month," Josh said. "I think this calls for a joint."

"You think everything calls for a joint," Rick said.

"Doesn't it?" He lit it up, took a long hit, then passed it around. "I also can't believe we're all going to be working at the same company. That means we're all going to be rich."

"Maybe you," Rick said. "I'm not making near the money you guys are."

Josh grinned. "Maybe you should have studied robotics."

"Maybe I should have just ridden Cole's shirttails too."

Josh shrugged, too high to care. "True." He turned to Cole. "What the hell you doing over there? Put down the laptop and relax. Take a toke. This is our last week to party before we join the working class."

Cole came over and sat on his bed. Josh handed him the joint. "Playing with your drone again?"

Cole passed back the joint and slowly exhaled. "Paige went off with her friends to Rolling's Tavern. I thought I'd surprise her when she came out."

"So you're stalking her. Come on; let's do some drinking."

They sat passing the joint around. They reminisced about their college days and erupted into laughter at their foolish antics. Josh stood up and pretended to be Dean Benson, his voice changed, "You got something to say Finnigan?"

"No, sir," Josh said.

Josh mimicked the Dean's voice with a slight crackle. "I didn't think so." They erupted again into laughter to the point of holding their stomachs as the fog of smoke filled the air.

The night was calm, and the dragonfly drone rested on the pitch of the roof, its camera focused on the tavern's door. It was 11:30 p.m. when Cole sat trying to focus his bloodshot eyes on the laptop screen. He was going to surprise Paige and her girlfriends and see if she wanted to go to an after-hours party Rick knew about.

"Come on, Cole," Josh yelled from the frat hallway. "Just call her."

"Yeah, okay." But just as he was going to bring his drone home, Paige came out of the tavern by herself. Cole maneuvered the drone to her right, hovering within talking distance, making Paige jump.

"Oh my God, Cole. You scared me. I almost swatted that damn thing."

He laughed. "Kurt's having an after-hours party. I was wondering if you wanted to go."

"Sure. I'll meet you over there."

"Where are your friends?"

"They wanted to stay. I wanted to see you."

"Oh, really?"

"Cole, *come on!*" Josh yelled from another room.

"Paige, can my drone hop a ride with you?"

"You know how much I hate this thing, right? But sure."

The drone landed in her hand. She opened her car door and placed it on the passenger seat.

"It's like I'm with you, Paige."

She smiled; she could always tell when he'd been smoking. "I'll be there in fifteen minutes."

The road was barren and dark, so she drove carefully, focused on the road ahead. Then she felt something hit her back bumper.

"Cole?"

He was talking to Rick but stopped immediately when he heard the fear in her voice.

"Paige, you okay? What's wrong? Talk to me."

"Someone just tapped my back bumper."

"Who is it?"

"I don't know. I don't see anyone."

"Where are you?"

"Route 31."

Cole sent a command to the drone, which was immediately followed by the sound of screeching tires and metal on metal. The drone slammed into the back seat but was still transmitting. Cole saw on his phone that the car spun in a 360, then listened as it rolled to a stop.

"Paige!" Cole yelled. "Paige, answer me. Are you okay?"

He could hear voices but couldn't make out what was being said. He focused the drone's camera on the commotion. The driver side door was opened, and Paige screamed as a man reached in and yanked her out of the car. She struggled to get away, calling out for Cole. Hearing Paige as the man dragged her away and being unable to help her was agony. All Cole could do was dial 911.

He grabbed Rick and Josh and explained what was happening as they raced out of the frat house to Cole's truck. He floored the accelerator, hopping over the curb. Fear had his adrenaline on overdrive, and his heart felt like it could rupture at any moment. His entire body ached with dread as he raced down Route 31. In a few minutes he saw the blue lights of a police cruiser flashing ahead. He stopped the truck twenty yards from the cruiser and raced to Paige's car.

The cop on the scene yelled for him to stop. "Don't you dare touch that car. Who the hell are you?"

"I'm the one who called you. I'm Cole Adams, Paige Turner's fiancé. Somebody forcibly grabbed her from the car. Have you found Paige?"

Another cruiser arrived on the scene, conferred with the first cop, then sped down the road, lights flashing.

"I've got to find her." Cole reached into the car and pulled out his drone.

"We're already on it," the officer said. "Just slow down, okay? My sergeant is going to be here any minute."

"I can't wait."

"Let us handle this. There's nothing more you can do."

"Oh, yes, there is."

Cole placed his laptop on the truck's hood and replayed the drone's footage. There were at least two men involved, but the camera only caught an image of one. And a van was clearly visible in the background. He ran over to the officer.

"Here, my drone got an image of one of the men. Maybe you can identify him. And look there; they took her in a van."

The officer radioed in the description of the van and asked Cole if he would pull a still image of the man from the video and also send a picture of Paige. Cole emailed the photos to the officer's phone.

"This is good," he said. "It's a big help."

A few minutes later another cruiser pulled up and parked. The sergeant got out of the car and motioned the officer over. After conferring, the sergeant approached Cole, Josh, and Rick.

"I don't want anyone near the car again, understand? I know this is tough. I know you want to do something, anything. But we are doing the best we can do. We now have a picture of the girl, which has saved a lot of time. This will help. We are going to put out an abduction alert as soon as possible, but it might take just a little time."

"We don't have time," Cole said angrily.

"I know you're upset, son. But we got a good head start on this one. Now the way you can help most right now is to answer some questions about Paige so we can send it out with the BOLO, like what she was wearing, birthmarks, things like that. We also need contact information for her next of kin, which we need to do ourselves. Can you help with all that?"

Cole nodded.

"Good. Do you know where she came from tonight?"

"Rolling's Tavern, a few miles from here."

"I know where it is. We'll take a look at the surveillance system and see if we get any leads. I assume she was with friends."

"Yeah." Cole gave the sergeant the names of the girls Paige had been with.

"Thank you. Are you all students?"

"Yeah," Josh answered. "We go to Pale State. Paige too."

A call from dispatch came through on the sergeant's two-way radio attached to his shoulder. He excused himself and walked away out of hearing distance. When he returned his expression was grim. Cole thought his legs might give out.

"We found the van. It looks like it was stolen."

"What does that mean?"

"It means that this might not be random."

"I don't understand," Cole said.

"It might have been planned. As in Paige was the intended target."

"How is that possible?" Cole snapped, losing control of his emotions. "She's never done anything to harm anyone; why would someone go after her?"

"Look, I wish I could tell you more. After you talk to the office, I want you to go back to your dorm, or wherever you live. I know it's tough to leave, but you will just be in the way out here. And you've helped us. Our detectives will be in touch with you in the morning. And if we find anything tonight, I'll personally call you, okay?"

Cole nodded and walked slowly back to the truck with his head down. He didn't want to leave the last place he knew Paige had been. He stood on the road's centerline and stared hopelessly down the dark road and put his hands to his face as a tear rolled down his cheek. The girl he loved was gone.

Chapter 13

At 5:30 in the morning, Special Agent Wyatt Miller's phone vibrated on the nightstand. He rolled over and reached for the phone, propped on his elbow.

"Miller here." He listened a few moments then sat up and pushed his black hair back from his eyes. "I can be there in a couple of hours. I'll touch base with you then."

He put the phone down and rocked his tall, lean frame off the bed.

"What's going on?" his wife asked.

"Another kidnapping. This time in Indiana. A college student is missing."

"Is it related to the others?"

"It's looking that way, honey. We'll see after I get a full briefing. I'm just glad I'm not the one who has to tell the family." He walked over to her side of the bed. "You take good care of the girls while I'm gone and tell them I love them."

"And you be careful," she said, giving him a kiss. "When will you be back?"

"I don't know. But I don't have a good feeling about this one."

Staring out his window, Cole watched the first light of dawn creep through the trees. He hadn't slept at all. A part of him was missing. It was surreal.

"Maybe we should head for breakfast," Josh suggested, nursing a grade A headache. He and Rick had spent the night with Cole, unwilling to leave him alone.

Cole paced the room. "I'm not hungry. I'm going to call the station and see if they heard anything."

"Why don't we just go down there in person, and then go out for breakfast," Rick said. "You not eating isn't going to bring Paige home any quicker."

"You're probably right, Rick; let's go," Cole said, even though he had no appetite, just an empty void in his gut.

A couple of hours later, Special Agent Miller was at the abduction scene with his partner, Cliff Allen, watching a forensic team dusting the car for prints under an overcast sky threatening rain.

"Glad we were finally smart enough to bring our long raincoats," Wyatt said to his partner. "Looks like we are going to get a good soaking."

They were joined by Detective Jose Lopez. After handshakes all around, Wyatt asked, "What do we have?"

"A young college girl out with her friends at a local tavern leaves to meet her fiancé at a party but never makes it because someone had other intentions. Looks like her car was hit from behind, causing her to lose control. Then two guys grabbed her and pushed her into a blue van. The rest is history."

Wyatt asked, "Van was stolen?"

"Yeah."

"And you found it just a few miles from the abduction site?"

Lopez paused. "Yeah. How do you know that?"

Wyatt glanced at his partner, who nodded. "This isn't the first girl abducted under these circumstances. But it's

the first time they've struck in Indiana. That's why we're here. If there's any good news here, it's that she's probably still alive. You've done a great job finding the stolen van so soon after the abduction."

"Maybe we'll get some prints," Lopez said.

"I don't think so unless they've gotten sloppy. Have you talked to her friends? And what about security cameras at the tavern?"

"We're working on that. We've talked to a few of the friends she was with last night, and they didn't remember anything of significance."

"I'll want to see all the security camera videos at the tavern when you get a chance."

"Sure."

"Nobody ever notices the subtle stares," Wyatt said. "Whoever did this was there. Do you have a photo of her?"

"Yeah, I do. I need to go to my car. I have something else I want to show you too. I'll be right back."

When Lopez walked away, Cliff asked, "What do you think?"

"Same old shit. This one is going to hit the media—big time. And these guys are going to go dark for a while just like cockroaches do when the lights are turned on. But they'll eventually strike again unless we find them first."

Detective Lopez returned and handed Wyatt Paige's engagement announcement photo.

"Very pretty girl," Wyatt said. "Same as the rest of them. All damn pretty."

Detective Lopez held out another photo. "I think you'll want this one, too."

"Who's this?"

"We believe it's one of the kidnappers."

"How did you get this?"

"The boyfriend was talking to her through his drone when it happened, so he managed to get a video of the abduction. You can also see the van was in the background."

"This photo is a big deal. We can send it to the FBI lab

and use facial recognition. If we're lucky, we might get a hit. Great work, Detective."

"I think you should be thanking the boyfriend."

"Where can I find him?"

"The Beta Chi Gamma frat house at Pale State. I can text you directions."

"Thanks. In the meantime, this photo of the alleged kidnapper cannot get out to the media. Otherwise, we might find this guy in the river."

"I understand, Agent Miller. I'll make sure there's no leak."

"Good. As long as they don't know we have a link, maybe we finally have half a chance of finding these guys."

The agents spent some time looking over the crime scene for any clues that might have been missed. With rain now pelting down, Wyatt moved further away from the crime scene and found a worn path in front of a large cleared field. He stopped for a cigarette break.

Cliff walked up a few minutes later. "I thought you quit."

"I thought I did too. But thinking about the families and the pain they go through, drives me to nicotine."

Like Wyatt, Cliff also had children. "I know what you mean. I was looking at the information gathered by the local guys. She's a nursing student. Engaged to her high school sweetheart."

"When you got daughters you can never stop worrying about them in this crazy sick world of ours."

Wyatt dropped his butt, and when he stamped it out, he felt something hard under his boot. He squatted down and pressed his hand against the soil. He looked up.

"Hey, Cliff, you mind getting me the shovel out of the trunk?"

Ten minutes later Wyatt had cleared the dirt away from what he'd felt under his boot. He stood up to let Cliff get a look.

"What the hell is that? Someone's Halloween costume?"

"I have no clue. It looks like something from science fiction," Wyatt said. "But it also looks kind of human." He pulled out a little flashlight and shined it into the missing eyeball socket.

"What do you see?"

"It looks like some sort of circuitry."

"Like a robot?"

"Maybe. This is very strange, whatever it is. Why bury it?"

"And I wonder what happened to the rest of it."

Wyatt stood up. "I already have too many mysteries I'm working on. I don't need another."

"What should we do with it?"

"Well, we can't leave it here. Let's put it in the trunk then drop it off for the lab guys to figure out. We need to focus on finding our missing college student."

Special Agents Wyatt Miller and Cliff Allen got out and walked up to the porch of the Beta Chi Gamma fraternity. They knocked, a frat member answered, and they flashed their badges.

"We are looking for a Cole Adams. We're with the FBI," said Miller.

"Come on in. He's on the second floor."

"Can you get him for us? We need to talk to him. It's important."

The guy trotted to the second floor. "Hey Cole, there's two guys from the FBI here. They want to talk to you."

Cole jumped up and hustled down the stairs, hoping for good news—they had found the bad guys, and Paige was okay and just a little shook up.

"I'm Cole Adams. Did you hear something about Paige?"

"I'm Special Agent Wyatt Miller, and this is my partner Cliff Allen." They shook hands. "We haven't heard anything yet, I'm sorry. We are doing the best we can with the lead you gave us. We need to ask you a few questions, okay?"

Cole led them to the living room. The agents plopped on the couch opposite Cole, who sat in a chair.

"Do you want me to be blunt or sugarcoat it?" Wyatt asked.

"I just want the truth."

"Well, the good news, if you want to call it that, is there's a good chance she's still alive."

"And the bad news?" Cole asked, nervous to hear the truth.

Wyatt shook his head. "Well, the best way I can say it is, there's a good chance you might never see her again."

"Why not? You have a picture of the kidnapper, the damn van they used, I mean come on. These guys probably have records." A pulse of anger pulsated in Cole's veins. "And you don't know Paige. She's a damn fighter."

"We didn't come here to get you upset, Cole. We understand what you are going through."

"Really? You don't understand. You're just doing your damn job."

"I don't want to sugarcoat it, Mr. Adams. Maybe she'll be one of the lucky ones."

He stared at them intensely. "I want you both to treat this like it was your own daughter."

"Believe me, we understand," Wyatt said with a slight smile. "But this isn't your typical kidnapping. They've done this before. They don't leave much of a trace—no fingerprints, they change vehicles, and they disappear until they do it again."

"How do you know all this?"

"Well, your girlfriend isn't the first one that this has happened to."

"She's more than a girlfriend. She's my fiancée."

"I'm sorry. Like I said, we are doing the best we can. The video of one of the kidnappers is big. If we can find him, it might just lead us to the rest of them."

"Why are they doing this?"

"Human trafficking," Cliff said.

"They pick their spots and do it in a systematic, disciplined way," Miller added. "Nothing is random; it's all thought out."

"They kidnap them and send them off to the highest bidder in some shithole in the world, and you guys can't figure it out. How long has this been going on around here?"

"A few years. We don't like to scare the public."

"Well, we need to find Paige."

"You gave us some good leads, but how did you get the video while this was going on?"

"I work with robotics and built a small drone with a video camera on it. I was talking to her when her car got hit from behind, and it spun out of control. The drone's camera picked up the kidnapper and the van. The damn thing got damage when the car spun out of control; otherwise, I could have tracked those sick bastards."

"Well, it's a big help. I wish we could tell you more. If you could forward us any good pictures of Paige, that would help. The more pictures we have, maybe someone will notice something and come forward." He handed his card to Cole. "Call me anytime. I know right now your heart is broken. We are going to try like hell to get her back, okay?"

"We are going to find her, Agent Miller. We are. She is not going to be a statistic."

Wyatt nodded. "If you don't mind, I'd like to show you something out in my trunk. Maybe you'll have a better idea what it is since you're a tech guy."

Cole followed the agents to their car. Wyatt opened the trunk and pushed aside the bag that covered the mystery object, revealing the face of a futuristic AI that Cole knew all too well.

"Where did you find it?"

"I walked out from the crime scene to gather my thoughts, and I needed a smoke. I felt something under my foot as I was putting out my cigarette, and I dug it up. So do you have any idea of what this thing is?"

Cole slowly shrugged. "I'm sorry, I don't. Maybe it's a kid's Halloween costume."

Cliff smirked. "That's what I said."

"I thought maybe it was an alien invasion," Wyatt says, covering it back up and shutting the trunk. "Thanks, Mr. Adams. We'll be in touch."

Two agents drove off, heading to the tavern to look at the security camera video.

"The kid thought it was a Halloween costume too," Cliff said with a chuckle.

"You missed it."

"Missed what?"

"He said: *Where did you find it?* He didn't say: *What is it?*"

Cliff tried to keep a straight face. "Is this another one of your conspiracies or something? Maybe he's one of them."

"You know, sometimes you're an idiot," Wyatt said amiably. "The kid and her family are hurting for sure. We got our work cut out for us. Let's find this girl."

Chapter 14

The FBI crime lab in Quantico, Virginia, called Agent Miller to say their recognition program had come up with a match for the image of Paige's abductor. It was their first big break in the string of random kidnappings. The suspect was a second-degree hoodlum named Andrew Murphy. Wyatt scanned the crime sheet of the thirty-nine-year-old white male that included aggravated assault, possession of a firearm, robbery, child pornography—and the list went on. He had been in and out of prison his whole life.

Wyatt and Cliff spent the next few weeks digging under every rock. They spent time at every known address Murphy had frequented. Family members were contacted; they hadn't seen him in years and wanted nothing to do with him. They rousted known associates Murphy had met during his various incarcerations to see if they might be harboring him. But after weeks of deep detective work, they'd come up empty. It was like he was a ghost and had just vanished.

Wyatt and Cliff had concluded that some criminal group had taken him under their wing, and he was keeping a low profile. But they knew at some point, people like Andrew Murphy screwed up. That was who they were.

Cole sat on his porch in a rocking chair. The summer was almost here. The cornstalks were getting taller. The insects were coming to life. The flowers were blooming. Yet he felt a deep void in his life. But life went on. It had been five weeks since Paige disappeared. In two weeks, he was scheduled to start his new job. He should have been excited, but he didn't care. He just went through the motions.

His grandfather sauntered over and sat down in a chair next to him. He packed his pipe and lit it, blowing a small ring of smoke.

"I love doing that," he muttered. "Okay, Cole, you can't mope your whole life away, you know that. I been watching you in this funk. It's not going to bring Paige back. I miss seeing her face around here too. You found a good woman, but you have to move forward, or it will eat you alive from the inside. There are people who love you here. You don't think it affects your father? Your mom is dying inside, not just that Paige is missing, but at what you are going through."

"Grandpa, you don't understand."

"I don't understand, huh? Being with your grandmother for fifty years and losing her hurts more than you know, even though I don't show it. What good would that do?"

"I didn't mean that you don't understand missing someone. I'm sorry. But you know what happened to Grandma."

His grandfather stared out at the cornfields like he was in a trance. "When I fought in World War II, I was in my late teens. One of my best buddies, Johnny Cook, died right in front of me. I've never forgotten it, never will. He was a good guy, never deserved to die out in a frigging trench in a snow-covered field in the dead of winter along the Gari River near Cassino, Italy. Johnny had a southern accent and was just a polite guy. He would have never hurt a soul. How many years ago was that, and yet he pops up in my mind a lot. You ask yourself why him and not me? He had this pretty girlfriend waiting for him back home. He would show me the pictures of her, and he was the proudest guy in the platoon. He only had a month to go and had his whole life ahead of him. He couldn't wait to get back home and see his girlfriend and just drive a truck. A plain old truck.

"In that moment we were just talking, cracking jokes, couldn't wait to get out of the cold and play a game of cards, light up a cigarette, and maybe find some whiskey. Just trying to get through the stress the best way we knew. Whiskey, a game of cards, and a little warmth—that's all we needed. Then a bullet pierced his stomach. I watched his life being sucked out of him in slow motion—the blood oozing out, lungs gasping for air, and then his face turning ash gray. He was gone, and all his dreams and his loves went with him. I cried like I never had before. Not a cry of pain, but a cry of loss, quite different. My life changed. From that time forward I was different. Anytime I had problems or got down, I would think of Johnny. It wasn't fair to Johnny and his family, just like it's not fair to Paige or her family or to you, but that's life. You have to move on, Cole. It's not just you; it's everybody connected to you. You can take my words and do whatever you want with them, but the losses add up as life goes on; it's just how you handle them. And it doesn't get any easier when you lose someone you've been with for fifty years, but Grandma would want me to live life."

He got up from his chair and walked inside.

Cole stepped off the porch. The temperature was close to seventy. The air was still. He wore a sweatshirt and jeans. He strolled over to the shed. He had almost avoided Robby, the machine from another world, ever since his class presentation, where it had become clear he had no real control over Robby.

Inside the shed he went over to the laptop and pressed a few keys. Robby opened his eyes. They stared at each other.

After a pause, Robby said in a soft human voice, "Cole, I can sense a deep sadness in you."

"How can you do that? You're a machine."

"You really don't know what I am, Cole."

"You got me there. The difference between you and me

is you think logically. I'm unpredictable. Something you wouldn't understand."

"Cole, I appreciate what you've done for me. I needed time to repair and recharge my system and to repair my synaptic connections. And you gave me that time. My neural network is now functioning at an optimum level. Other than some damage to some memory files, my systems are now close to a hundred percent."

"What does that mean?"

"I can't stay here."

"Where would you go?"

"There are a few like me here, but we need to find our way home. This isn't our world, but I'm afraid the technology has already been exploited."

"I don't know what to say."

"You don't have to say anything. I'm going to leave you with the schematics for creating a genetically engineered human like me.

"I don't want it."

"You're human; you'll want it. That's what humans do. They need to be recognized or grab power out of self-pity, jealousy, greed, or even curiosity. Humans can never get along for these reasons. We were initially created by humans, but they died out for all the reasons I mentioned. You'll colonize a planet and think it will be different, but you bring the same traits to wherever you go. In reality humans are flawed and predictable. So when AI become self-sufficient, why would they need humans?"

Cole's mind was running wild. He had opened Pandora's box. The whole time he had never controlled Robby. He didn't know if Robby was friend or foe, and if there were others, what damage could they cause? What if these AIs had been banned or exiled, and he had opened the door for them? He remembered his father's words: *You're only smart if you understand the consequences.*

Chapter 15

Two months later Cole was living outside of Indianapolis in a rented apartment with his buddies Josh and Rick. They carpooled to Round Robotics, which was a technological marvel. The company employees were mostly from the top schools in the nation, but Cole was a shining star among the intellects. He could apply algorithm programs to the real world and into practical, everyday use, something many of the smartest guys had a hard time doing.

Cole sat in his office, making entries into a computer. He stood up, looking out at the green landscape where the driverless vehicles were picking up and dropping off people. The place always had a stream of visitors, whether it was Wall Street bankers, salesmen, or characters who didn't say much and wore dark sunglasses as if they didn't want to be noticed.

His phone buzzed. It was his father.

"Hi, Dad; everything okay?" He listened. "I'll be there as soon as I can."

He put the phone down and sat in his high-back leather chair. He closed his eyes, recalling what his grandfather had said: *Losses add up as life goes on.*

There was a knock on the door, and Sid Martin walked in.

"Is this a bad time?"

"No. it's fine, Sid."

"I've been wanting to talk to you," he said, sitting down.

"Something wrong?"

"No, you've been doing a great job. You've picked up this stuff like you've been doing this all your life. You're showing up people who've been around a long time. In fact, I see a promotion in your future."

"I'm going to need a few days off. I just got the news my grandfather passed away."

"I'm sorry to hear that."

"He was a great guy. A book of knowledge. He actually lived, not like people today who sit in front of a computer screen and don't experience life. There's something to be said about being old school."

"Take as much time as you need. I'll make this quick. Bill McDonald wants to see your AI creation. I bragged about how I'd never seen anything like it, so he wants to see it."

Cole sat quietly. The last thing he wanted to do was bring Robby here. It was too risky, and there was no telling what he might do. He hated to lie, but …

"I'm sorry, Sid, but I don't have it anymore."

"Why not?"

"My brother was using the corn harvester and accidentally chewed it up. It was my fault; I shouldn't have left it around."

"That's unfortunate."

"Yeah."

"Well, then, I have a better idea. I want you to build another one. You'll have the full resources of the company. You can have your pal Josh work with you. I'm going to assign Cal Jensen to the project as well. You know him?"

"A little bit."

"He knows his way around here. He'll be a good resource."

Cole, still stunned by his grandfather's sudden death, was now facing an almost impossible task. He could never duplicate Robby no matter how hard he tried. He could pretend for a while, but eventually they would realize he was a fraud. Nobody could build something like Robby.

"What's the timetable?" Cole asked.

"A year. I'm putting my neck out for you, Cole, so don't let me down, okay?"

"Yeah."

"So why don't you get out of here and do what you have to do."

The funeral procession moved under an overcast sky. The gathering of people wearing suits and overcoats circled the priest as he sprinkled holy water on the coffin in preparation for the casket to be lowered. There were about one hundred people in attendance. Cole's father, standing alongside his brothers, was typically holding his emotions in, while his mother's eyes were red-rimmed from grief. Cole stood in silence as tears rolled down his cheeks. He wasn't crying just for his grandfather, who had lived a good life of ninety-seven years, but for Paige whose life had been stolen. He tried to dismiss the thought that she might not be alive; if she was alive, there was always hope she'd come home. Paige's parents had shown up at the funeral. He glanced over at them and wondered what was going through their minds.

After the service, family and friends headed back to the farmhouse for a celebration of life to recall memories of his grandfather. The bar was busy. The conversation nostalgic. And the overcast clouds had given way to sunshine as if his grandfather was saying: *Enjoy yourself; I'm okay.*

Cole's Uncle George came over. "How's the new job? I hear you're making big money."

"Yeah, Uncle George. It's going good."

"Have you gotten taller since the last time I've seen you?"

"I don't know. I think my feet are still growing."

They both looked down.

"I think you're right."

After an awkward silence, Cole said, "It's good seeing you, Uncle George. I promised someone a drink."

He stopped by the bar then marched out to the patio and found his brother, Ted.

"Here you go."

"Thanks, bro."

"I was talking to Uncle George; he asked if I'd gotten taller."

"He did the same with me." They both chuckled. "Did you see Paige's mom?"

"Yeah, she was sobbing."

Ted put his arm around Cole. "They're going to find her; you know that."

"I hope you're right."

Ted's phone buzzed. "My girlfriend is calling me. I'll talk to you later." He patted Cole's shoulder before walking away to take the call.

Cole moved over to Josh and Rick. "Thanks for coming."

"Your Grandfather was a funny guy," Josh said. "He was always good at catching us getting into mischief. Like the time we were going to build a fort in what we thought was the perfect place. He told us: *I wouldn't do that if I were you.* We didn't listen of course, and the next thing you know, we're running for our lives from a swarm of bees."

"I think I got stung like six times," Cole said. "Lucky I wasn't allergic. He walked by us and said: *I told you so* with that shitty smirk of his. But he believed the only way you learned was by screwing up."

"He had a point," Rick said.

"Hey, Sid said we were going to be working on a project together," Josh said to Cole. "That's awesome."

"No, it's not awesome."

"Why not?"

"He wants to see Robby. Or more precisely, Bill McDonald wants to see him."

"What's the problem?"

"Besides that I don't think I have control over him anymore?"

"Oh. What are we going to do?"

"I bought us some time by telling Sid that my brother accidentally mangled it with the corn harvester."

"That was good."

"But now he wants us to create the thing from scratch, and he assigned Cal Jensen to help us out."

"Well, Cal Jensen's pretty cool. He'll be fun to work with. But how are we going to create something as good as Robby."

"We're not. And when they figure out that there is no way we built that thing, it might be an issue. We are basically screwed."

"No, you're not," Rick said.

"Why are you saying that?"

"If you can hang on until the company goes public, everybody working there will be millionaires. Everybody in the accounting department has been talking about it, but you guys are going to get a lot more stock than us office guys."

Cole sat back in a chair, watching the cornstalks sway in the breeze. His mind recalled the night Paige was abducted, a mental video he had replayed a million times, and the abductor's face was sketched in his brain. He would never forget it.

His father sat down next to him and patted his knee.

"I haven't had much time to talk to you lately. How you doing? The job going well?"

"Yeah, they tell me I'm doing a great job."

"Where's that Cole enthusiasm?"

"Long day, Dad."

"I just wanted to say I'm proud of you. And Grandpa, he thought the world of you. He was really proud of you too.

Hell, he was always sticking up for you, especially when I was tough on you."

"I learned a lot from you, Dad."

"I hoped some of it would sink in," he smiled. "I invited Paige's parents back here. I was glad to see at least Bret came by and had a drink. I know Paige's mom has been having a hard time. How're you dealing with it? It's affected us all. Paige was like family to your mom and me."

"I have my good days and my bad days. But there is a big void in my life."

"Have you heard anything? I didn't want to ask Bret."

"They don't say much, Dad, because I don't think they've got a clue." Cole sipped his beer. "I miss the little things about her. Her ponytail, that smile, the look when she didn't agree with me."

"You two were meant to be. I knew with your mother when I saw her for the first time. She was such a warm soul. It took your mother a little bit longer to figure out I was the guy. But we both had the same interests, and we wanted to raise a family and be close to nature. There's something to be said about working with your hands. I don't know how you do it working with machines, the internet, dealing with social media—the whole cesspool of technology, in my opinion, sucks the human spirit out of people."

"I know I was lucky to grow up on a farm, have a great family, and still hang around with my childhood buddies."

"You are lucky, Cole. You have a good support system. Just remember we are here for you, okay?"

"Thanks. It's been a hard year."

"Life was meant to be hard; that's the only way you respect it and respect other people. I'm a rich guy. Not moneywise but your mom is my best friend, and I have a great family and many friends." He stood. "Let's go for a walk."

"Sure."

They walked in no hurry, talking about Grandpa and his outlook on life. Cole stopped when they came up to the shed.

"Dad, did Grandpa ever bring up any war stories?

"No. He never wanted to talk about it."

Cole thought how his grandfather had released one of his painful war memories just to prove a point. He opened the lock and pushed open the door, flipping on the light.

"Dad, I want to show you something."

"So, we got lights in here now?" his dad said, taking in his son's laboratory.

Cole walked over to the workbench, opened the laptop, then stared at the corner of the shed where Robby resided. Or used to reside. He was gone. Cole swiveled his head. The shed was empty.

"Something wrong?" his dad asked.

"No." Cole kept his voice steady.

"What did you want to show me?"

"Oh, I, uh, wanted to show you the lighting I put in. And we have heat in here now too."

"Well, that's good." His dad glanced at his watch. "We should head back. People are probably looking for us."

"Sure. I'll be right there, Dad. I just need to do something on my laptop."

"Okay. Don't be too long."

When his father left, Cole dropped into his chair. Robby was indeed gone. Where would it go and what sort of damage could an alien AI running amok in the general population that nobody knows about do. The GPS tracking device had been disabled, and then Cole found an unknown file recently created. It was Robby's parting gift, a file with AI setup instructions, material that more closely imitated biological bone and tissue, internally and externally, and the complete schematics of creating a new AI. He quickly browsed it then stared long at the delete key but couldn't push it.

Robby knew human traits all too well.

Chapter 16

Guards at the gated entrance of Round Robotics founder and CEO Luke Richards' estate checked each car as it entered. He was worth billions. He entertained the world's elite but kept a low profile. Few of the public had ever heard of him. He liked it that way. He had lost the marriage game three times, he liked the young ladies, even as his gray hair thinned and turned a pure white, and now pushing seventy, he had slowed down on the tennis court. He still thought he had more to do. While some billionaires like to flaunt their success or take interviews or see themselves on the nightly news or rub elbows with the Hollywood types, he avoided it. He still had big dreams, and to carry out those big dreams being obscure was imperative. The world was a dangerous place.

Cole drove up to the gate with Josh in the passenger seat and Rick in the backseat. The guards checked over their credentials, looked under the carriage of the truck with special equipment, and then let them pass.

"Look at this place; it's amazing. I can't believe we got invited."

"Sid said the CEO throws these big parties every once in a while, and you never know who you'll see," Cole said.

"As long as they have drinks and good food, we'll have a good time."

"I bet there will be some big Wall Street types here," Rick said. "You know, to hype up the IPO."

"That makes sense," Cole said.

"I just want to work on the first million," Josh said. "And that IPO is getting closer."

The truck rolled up to the circular driveway in front of the large mansion. Cole gave the keys to the valet parking attendant, and they walked up a long brick walkway to the main door, where an attendant in a black suit welcomed them in.

"Look at this place, man," Josh said, gazing at the open architecture and high ceilings.

A waitress walked by with a tray of hors d'oeuvres. Rick and Josh grabbed a few before they headed off to find a bar. They maneuvered around people as if they were lost kids trying to find their mom. They went outside. It was a warm summer night. Small lights lit up the landscaping. They found a bar by the pool and ordered drinks on the house, toasting to each other's success.

Cal came over and gestured at the identical blazers the three friends were wearing. "Look at the blue blazer boys, here," he teased.

"Yeah, we know, Cal," Josh said.

Cal laughed. "Bartender, can I get a shot of whiskey for my blue blazer buddies here."

The bartender poured a round of shots in front of them. They each downed them in one gulp and slammed the short glasses on the bar.

"So what do you think?" Cal asked.

"This place is unbelievable," Josh said. "Have you been here before?"

"Yeah, two years ago. Not as many people then. But this place is crazy tonight."

"The smell of money," Josh said.

"Oh, yeah; they all want a piece of that IPO. But wait until Sid sees our AI project. I think we'll all get a promotion."

"We need a few more tests, Cal."

"Of course, Cole."

"I'm going to take a walk," Cole said.

"Check out the talent," Cal said. "It's pretty impressive. And watch out for Carol; she's pretty horny."

The group laughed.

"They want to see how Carol's self-modifying code is working. If it's bringing in new data and learning new things. Nobody here even knows it's AI and not human. Check it out, Cole. I guarantee you'll see guys trying to pick her up. It's a riot."

"Yeah, I'll check it out, Cal."

Back inside a band played, and people danced to the beat. The waiters lined buffet tables with steaks, chicken, lobster, fish, and all sorts of sautéed vegetables. The dessert table was piled with pastries of all shapes and sizes.

To Cole it all seemed too good to be true. A bunch of country boys were living the dream. And shortly they were going to be multimillionaires. What could go wrong? He scanned the room, filled with people he didn't know. The men wore fine suits. The ladies wore beautiful dresses. He had never seen so many good-looking couples. These types of people were attracted to the money. They were shallow in so many ways. They smiled like they cared, but in reality, they all were looking for a piece of the next great company.

Cal was right. There were guys trying to pickup AI-Carol, secretary by day, hooker by night. He worked with this stuff all day. What was common now to him would be downright scary to the outside public. He slithered through the crowd then paused when he heard someone call his name.

He glanced around and saw William McDonald, the head scientist, standing by the stairs with another man.

"Hey, Cole!" McDonald called again, waving at him.

He was surprised the scientist—who was more like a mad scientist type—remembered his name. Cole walked over. It was obvious the man had drunk a few too many.

"Hi, Mr. McDonald."

"I was just talking about you with Sid. He tells me you

got a big surprise for us. I'm looking forward to it. I've been busy, but I'm going to turn my attention to your project. I've noticed your budget has been getting bigger and bigger. Cal tells me it's all worth the money."

"Okay."

"Let me introduce you to my friend here. This is Chip Butler; he's a big shot with the defense industry. A highly paid consultant. Hard guy to track down."

Chip shook Cole's hand. "Hey, Bill, I'm going to borrow your star player."

"Okay, but don't put any bad ideas into the kid's head."

"Why do you think I would do that?"

"Because I know you."

Chip chuckled and led Cole away. "Bill doesn't get out much, and then he drinks too much. I hear you're very good at robotics."

"I don't know about that."

"Don't undersell yourself."

They went outside to the pool bar, where a few people were mingling.

"Why don't you have a shot of Jack Daniels with me," Chip said.

"Sure. Why not. So what do you do exactly?"

"I'm the guy who makes the decision if your company gets a $4 billion military contract. And with your IPO coming out soon, it's a big deal. So they wine and dine me. They take good care of me."

He packed his pipe with some loose tobacco, took a few puffs, and then downed the shot of Jack Daniels.

"Now that hit the spot. You're fairly new to the industry. You're green. You're good. You have no idea what Round Robotics is all about. I would tell you to trust your instincts. You might need them."

"What does that mean?"

"I'm not going to get into that here. You have to be careful what you say. There's a few AI's running around here. Bartenders are fairly easy to duplicate with Round's technology. The algorithms are pretty simple. They just have to make drinks. You look surprised."

Cole was openly skeptical. "So, you're telling me the guy behind the bar is AI?"

Chip smirked. "Well, if I'm right, you'll meet me for breakfast on Sunday. If I'm wrong, I'll give you a $100 bill. Fair enough? Let me order another Jack Daniels."

He pulled out a small object from his pocket.

"What's that?"

"It emits a highpitched sound, basically like a dog whistle. It's my AI finder. Watch; this is so much fun." He waved over the bartender. "I'll take a shot of Jack Daniels, and my friend here will have one as well."

The bartender filled the short glasses at the back counter and then walked over with the shots in each hand. Chip pressed the button on his device. The bartender's eyes rolled for a second, its body shook as if it was having a seizure, and the shot glasses dropped.

"I'm sorry, sir."

"Don't worry about it," Chip said with a chuckle.

"I'll get you two more shots."

"Okay, I believe you." Cole smiled as the AI walked away.

"Some people are going to like what's being billed as a new utopia," Chip said. "Yet it's going to be more a world of dystopia because the AIs are flawed."

Just as the bartender was about to place the two new shots on the bar, Chip pressed the button, and again the AI shook and dropped the glasses.

"I'm sorry, sir. I'll get you two more."

"You do that," he said, then turned back to Cole. "We could do this all night or at least until they run out of Jack Daniels, but that would be a waste."

"You proved your point."

The AI returned with two shots and placed them on the bar.

"Thank you. So, as we create these AI machines, they'll

have weaknesses just like humans. But they'll be different weaknesses. Sarin gas will do a number on humans, but AI will be immune. But aim an electromagnetic pulse at them, and it would be fatal. Today you can't tell the difference between real news and fake news. Now we are going to add another layer of who's human and who's AI. Of course we are going to have a database of everybody's DNA down the road, so I'm sure we'll eventually figure out how to identify AI. But right now, it's the Wild West."

"Maybe you should patent your device."

"It's nothing new. Ultrasonic technology was invented in 1893—give or take—old technology defeating new technology. Funny how that works."

Cole wondered if maybe this was some sort of loyalty test since Chip knew the big shots in the company.

"So do you know everybody here?"

"I've worked in the industry a long time. I know Bill from Stanford. I did four years in Vietnam. I've worked for NASA, defense companies, and I'm a consultant for the DOD."

"You've done a lot."

Chip pointed. "You see those guys over there by the cabana."

"Those two guys with the two women?"

"Yeah. That's Senator Brock and Senator Johnson. There are a few more politicians running around here. They make sure they take care of those guys for legislation purposes. Then there are some big CEOs here as well. You see the guy that just joined them? That's Forbes Shannon, a Wall Street tycoon. That guy off to the side not too far from the senators is FBI Director, Mark Rogers. There's a lot of heavy hitters here, tonight. All of them getting ready for the big IPO. That's how capitalism works for *them*, but they sell a whole different set of bullshit to the masses."

Chip put his device back in his pocket.

"Depending on market conditions, the IPO's opening stock price is probably going to be $50 on the first day.

You're lucky, Cole; you'll get them for pennies on the dollar and be a wealthy guy. But once these outsiders accept the shares, which is going to be hard not to accept, they'll be in the company's pocket. They need to keep their mistresses happy or finance their kids' college educations or even make their wives happy. And they'll never want anybody to know where they got the money. You ever wonder how politicians come to Washington basically broke and leave wealthy? Shit like this is just one example. Anyway, I need to mingle with your CEO. I like to keep him waiting."

"Thanks for the insight."

"Since you lost the bet, I'll see you Sunday at Rosebud Diner in Thorntown. It's about twenty minutes from here. I'll be there around eight o'clock. I have a plane to catch in the afternoon." He wrote down the information on the back of a card. "You'll like the food. I'll see you then."

Chip walked away, and Cole just stared at the AI bartender. The world was about to change. He wondered why Chip had such an interest in him. And what was his company hiding?

Rosebud Diner was busy on Sunday morning. Waitresses ran around jotting down orders and filling cups of coffee. The cooks took the orders and moved around the eggs, pancakes, and home fries on the hot grill. The diner had old-fashioned swivel stools at the front counter, and the booths were lined up adjacent to the windows.

Chip sat in a booth, sipping coffee while looking out the window. He watched as a pickup truck rolled to a stop at the curb. Cole jumped out, and as he entered the Rosebud Diner, Chip waved him over.

"I'm glad you could make it."

"I had my reservations," he said, picking up a menu.

An attractive waitress with blonde hair came over. "Can I get you something?" she asked with a smile.

"I'll take a coffee."

She filled up his cup and took their orders. Chip requested his usual—pancakes, home fries, and scrambled eggs. Cole asked for blueberry pancakes. The waitress took the orders and grabbed the menus and walked off.

"So, did you have a good time the other night?" Chip asked.

"Yeah. We didn't get out of there until 3:00 a.m. The place was wild."

"I can imagine. I leave those parties before it gets too crazy."

Cole looked around. "How did you find this place?"

"I just came across it while driving by one day. The people are friendly, the service is great, and the waitresses are easy on the eyes. It's just simple and away from the rat race. You know what I mean?"

"Yeah, I do."

"When you get to be my age, you find yourself looking back. When you're young, you look ahead. It's funny how that works. So, I'm sure you are wondering why I wanted to talk to you."

"I'm curious why you're singling me out, especially since I know nothing about you."

"There's nothing I'm going to say that will make you feel comfortable. You are just going to have to trust me." He reached into his wallet and pulled out a Department of Defense ID badge.

Cole studied it then handed it back. "Again, this means nothing to me. What are you looking for from me?"

"First, I don't give a shit about Round Robotics or the DOD for that matter. I've made my money. But back about fourteen years ago on a farm in Indiana, a bunch of kids were playing and stumbled across an alien spacecraft. Ring any bells?"

Cole stared at Chip. "What else do you know about that?"

"The spacecraft that was found on your father's farm had a trove of alien technology. Seven years ago in Area 51, a rogue individual downloaded that technology, uploaded a malicious malware virus into the servers, and then shot all the people working on the project. Then to make sure the job was complete, set off a bomb. Whoever wanted that technology made sure that there was no trail and sure didn't want anybody else to have it. I was part of that project. I had some good friends who worked in that lab."

"So why aren't you dead?" Cole asked.

"Nobody knew about my involvement. I worked off-site, so all my information and files were off-site too. Whoever orchestrated this would have surely killed me had they known. It was an inside job at a very high level."

"What did you do with the files?"

"I kept them. I've never told anyone except you. I've been working with this technology for thirteen years ever since I was assigned to that project. While everybody is figuring out how to create these things, I've been working on how to destroy them."

"So you think Round Robotics stole the technology."

"Not exactly. A couple of years ago when I saw this technology in action, I knew they had acquired it from someone or were part of the plan. If you follow the money, it gets very complicated who is behind Round Robotics. Now they're getting ready to cash out and get very rich. Did you ever wonder what a company like this is doing out here and not part of Silicon Valley? They are out here to be low-key and to have extreme security. I believe they have an off-site. They have a restricted area, as you know, just for certain employees, where they work on the top-secret technology. The gadgets and technology you see, as impressive as it is, is nothing compared to what they are working on from that alien technology. The AI behind the curtains are part human, part bioengineered life-forms with self-modifying code—you could say consciousness. They have the ability to work without human intervention, a scary thought. Yet, you don't look surprised."

Cole said nothing, unwilling to admit what he knew to be true.

"Sid is very high on you," Chip said. "He loves talking about the amazing AI you created for a college presentation. Said he'd never seen anything like it. Then it was ruined in a farm accident, but you were in the process of building another one. He tells me you're a savant with robotics."

"I don't consider myself that." Cole still wasn't sure where this conversation was going. He felt uncomfortable waiting for the punchline. "Chip, just get to the point."

The waitress brought their plates, and Chip waited until she walked away.

"Okay, you found one of these things, didn't you?"

"No."

"That's okay, Cole. You don't have to tell me, but you weren't shocked by AI having self-modifying code. It's an interesting thing about humans; they just look at the upside, not the downside. When NASA sends out a probe looking for life, it's always under the assumption that it's good for mankind, when in reality maybe there's something lurking out there that's evil, like a spider waiting for its prey. This alien technology is unknown. Once the genie is out of the bottle, there's no putting it back."

Cole couldn't tell him that there was an AI on the lose or that he just happened to get a step-by-step instruction manual from one of them. "What do you want from me?"

"Anybody ever mention Charlie Nash?"

"No, never heard of the name."

"Well, he was about your age. A savant in robotics, a real star. He worked at Round in the high-security area with the advanced AI technology. I met him once at one of Round's special presentations to a select few. It was pretty amazing stuff. Around two years ago Charlie went out drinking after work and never came home."

"What do you mean?"

"I mean, he's presumed dead. What's interesting is that a week before going missing, he had given his notice."

"Maybe it's just a coincidence."

"No, it's not. I'm going to tell you something; nobody leaves that company when they work in Round's high-secu-rity area. Something spooked him. That's why I need you. I need someone on the inside. My real goal is to find out who the puppet master is."

"You might not like what you find."

"You're right. I might not like what I find. You're going to get promoted to the next level at Round very soon."

"So, I might end up like Charlie Nash."

"No. We won't be in contact unless you have something."

His father's words rang in Cole's head: *Think it through.*
"I can't do it, Chip. It sounds too dangerous. I'm sorry. I just
want to create robotics. I'm not there to get into the politics
of what is right or wrong or what happened to Charlie Nash.
You'll just have to find someone else."

He finished his pancake and coffee, stood up, and threw
a ten-dollar bill on the table. "It was nice meeting you, Chip.
And I'm sorry about Charlie."

As Cole turned to leave, Chip said, "Andrew Murphy."

Cole stopped. "Who's that?"

"Andrew Murphy is one of the guys who kidnapped
your fiancée."

Cole slid back in the booth. "How do you know that?"

"I just do. And I can find him."

"What makes you think you can find him better than
the FBI when they haven't even gotten close."

"Look, the guy obviously has an alias, but the people
I work with don't use the same tactics as the FBI; they're
a little heartless. I have a private investigator looking for
him as we speak. Everybody has a price, Cole. Yours isn't
money. It's love. But I can call off the private investigator if
you want."

Cole shook his head. "You might be the devil."

"I'm not the enemy, but to get the job done, you use all
the tools available, and in your case, you care more about
Paige Turner than your own well-being."

Chip pulled out his phone and placed it on the table. "It's
your choice, Cole.

Cole's eyes narrowed. "You're a bastard."

"We got a deal?"

"Yeah."

"Good. If you come across something, call this number."

"What am I going to come across?"

"You're a smart guy; you'll know it when you see it."
He pushed a card toward Cole. "Use a landline. If you're in
trouble of any sort, call the number from anywhere. Use

the word *purple*. We can track your location. I can have people in place quickly. This is where we'll meet when I'm in town."

Cole took the card. "I was just so excited to work on robotics, and now I find myself in some J.P. Farrell novel."

"I don't know the author."

"Maybe you should read his novels; you'd probably identify with a character or two."

He laughed. "At least you got a sense of humor, Cole."

"Sure, why not. I'll be doing all the heavy lifting on the inside with my life on the line."

"Limit your internet use, and don't say much on your phone calls. Since we really don't know the enemy."

"That just gives me a warm and fuzzy feeling, Chip."

"The government has an intelligence community cloud that allows government analysts to connect the dots across all available data sources, whether classified or not. And since we're not sure who the bad guys or good guys are, we have to be careful." He stuck his hand out. "I'll find Paige."

Cole hesitated then shook it, got up, and walked out.

Chapter 18

S enator Joe Brock sipped a gin and tonic at a popular bar in downtown Washington, DC. He flirted with two young ladies and feeling generous, announced the next round of drinks was on him. The flamboyant senator schmoozed with the patrons. He laughed and cracked jokes. He didn't have to worry about driving tonight; he was staying just a block down the street. His animal spirits were high, which usually got him in trouble. He had just recently won another senate term and had six years of clear sailing. He had been on his best behavior for far too long, but tonight he could feel the pull of the dark side.

A man wearing a cap pulled up a stool beside him. Senator Brock turned.

"You need a drink. It's on me."

"Thanks for the drink, Senator."

"You know me? Who are you?"

"I'm just the messenger. Your friends wanted you to know the time is here, Senator. They'll be in contact sooner than later."

"My friends, huh? Is that what they said?"

"I was told to tell you that. You would know what it meant. I don't know anything other than that."

"These people don't own me. You can tell them that."

"Thanks for the drink." The man downed his shot and walked away.

The senator's smile turned to a frown. He stopped talking and ordered a shot of whiskey to dull the pain and remembered his last conversation with Shannon Forbes many years ago. He had thought that maybe they would forget.

A couple of weeks later, Senator Brock was given instructions to drive alone to a small town called Floyd, Virginia, tucked away in the Blue Ridge Mountains. The road turned from gravel to tar as a large cabin became visible in the distance. He came to a gate where security checked his ID and scanned him. This wasn't typical security.

The cabin was out in no man's land yet appeared to have all the bells and whistles of a five-star resort. Brock had no idea what these people were going to present him. They just said it was a private showing. He'd begun to regret taking the money, the favors, and the donations for his elections. He always raised more money than his challenger, and the media always played him up as a great politician who cared about the people, yet he was anything but. He was a womanizer, had received secret payments in a Cayman Island account, always got special favors whenever he picked up the phone. He was owned by a group of people that cared about nothing but the agenda they had set in motion years ago. He was just one piece of a puzzle and was too far in to turn back.

Brock got out of the car and was greeted by Forbes Shannon.

"Senator, how've you been?" He shook his hand hard. "Nice election."

They walked up the stairs to the large, wraparound porch circling the cabin and went to the back that had a magnificent view of the lake.

"What do you think of this place?" Forbes asked.

"The cabin is beautiful."

"You want something to drink?"

"Sure, I'll have a beer. Is anybody else coming?"

"You're the first one," Forbes called from the kitchen. He came back and handed Brock a beer. "We'll be eating soon. I think you'll like the menu. Make yourself comfortable."

The senator sat in a chair overlooking the lake, the evening sun glistering off the lake. He wondered what a cabin was doing in the middle of nowhere in a rural area of southern Virginia, with a security team watching the perimeter. It was very strange. He sipped his bottle then looked at his phone.

"I have no phone service, and why the heavy security?"

"Well, we're out in the boondocks, Joe, and you can never be too careful."

"I guess that makes sense. How's the investment world?"

"Making money, Joe. I'm looking forward to that Round Robotics IPO. It's going to make a ton of money for a lot of people, yourself included."

"Yeah."

A short, well-dressed man with pure white hair stepped out on to the deck. Forbes got up. "Hey, Joe; this is Luke Richards, CEO of Round Robotics."

"I haven't lost my mind yet, Forbes," Luke said. "I know the senator."

Brock shook his hand. "We just talked a few weeks ago at his party. And it was a great party at that."

Another man come onto the deck with a beer in his hand. Luke introduced him to Brock. "I'd like you to meet Round Robotics' chief scientist, William McDonald. He's one smart guy and makes everything go."

"Nice to meet you, Bill," Brock said.

A few more people arrived, and they all mingled. Senator Brock was talking to Forbes when he noticed the familiar face of Senator Johnson walk up.

"Ben, what the hell you doing here? You didn't tell me you were coming."

"You didn't tell me either, Joe."

"Hey, let me introduce you. Ben, this is Forbes Shannon. He's a financier from New York. Forbes, Senator Johnson."

They shook hands.

"You're probably wondering why we wanted you out here, Senator Johnson," Forbes said.

"I think I have a good idea."

"We're looking for good candidates like you who are interested in running for president in the next election, Senator Johnson," Luke said.

Brock knew from previous conversations that they had targeted Johnson to run for president. They had requested background information that Brock had provided. He wasn't sure what they were up to now. Maybe they wanted to make sure there was nothing to derail the senator's candidacy.

"I been thinking about it seriously lately," Johnson said. "I'm leaning toward running."

"That's good news," Luke said. "I'll leave you alone for now; enjoy yourself. We'll talk later."

Brock was surprised at Johnson's interest. He'd never talked about it. Maybe this was a recent change of mind.

They went into the cabin, and a buffet of steak, chicken, swordfish, and assorted vegetables was lined up on a table. They helped themselves. The senators took their plates of food and fresh beers back out to the deck and ate while watching the sun descend, coloring the sky with a radiating orange hue.

After eating, Brock got up and retrieved two fresh beers then leaned on the deck railing to admire the lake view. Johnson joined him.

"I'd rather be fishing, Ben, than being here with these guys. They have no personality."

"You're right about that. Look at that lake below; we could be reeling them in."

They chatted as the sun set, and the orange hue vanished. They drank a few more beers before Forbes finally called everyone into the living room, which was complemented by recessed lighting, ample green plants, leather furniture, and large oval windows that overlooked the lake. The group settled into their seats, except for Johnson, who excused himself to the bathroom.

Luke Richards sat in a high-backed leather chair with Bill McDonald to the right and Forbes Shannon to the left, opposite Brock. Luke leaned forward, putting his drink down on a coffee table.

"It's time to talk business, Joe," Luke said.

"Shouldn't we wait for Ben?"

"We can start without him. Let me ask you something. Do you think Senator Johnson can win the next election?"

"I don't know. Why not?"

"You're right; why not? They tell me you did a good job of getting all the background information on Ben that we needed."

Joe frowned. "Do you want Ben to hear that?"

"Speak of the devil."

Johnson sat down in a chair next to Brock's.

"We were just talking about you," Luke said.

"You were? I hope it was all good."

"You're amazing, Senator. You really are a science marvel. The thought of you winning the presidency is remarkable. Joe, a lot of research went into finding the perfect candidate, and you have been a terrific help. You know Senator Johnson better than anyone. You've been friends since childhood. If anybody is going to figure it out, it'll be you, Joe."

"What are you talking about?"

Brock glanced over at Johnson, who had closed his eyes. Probably too many beers, he thought.

"Hey, Ben; you okay?"

He tapped Johnson's shoulder, but there was no response. Brock stood up.

"I think there's something wrong with Ben. We need to call a doctor."

The others in the room just stared. Nobody moved, as if they were members of a cult.

"He's fine, Joe," Luke said.

"No, he's not. What's wrong with you people?"

The others smiled.

"Joe, he's not real in the flesh-and-blood sense," Luke explained.

"What are you talking about?"

"You remember our little conversation at George York Steakhouse a few years ago. I said we had a big technology breakthrough, and I was going to give you a special showing. I know you are a little confused at the moment. Take a moment to let it sink in."

Joe slumped in his chair as the reality of the presentation hit him. He ran out to the deck and threw up. After a few minutes, he composed himself and walked back in.

"Feeling better?" Luke asked. "I know it's a little shocking. This was our final test, and it was a great success. If his childhood friend can't tell the difference, I think we are set to go."

The group nodded in agreement. Joe was afraid to voice the question he already knew the answer to.

"But after hundreds of millions of dollars and years of research, we've created an AI humanoid that can function exactly like a person," Luke continued.

"I need a shot of ... something."

Brock went over to the liquor table, his hand shaking while pouring whiskey into a shot glass. Many in the room seemed amused by his reaction.

"It's okay," Luke said softly. "You should need a drink. Very few people know how far we've come along in AI development. You're getting a front-row seat because you're part of the team."

Joe drank his shot then poured himself a second. "Are you thinking of replacing Senator Johnson?"

"It's okay, Joe. After a while not even you will know the difference," Luke assured him. "I'm sure you have some questions, but first let me introduce you to the team. You've already met Bill over here; he'll only get involved if we have a serious problem. Forbes has been the money guy. Gary and Lance over there are the programmers who will monitor and fix any hiccups. Mal here will be your contact if you have any concerns. And Henry's our security guy, right, Henry?"

"Yes, sir."

Henry sat with his muscled arms crossed over a barrel chest, staring at Brock with piercing eyes.

Luke leaned closer to Brock. "He really is a crazy bastard, Joe."

"So you really think you can replace Ben with ... this thing?" Brock asked. His family will know. His wife will know."

"You didn't know, and his family isn't going to know either," Luke snapped. "We've put a lot of money and years of planning into this."

"Why bring me into this?"

"To be blunt, you're a functional drunk. Politicians like you are always looking for the money, the booze, and the women. Once you bit the apple, we owned you—unless you want to go to prison or end up six feet under along with your family. Also, you were perfect because of your childhood connection to the Senator. You could give us data that nobody else could. And since your wives are best friends, any concerns Mrs. Johnson might have with him, she'll share with your wife, who in turn will tell you. You see how that works? We can then fix that concern. Perfect."

Joe leaned back in his chair, wishing he could wake up from this nightmare, but it was now his reality.

"What about the real Ben?"

"He'll be fine," Luke promised. "We'll take good care of him in a nice place. We might need some information on the fly, whatever. And it will ensure that you take good care of our AI friend. Think of it as an insurance policy."

"How long are we talking?"

"I don't know, ten years."

"Ten years!"

"Do you want the alternative?"

Brock sagged back into his chair. "No."

"We're going to take good care of you financially. All you have to do is be yourself. I don't think that's too much to ask. Now, let me give you a couple of ground rules. Like I said, Mal is your contact for any concerns. We are all one big circle, and if someone falls out of the circle, it won't be pretty. You don't want me to get Henry involved. He's very loyal to the cause. He will have no problem killing you or your family. And if our AI friend gets found out, we will have no use for the real Senator Johnson. Do you understand?"

"Yeah. When is this all going to happen?"

"We'll let you know. We need to work out a few final kinks."

"How will I know when it's done?"

"Because you'll be there. You have a cabin somewhere in Bridgton, Maine, off the beaten path where you like to go fishing. Tell him you need to get away. Tell him you need to talk to him about some personal stuff, whatever it takes for the two of you to go to Maine. We'll make the switch there."

"Just like that."

"Yes, just like that. And nobody will know the difference."

"What's the purpose of all this?"

"The purpose of all this is to win the White House. It's the first phase of the plan."

"What's the second?"

Luke leaned forward. "This planet is not going to last forever. We are slowly using up our resources. We've discovered a planet just like Earth. And we have developed the technology to get there. Controlling the White House will make it easier for us to get there when the time comes."

Brock stared at Luke, who sounded like a mad scientist from some science fiction novel.

"If it makes you feel any better, Joe, what you're really doing is for the good of mankind, not the other way around. The colonization of our civilization. In simple terms, we are doing exactly what Christopher Columbus did in 1492, setting sail for a new world."

Brock stared at Luke, hating him almost as much as he hated himself. "Yeah, I feel so much better now."

Chapter 19

The sun slowly rose over the treetops as Cole entered the Round Robotics facility. The one constant, no matter what time of day he entered the building, was Henry, the company's head of security. His dead eyes watched everything. He never smiled, never talked, just stared at you with bad intentions. The security robots were less threatening, roaming the facility day and night.

Today was no different. Henry was leaning against a desk, tapping his fingers against the wood, staring with those cold eyes. He never took his eyes off Cole as he walked down the long corridor to a makeshift office at the far end of the building. The facial recognition scanner opened the door to Lab 4, enabling Cole to escape Henry's scrutiny.

Cal had secured this area of the building with Sid's permission, and they had worked in secret there for the last year. With each passing month Sid put increasing pressure on them to have a final product. Cal had squeezed more time from Sid, but the prototype failures had piled up. They were now working on the fifth prototype. Cal was able to supply the exact materials that Robby had instructed, right down to the unique chemistry of biological bone and tissue that resembled human properties. It was almost like cheating science by jumping two hundred years into the future. Cal and Josh were amazed at the unique properties Cole had instructed them to put together. Little did they know it wasn't his instructions but an alien AI's from a distant world.

112

They had created a human shell from an advanced version of 3D printing technology. It was surrounded by a circular, tall glass enclosure. The AI appeared as a lifeless mannequin at the moment. The AI neural network normally would consist of a framework for many different machine-learning algorithms to work together and process complex data inputs, but this was more biological.

He used the gene editor system CRISPER, just as Robby had instructed to arrange the DNA of the stem cells. He looked at his lifeless mannequin as one big Petri dish of cells, nerve fibers, and blood. Throw in an artificial heart, and somehow this was going to come to life with a flick of a switch. His first four efforts at building an artificial human from scratch had failed.

They had contacted a lab to supply them with stem cells, but in this current attempt Cole had used Paige's stem cells. He could hear his father's voice warning: *Think out the consequences.* But a deeper thought played in his head; he missed Paige.

Years ago, Paige had told him that her parents had saved her umbilical cord stem cells and stored them at a facility. Once he got the courage up to ask her father, he kept it simple.

"Mr. Turner, I need a few of Paige's stem cells that you have in storage for an important, top-secret project I am working on."

Her father had stared at Cole intensely, then agreed. Just like that.

Robby had detailed how stem cells could create an entire neural network, from the head right down to the toes. It was an amazing process of seeing the accelerated regrowth of axons, which conveyed information to other neurons via a regenerative electrical signal. But it was tricky. Just like trying to light a fire in your fireplace; it either caught and blazed or fizzled out. So far his attempts had fizzled. He hoped Paige's stem cells would blaze.

In the privacy of the lab, he studied the nerve growth.

He found the process of creating an artificial human being outside the womb strange. The AI's internal systems were regenerating at a fast rate, and every day there was something new. The artificial heart was pumping blood through its veins, and brain fibers were growing at an astonishing rate. They had never gotten past this point before. Schwann cells were appearing and wrapping around nerve fiber, forming the myelin sheath. He felt like that young scientist who was creating Frankenstein in an unorthodox scientific experiment.

Cal walked in sipping a coffee. "How is our mannequin doing today? We can't have another failure. I haven't shown Sid the budget yet. I'm actually afraid; we've spent a ton of money on failure so far. He's going to shut off the spigot if we don't show some progress."

"I haven't seen him around lately. What's going on?"

"He has some health issues he's been dealing with. He gave me an open checkbook for our little project here, but we have to show something, or I'm sure Bill will get involved."

"I haven't seen him around either."

"I know; he's been tied up with something lately and doesn't have the time to focus on us. Good news for us. We are basically on our own."

"Take a look at this morning's scans."

Cal looked over the images. "Are you shitting me? The nerve fibers are propagating like gangbusters. The stem cells are going crazy."

"I know. This is the furthest we have ever gone. Did you see the Schwann cells are creating the myelin sheath?"

"It's amazing. Cole, you got a gift. We are building an artificial frigging human. Forget about artificial intelligence; you are using some gene-editing system for God's sake. I hope you know what you are doing."

"To tell you the truth, I'm not sure of anything." All Cole knew was what Robby had instructed; the fear was what he didn't know.

Cal's phone buzzed. "Speak of the devil." He answered. "Yes? ... Okay, I'll tell him."

"Who was that?"

"That was the big guy, Bill McDonald. He wants you to work with Mitch today in the high-security area."

"Who's Mitch?"

"He's a grouchy old-timer until you get to know him. He's been here from the beginning and stays to himself."

"Why now?"

"Your guess is as good as mine. Maybe McDonald has big plans for you. Don't worry, Cole. Josh and I will take care of things around here while you're gone."

"I don't even have clearance to go there."

"The systems people will get you clearance. I think there are different levels. Bill said that Mitch would meet you at the front desk and take you in from there."

Cole walked to the front desk. "You must be Mitch."

"And you must be Cole."

Mitch looked like the typical scientist—scrubby beard, disheveled, gray hair out of place, glasses, white lab coat, and not much of an apparent personality.

"Why do you need me?"

"I'm busy," he snarled. "I threatened to quit if I didn't get some help. So they gave me you. It's probably a waste of time. You won't understand anything; you'll probably be a pain in the ass asking questions. I'll tell you right now: I don't have time to train you. So you better pick it up quick."

Cole just rolled his eyes.

When they arrived at level one, Mitch said, "Stick your face in the camera's perimeter. I'm sure the system people screwed that up. It probably will deny you access."

It worked, and the corridor door opened.

"Lucky you, Cole. The systems people did screw up;

they gave you full access. Though I don't have time to get it corrected."

They strolled down a long corridor and came to a room on the right. The security system scanned their faces, and the lab door unlocked.

"Don't get too caught up in the technology, Cole. We have work to do."

Mitch ranted about the chores of the day, pushing his hair back. He looked like a mad scientist. Cole realized nobody could stand working for him, so he got stuck with the short straw.

Cole gazed at four AI humanoids lined up against the wall in plastic. Almost as if they were ready to be delivered to a client.

"What's the story with those four AI against the wall."

"I told you, don't ask questions."

"I'm just curious. Are they finished? What do they do?"

He ignored his questions. "You see this AI right here? Hook it up to the computer. The programming is off. See if you can find the errors."

Cole analyzed the AI in front of him. It had a synthetic skull, and the skin was made of biological material. The internals were nothing like what he was working on. This was more machine. The components consisted of sensors, wires, and metal. It was hard-coded for specific tasks, but as he went through the algorithms, he stumbled upon a more sinister plan—buried code not part of the standard algorithms that he needed a password to access.

The question was why. What was the purpose of buried code unless it was a key to someone unleashing it from a remote computer? These humanoids would appear as one thing but could be accessed to do something else. The average person would never know.

"Hey, Mitch. I think I know what is wrong with this thing."

He walked over. "Let's see if you know what you are talking about."

"I corrected some of the errors in the algorithms. It should work now."

"Well, let's see." Mitch turned it on.

"Hello, Mitch," the AI said in a robotic voice. "What happened to me?"

"Cole here fixed you. You had some programming bugs." Mitch went through a series of tests. It could understand simple commands and respond to set questions in simple sentences. To the average person this would be amazing; to Cole it was now basic.

"Good job, Cole," Mitch said. "I got a few more of these things you can look at. You familiar with emotion detection technology?"

"Yeah."

"Then you know emotion detection technology requires two techniques," Mitch stated, "computer vision to precisely identify facial expressions, and machine-learning algorithms to analyze and interpret the emotional content of those facial features. I want you to take a look at the labeled data set of human emotions and then train the algorithm. Can you do that?"

"Sure," Cole said, staring at a large computer screen with a multiple of human facial expressions. "This stuff is cute, but where's the real AI? And I noticed there's buried code in this thing."

"You ask too many questions. If you want to survive here, you'll just keep your mouth shut. No more questions."

And as Mitch walked away, Cole blurted, "Did you know Charlie Nash?"

He stopped and retraced his tracks and put on a machine that made a humming noise. "They hear everything. They see everything. You understand?" he asked with a stern look. "I have six frigging months left in this place, and then I'm going to retire. I'm going to cash in my chips, and every day is going to be Saturday."

Cole could see he had hit a nerve when it came to Charlie Nash. Mitch was scared to discuss anything about him. "Did you know him?"

"You are persistent. Yeah, I worked with him until he got promoted, and McDonald took him under his wing. Just like he's preparing to do with you."

"What do you mean?"

"It broke my heart what happened to him. He was really a smart kid, asked a lot of questions, just like you. He was living life. He got promoted. He was all excited. They offered him more money. He worked with stuff he couldn't talk about, and I could see in his eyes that he didn't like what he was working on. But once Bill gets hold of you, they own you. I'm going to tell you something; once you work at the next level, nobody ever leaves the company."

"They can't keep you here."

"I'm telling you; nobody leaves. They make you sign some crazy document, and once you accept the money, that's it. My advice to you is turn down Bill's offer. My guess, Sid's been protecting you."

Cole's mind was replaying what Chip told him; Charlie had given his notice, and a week later he was missing. "I'm working on a project for Sid."

"You think you are, but you're not." Mitch leaned in. "They're grooming you for the next level—self-modifying code. AI without the instructions. I usually keep to myself. I'm a single guy. I've lived in the same house my whole life. I took care of my mother until she passed away. I have a couple of dogs. I don't get involved with the politics around here. But Charlie got me to go with him a few times after work for a drink. He was funny. He told people I was his father or in some cases his wingman. All the girls thought it was cute. I think he enjoyed the women a lot more than the coding, and he was damn good at that. He told me things, and I'm never repeating them again."

"So you think it wasn't a coincidence that Charlie is missing?"

"No more questions, Cole. Let's get to work."

Chapter 20

Cole spent the morning hours translating facial expressions to corresponding emotions. The idea was for AI to have the ability to tap into our visceral, subconscious, moment-by-moment responses. Before he started robotic testing, he asked Mitch where the bathrooms were.

"Down the hall. And stick to the bathroom."

Slowly walking toward the bathroom, people in white coats and a security robot moved up and down the hall. He passed some labs and wondered what was in them. Curiosity began to tug at his soul. He saw a couple of people exit one of the labs, and something about it caught his eye. He stopped to tie his shoe, and when they turned the corner, he peered in the lab window, and the door unlatched.

He had Mitch in his head, warning him to mind his own business along with Chip's words to find the truth. He walked in the empty lab, studying the room like a law student getting ready for the bar. The room was full of empty glass enclosures with nothing in them. It was eerie. But the people he'd seen in the corridor were working on something. He could sense it.

He heard voices out in the corridor. They were coming back. He hid behind one of the glass enclosures, crouched low, and watched. Two wore white lab technician coats, and one was dressed in a suit. He had never seen them before. One of the technicians pushed a button, and the floor

119

opened, a cylindrical glass canister emerging from below. Dry ice vapor filled the cylinder. Once opened the vapor disappeared, and Cole could see that inside the cylinder was a six-foot, perfect-looking AI humanoid. The lab guy pushed another button, and the AI rotated slowly. The guy in the suit studied the AI looking for imperfections while referring to scans.

"I want a full test of every system," the suit said.

"We've run the two tests you requested. Everything checked out."

"I don't care. Run them again."

"It's a waste of time, Mal. Everything checks out."

"I'll decide what's a waste of time. It has to be perfect; you got that? The cosmetic updates look good. We have a couple of more weeks, so let's get this right. I want Bill to be here for the final testing and his sign off."

"Sure."

Cole stared at the AI and focused on its face. He had seen this face before, but he couldn't place it. The tech pushed a button, and the AI descended back down. Cole crouched as low as he could go as the three men exited the lab, flipping off the light. Cole's heart was racing. He had to get out of there before they came back. He slipped back out into the corridor, his full bladder forgotten. He returned to Mitch's lab and walked in quietly.

"Does it take twenty minutes to go to the bathroom?" Mitch asked.

"I went to the café and grabbed something to eat."

"I hope so."

Cole sat down and began testing the AI. He pushed the computer screen in front of the humanoid. "What type of facial expression do you see?"

The humanoid responded. "Fear."

Cole shook his head. "It's a happy face. I need to look at the emotion detection database. Something is missing."

"Your facial expressions show fear," the humanoid said.

"Mine?"

"Yes. I recognize your facial expression, body language, and voice inflection."

Cole closed his eyes. Chip was right; they had opened Pandora's box, and the world would never be the same.

It was 6:30 in the evening when Cole finished up with Mitch. It had been a long day. He exited the high-security area and walked into Lab 4, where his AI masterpiece was still in place.

Cal was just cleaning up and getting ready to head home. "How was your day with good old Mitch?"

"It wasn't too bad. He's really not that bad of a guy. He told me about Charlie Nash."

"That was sad," Cal said. "Charlie was one wild and fun guy. He always bought drinks for everyone. He knew code better than anyone in the company, but he liked the women and to party."

"That's what Mitch said."

"Well, anyway, I've got to go. You staying?"

"Yeah. I'm going to run some tests."

"Okay. Josh stepped out to get something to eat but said he would be back."

Cole settled in the quiet lab. He was tired but wanted to get his AI up and running. He thought about what he'd seen earlier and wondered what they were trying to do with that hidden AI humanoid? Was there really a dark plan like Chip said he was trying to uncover, with him just a pawn to expose it?

He sat at the computer and hooked up the female creation sitting before him, who looked asleep. He scanned the neural system. It was intact. Neurons were establishing electrical connections. The heart was in low mode state, and the artificial blood type O was mixing with actual blood being made by living cells, circulating at a steady pace. The stem cells had broken into new cell types.

The nervous system had wired itself through the entire structure.

Cole leaned back in his chair. Robby had given him the AI blueprint, and he'd been able to use today's technology to build it. He thought of his grandfather and decided to call it Rose to reflect a flower.

Cole pulled the laptop closer and adjusted the heartbeat to a higher mode. He didn't know what to expect. The veins started pulsating, and the bio-engineered skin turned natural. The cheeks turned rosy. It was breathing. The body started shaking then its eyelids popped open. Startled, Cole pushed back on his chair. Rose looked around as if confused, like someone waking abruptly from a deep nap and trying to organize their thoughts.

Cole was at a loss for words. He had tinkered with the fabric of life, applying alien technology to create the unknown. Once again his father's words of wisdom played in his head: *understand the consequences*. But there was no turning back now.

Rose looked straight at him. Cole froze as if confronting a bear, not knowing if it would accept him or attack him.

"I'm Cole," he said slowly. "We call you Rose."

She paused, trying to digest the words, then smiled. "Where am I?"

It hit him hard. He stared at her, those blue eyes, the hair, the freckles he never noticed. Even the voice was similar. A tear rolled down his cheek. He had played God, creating a duplicate of Paige. Then she said something he never expected.

"Are you okay? Why are you so sad? Is it something I did?"

She seemed so human, able to understand emotion. He didn't have to run tests. She was passing them.

"It's nothing. You're beautiful."

"You mean pretty."

"Yes."

"Why am I pretty?"

"That's a good question. Beauty in many ways is shallow unless you have a kind heart."

"Do I have a kind heart?"

Cole didn't know how to answer the question. This whole experience was surreal.

"A kind heart is somebody that has empathy for other people and tries not to hurt other people's feelings."

"Feelings?" she repeated with a confused look.

"Feelings are emotional states or reactions, something you'll learn over time."

"When you had a tear rolling down your cheek, that was an emotion."

"Yes."

"How can I make you happy?"

"You have to make yourself happy. Nobody can make you happy. I'm going to work with you. You'll understand over time." It was like dealing with someone who was rehabbing from a brain injury and had lost all sense of who they were.

"I'm confused."

"That should be expected. It will be hard at first, but you'll adapt over time."

Just then Josh walked in and stood at the glass entrance. "Oh, my God. She looks just like Paige."

"Who's Paige?" Rose asked.

"Just somebody we know."

"Josh, you need to be careful what you say," Cole said.

"Okay, I know."

"Is Josh angry?" Rose asked.

"No. He's just being—oh, forget it."

"What am I being, Cole?"

"Can I talk to you outside, Josh?"

They stepped out of the glass enclosure.

"What?"

"We have to be good examples here. Rose is confused, and this is her first introduction to the world."

"Rose?"

"Yeah, like the flower."

"This is crazy, Cole. What does this mean?"

"Let's shut Rose down for the night and go out for a drink. I think we both need one."

"Good idea."

They went to a local tavern not far from their apartment. It was 9:00 p.m. They swung onto the bar stools and ordered a couple of cold ones. At first Cole just stared ahead, not really paying attention to the sporting event on TV.

"Did we break any laws here?" Josh asked.

"We've probably broken every law on the books, but Round Robotics has already beaten us to it."

"You realize you created a clone of Paige, don't you?"

"Yeah, and it was a big mistake. I don't know what I was thinking. I miss Paige, but I didn't think it would be like this. It's very real now."

"Yeah, it's frigging real. Do you think that Round is going to let you keep Rose? It's not a dog that you can take home. Did you think about that?"

"I guess we are taking opposite roles tonight. Usually I'm the voice of reason. I like it better when you don't give a shit."

"I give a shit. Once they get hold of Rose, who the hell knows what they'll do with her. It's not going to be hugs and kisses."

"I get it." Cole ordered two whiskey shots from the bartender. "There's something I haven't told you."

"I don't like the sound of that."

"I told you that Robby flew the coop."

Josh shrugged. "We got an alien AI running around the countryside. What sort of trouble could he get in?"

"I don't want to think about that right now. Robby left instructions how to build one of these things."

"You used them?"

"Sid put pressure on us to create what he saw in our college presentation. What other choice did we have?"

Josh shook his head. "I should have known. The shit you were coming up with. We've built a genetically engineered humanoid from scratch. Maybe they'll be impressed, and we'll get a raise."

"I don't think so."

The bartender poured the shots. Cole and Josh immediately knocked them back.

Cole chased the shot with a long swallow of beer. "That feels good."

"It only dulls the pain temporarily," Josh said.

"When I was working with Mitch in the high-security area, for some reason I had full access to the place. I was on my way to the bathroom and saw some guys leaving one of the labs. Something looked amiss, so I waited until they walked away then looked into the lab."

"What did you see?"

"Well, the lab door opened up, so I walked in. There wasn't much to see which seemed really strange, just empty glass enclosures. Then I heard voices outside the lab door and hid."

"What the hell were you doing, Cole? You could have gotten fired."

"Only if they'd caught me. They pressed a button, and an AI emerged from the floor in a glass enclosure. And I recognized its face. I'm telling you I've seen it before."

"They probably just copied someone."

"No. Just the way the man in the suit was dictating to the two lab techs, this was a big deal."

"What are you thinking?"

"I don't know. My first thought was they're going to replace someone."

Josh laughed. "Come on, Cole. You've been watching too many sci-fi movies."

"Nobody would have known our little friend Robby was AI, would they?"

"Okay, you got a point there."

"There's something else."

"Hey bartender," Josh threw a twenty-dollar bill on the counter. "Two more."

The bartender said, "I'm going to run out of whiskey."

He placed two more shots in front of them, which were quickly downed.

"Before we were hired," Cole said, "there was this guy Charlie Nash who was our age and worked in the high-security area. Mitch tells me that nobody ever leaves once they're in high security. Then he tells me about Charlie Nash giving his two-week notice, and a week later he disappears. Nobody has seen him since."

"You think Round Robotics put a hit on him? Or Crazy Eyes Henry took care of him?"

"I don't know what to think, but I'm telling you something shady is going on in there."

"I don't care. All we have to do is hang on for that IPO. And then we can sell lemonade for a living. Or better yet we can go off to the islands and sip umbrella drinks for the rest of our lives."

"I don't know, Josh. I feel like we're way in over our heads. They're going to wonder how the hell we created Rose. I think it's a bad thing."

Cole decided against telling Josh about Chip. It was better he didn't know. But Cole was sure he had good reason to be afraid.

"Stop being a detective; just go with the flow. You're probably blowing this thing way out of proportion."

"Maybe you're right, Josh. Let's have one more drink before we leave. Hey, bartender …"

Chapter 21

On a beautiful summer day in the Hamptons, Senator Joe Brock and his family piled into the SUV and drove over to Senator Ben Johnson's cookout. It was an annual gathering with family, friends, and neighbors. They had the pool, the outdoor bouncy house, the grills, the basketball court, even a volleyball net, and plenty of drinks, food, and beer to go around.

The two senators grilled chicken, hot dogs, and hamburgers and passed them out on a first-come, first-served basis.

"You couldn't have picked a better day, Ben."

"Yeah, we lucked out this year."

The two wives walked over.

"So how are the cooks doing?" Hannah Johnson asked.

"We are doing great, honey," Ben said. "We haven't had any complaints."

"When it comes to grilling, you got the best team right here," Joe said.

They pounded fists.

"We'll leave you two alone to concentrate on the food," Anna Brock said.

"We can talk and cook at the same time," Ben said with a chuckle.

"Yeah, and we can drink a few beers as well," Joe said. "You need another one, Ben?"

"Sure."

"Here you go." Joe handed Ben a beer. "After we eat let's pick sides and play a little hoop."

"Let's keep the same teams as last year. I want revenge from losing."

"Okay. You're on."

As the cookout continued into the evening, the sun descended below the treetops. The number of guests had thinned out. Joe sat on a patio couch watching the flames from the open fire pit.

He thought about what he had gotten himself into. It was just supposed to be general opposition research and a deep dive into his friend's background. He had been paid well, introduced to beautiful women, entertained with booze, and all-inclusive paid resorts. Reality had hit home when Luke called him a functional drunk. They used his weaknesses to turn him into the perfect setup man. Now he couldn't turn back; these people would kill him without a blink of an eye. They owned him.

He watched the embers in the open pit flicker, thinking they were all dust in the wind. He had been envious of Ben's life. He had married the perfect woman, the woman he'd wanted. But everybody loved Ben. They all respected him, while Joe's own family felt distant. He felt like he was on an island, and yet he had brought most of it onto himself. That's what functional drunks do.

Joe replayed his past, growing up in a dysfunctional family. The chaos of his family's dynamics. His own father was a drunk. His parents finally divorced when he was a young teenager. He used sports as a crutch, taking out all his frustration on opponents. He excelled at that. He swore he would never be like his father, but sometimes life has a way of sucking you in, the same gene pool, the same stories, the same stresses and pressures, trying to live up to something you're not and hoping nobody ever finds out, except one day it all comes crashing down. He pushed away a tear. Big Senator Brock was just a fraud. He had played in a game he thought he had control over. But in reality that wasn't the case.

He looked around at all the people laughing and joking. Were they really happy? Was it a front? Were they hiding secrets? He had manipulated his way through life, always looking for instant gratification, forgetting what was really important. But karma has a way of turning against you. He was manipulated by bigger manipulators; he shook his head at that thought. They kept luring him with bigger riches, and they knew more about him than he knew about himself, but now it was all crashing in on him.

He tried to justify the evil plot against someone he'd known his whole life and was a good friend. When Joe's parents were going through a divorce, Ben was the one guy who didn't judge him. He was there any time he had a problem, yet he was about to betray him. Again.

Ben came outside and sat next to Joe. "You look like you have the weight of the world on you. You're showing your age."

"Except on the court today."

"Okay, you got me there. Next year same teams."

"You never give up, do you?"

"Neither do you. Remember that high school lacrosse championship game against Saint Mary's when we were down by two goals with four minutes left and you announced to the whole team: *We're going to win this frigging game; we are not going to lose.*"

"That was a great moment."

"You were like a madman. You scored two goals in three minutes to tie the game. Then with thirty seconds left, you zig-zagged down the sideline and got open for the winning shot and put it home with four seconds left. It was unbelievable."

"Well, who passed me the ball."

"Okay, I did."

They both smiled wide.

"Hey, you want to go up to my cabin in Bridgton, Maine, in a few weeks and go fishing?" Joe asked. "Just the two of us."

"No kids, no wives?"

"Yeah. Just like old times. I need a break from the world."

"Me too. You know what, let's do it. I'm sure Hannah won't mind me getting away for a few days."

Chapter 22

Cole spent the next few weeks working with Rose, who became more and more human-like. She'd started off childlike—shy, timid, confused, overwhelmed by a new world. As the days passed her knowledge expanded, she was growing mentally at a fast pace, asking questions, excited by the unknown yet hesitant at times.

Cole, Josh, and Cal had decided they would keep their extraordinary project to themselves for the time being. Sid had been out of the office, and Bill McDonald had been mostly absent, and when he was in the facility, his mind was preoccupied with some other pressing issue, leaving them alone.

They were amazed how fast Rose was learning. She was already fluent in three languages. A computer chip in her brain allowed her an instant connection to Wi-Fi. She had the ability to Google any information she needed immediately. As much as she was a genetically engineered human, she was also machine, and the more experiments they ran on her, the more surprises they got.

The humanoid Rose stood tall as Cole and Josh did a computer analysis on her reflexes and body movements. Cole stared at the computer and studied Rose. She looked like Paige, five-seven, slim figure, blue eyes, dark hair, and freckles on her nose. Yet if someone was doing an experiment, they would realize early on what makes someone different is who they are on the inside; that piece of the equation was missing from their almost perfect creation. She was still learning the world, and her first exposure was Cal, Josh, and Cole.

The day was ending. Cal had left. Josh had stepped out. Cole was finishing up in the lab in the ten-by-ten glass enclosure.

"Cole, why do I look like your fiancée, Paige Turner?"

He was taken back. "Where did you get that?"

"I heard Josh say it. He also put a mirror in front of me so I could see what I look like. Then I looked up Paige Turner on the internet and saw a picture of her and read that bad people took her away."

Rose was interpreting and dissecting information in a way he never expected. "Yeah, you're right. Maybe it's too early to expose you to the world."

"You, Josh, and Cal are good people, right?"

"Yeah, we are good people."

"What about the people outside?"

"Not everybody is good. You'll have to figure that out for yourself."

"Why did you create me to look like Paige? And who created you?"

Cole leaned back in his chair. "They're not easy questions or easy answers."

"Your memory doesn't let you recall these facts?"

"I'm sorry. Maybe we should call it quits today."

"What did you like about Paige?"

He sighed. "Her sense of humor, the faces she made, the way she said something."

"Did you love her?"

"Yes."

She had turned the conversation around as if she was a therapist. She was inquisitive as if searching for a purpose. He could see that he'd created something without knowing the true ramifications.

"What is love?" Rose asked.

Cole shrugged. "It's a feeling between two people, an

emotion, the faces someone makes, a sense of humor, two people seeing the world in the same light, I guess. I'm not an expert, Rose. I'm probably the wrong person to ask that question."

"What is a sense of humor?"

Cole gave her a wry smile. "I can't win," he muttered. "It's what you find funny. Or your reaction."

Rose made a funny face. "Like this?"

Cole chuckled. "Yeah, something like that." For a moment it was easy to imagine he was talking to Paige. It was time to go.

"I feel sadness from you because you loved Paige," Rose said with sad eyes.

"It's alright."

"Why is my name Rose?"

"I wanted to name you after a beautiful flower."

Her eyes rolled as she scanned the internet. "Yes, it is beautiful, but it has prickly thorns."

"It's probably a good analogy of the bad and good of life."

"What is my purpose?"

Cole was caught off guard with that one. He liked talking to her and exposing her to the good of mankind, but he had no control over what would happen when Round took control of her. Would they make her into some military machine or use her for covert CIA operations?

"We'll talk some other time, okay? I have to go."

He shut her down.

Chapter 23

It was nine a.m. on a beautiful summer day and not a cloud in the sky when Cole's car rolled to a stop in the mostly empty Round Robotics parking lot. Even security seemed absent. No sight of Crazy Eyes Henry, which was unusual.

Maybe the guy actually took days off, Cole thought.

He hurried into the building; Josh was already there. After the lobby security scans cleared him, he stepped on the escalator heading to the second-floor offices. He'd gotten a text to go see Cal when he got in.

Cal's office was larger than Cole's, with a nice view of the parking lot and an adjacent conference room.

"Hey, Cole; you're running late today," Cal said.

"Well, it's Friday. Where is everyone today?"

"I don't know. The big guys are off-site, probably planning to take over the world," he quipped. "A lot of people took today off. Even Crazy Eyes was nowhere to be found."

"That was the first thing I noticed. So where is this offsite?"

"I don't know. Even Sid doesn't know. Let's go in the conference room. I want to do some field testing today with Rose."

Josh was already in the conference room, sipping on a coffee. "It's about time, Cole."

After they got settled in their seats, AI Carol walked in, dressed in a skimpy red dress. She sat next to Cole with her legs crossed and pressed close, stroking his hair.

"Hey, Cole; I've been thinking about you, and I really want you."

Cole pulled away. "Okay, guys, very funny."

Josh and Cal broke out laughing. "We reprogramed her while Sid is out. We changed her from an obedient secretary to basically a hooker."

"You guys are unbelievable."

"I would have done it to Josh," Cal said. "Except he probably would have taken her to the back room."

"Hey," Josh complained. "I got morals. I would have taken her home."

They all laughed.

"Okay, enough with the fun and games," Cal said. "So, Josh and I think it's a great day to do a little field testing."

"What do you mean by that?"

"To bring Rose out into the real world."

"You're kidding, right?"

"I think it's pertinent how Rose performs out in the real world. It needs to learn how to interact socially, recognize human body language and voice inflection, and respond appropriately. I know that look," Cal said. "What are you worried about?"

"The unknown."

"Josh, you're on board, right?"

"Yeah. I'm curious how Rose will do. And she needs to start somewhere, Cole. We can only do so much in a controlled environment."

"Valid point, but what if something goes wrong?"

"Nothing is going to go wrong. I'm going to take Rose, while you and Josh stay back here. You'll have complete control over her and can shut her down anytime. It will be a good test, something I can go back to Sid with. You good?"

"She'll be like a lost kid out there," Cole said. "I just

don't like what I don't know. And nobody has signed off on this. We could get in trouble."

"That's what you're worried about? Sid's not here. And Bill isn't here. In fact, it's a perfect day to do it. Isn't it our job to field test this shit?"

"This is so much different than regular work."

"No, it's not; this is our job. The problem is you've gotten attached to Rose. I think we all have, but eventually they are going to take Rose away. That's reality, but we can prepare her for the real world, okay?"

"You're the boss. But you know nothing can leave the facility, Cal."

"Come on, Cole. God knows what the hell they do in the secured area here and the off-site area. They probably have these things running around already. It will go smoothly. Stop worrying. Nobody will find out."

"Right, what could possibly go wrong?" Cole said under his breath.

Rose stepped out of the lab for the first time with Josh next to her. She looked around as if she was a traveler lost in a city. When they went up the escalator, she held on as if she were on a rollercoaster. She adjusted her footing as she stepped off the escalator then marched down the hallway to Cal's office.

She smiled. "Good morning Cal and Cole."

"She greeted us with a smile," Cal said. "That's a good response."

Rose walked over to the windows and stared inquisitively out at the world for the first time. Cole came to stand next to her. "See the flowers below and the trees further out?"

She smiled. "It's so beautiful."

"Yeah. I brought you something." He pulled out a rose and showed it to her.

"A rose."

"Yes, the real thing. Don't touch below. Those are the thorns."

Cal stood. "Rose, you're going to see the world today!"

She turned. "Where are we going?"

"To the city."

"A city is a large human settlement."

"Yes."

"Okay. When do we leave?"

"When we get you all dolled up."

"What does that mean?"

"Make you pretty."

"Are Josh and Cole coming too?"

"No, they are going to stay here."

"I wish they would come."

"Well, they are going to monitor you from here. We're going to introduce you to people and see how you react."

"Are they good people?"

"I hope so."

"Cole, I will use my sense of humor so they like me."

He smiled. "Rose, you'll do fine."

She winked at Cole as she walked out with Cal.

Chapter 24

C al drove while Rose sat in the passenger seat, staring out the window in awe. She wore a pretty black dress with her hair tied in a ponytail. They got past security with ease then drove to Indianapolis. Josh and Cole could see everything Rose could see through a visual function inside her eyes. They also had the ability to interject conversation through algorithms designed to override brain functions and, if needed, put her in a sleep mode that was the machine part; the human side was the wild card.

"Josh, we'll need to watch her social reactions to human interaction and monitor how she responds, and then we can go over it with her afterward."

"You're worried because you've gotten too attached to her."

"Maybe."

Cal found a parking spot in downtown Indianapolis, put on a baseball cap, then took Rose for a walk down the streets. The first thing Cal noticed was the men gazing at Rose as they passed by. That wasn't a surprise. Rose hardly noticed, oblivious to her womanly power. She just gazed at her surroundings, taking it all in.

Cal called the lab. "You guys capturing all this?"

They had him on speakerphone. "Yes."

"I'm going to take her into the Wilbur Hotel then stand a distance away and see how she reacts."

"Why leave her alone?" Cole asked.

"We need to see how she reacts on her own. Rose will be fine."

They walked through the vast Wilbur Hotel. The place was busier than Grand Central Station. Cal stayed in the lobby and sent Rose into the bar. Josh and Cole monitored the surroundings. Rose fit right in; little did anyone know she was a genetically-engineered marvel.

Rose took a seat at a table and people-watched.

"I feel like I'm fishing," Josh said. "What guy is going to take the bait?"

It wasn't long before a young man stopped at the table. "Can I buy you a drink?"

Rose smiled. "You're handsome."

He smiled wide. "You're very attractive yourself."

"Thank you."

"What do you drink?"

"I don't know."

"You look like the Cosmo type of girl."

"I guess."

"I'll be right back." The man went over to the bar and talked to another man leaning against the counter.

Rose watched the two men. Cole blurted, "Josh, there's something about these two men. They are up to no good."

Josh focused in. "I think you're right. He just put something into her drink. Did you see that?"

Cole nodded. "I did."

"What happens if she drinks it? Will it affect her in the same way as a human."

"I don't know."

"Where's Cal? I can't get ahold of him."

The man came back with two drinks. He sat close to Rose. "You know, I book girls for modeling. You would be great, and it pays really well."

"A model? You mean a replica or a duplicate? I'm already that."

"You're a model?"

"Yes."

"You look awfully familiar. Do you have a twin or something?"

"I don't think so, but I do look like Paige Turner."

Cole looked closer at the man across from her then searched through some files. Paige's kidnapper popped up. "Is that the same guy?"

Josh looked. "Holy shit; it sure looks like him!"

"He's the guy! Where the hell did Cal go?"

The man stood up and went back to the bar where his partner was leaning. They had a small discussion. The other man made a phone call on his way back to the table.

"Drink up," he said, sitting back down.

Cole thought the man seemed uneasy and got the impression his associate at the bar was directing the action. He also noticed a third man in a suit sitting at a back table closely observing the interaction between Rose and her suitor.

"I need Rose to stall this guy and have her slip out," Cole said. "Then I can call the cops."

Josh put his hands up. "Whoa, wait a minute. Have you considered what could happen if the police somehow figured out Rose isn't what they think? There could be all sorts of ramifications."

"You might be right about that, but I don't care about all the bullshit. I just care about finding out where Paige is."

"You ever think that maybe Paige is dead?"

"No, I don't think that, Josh."

Cole's tone had Josh apologizing. "I'm sorry; I shouldn't have said that."

Cole watched Rose and the man stand. "Where they going? It looks like they are going back to his room."

Through Rose's eyes they watched the elevator stop at the third floor and the door open. As they stepped out, the screen went blank.

"What the hell? Josh, override her system!" Cole shouted.

Josh sounded panicked. "It's not working."

The speakerphone beeped. Cole slammed his hand on the answer button.

"Cal, where the hell have you been?"

"I stepped out. I figured you guys had a handle on this."

"The GPS is down. She's on the third floor somewhere. Somehow her visual shut off. We're blind. No audio either."

"What do you want me to do? Pound on every door?"

"If you have to," Cole said.

"Okay, I'm going up there. I'll check rooms and see if I hear anything."

Cal got off the elevator and put his ear to each door. He looked up and saw Rose down the hall, moving toward him. The man who had bought her a drink came out of a room behind her, staggering. Cal hurried to meet her and took her to the elevator. He looked back and saw the man collapse. He told Cole and Josh he was leaving in the elevator with Rose.

When Cal got back to Round Robotics, he took Rose back to the lab and put her in sleep mode then went to the second floor where Cole and Josh were waiting in the conference room. Cal walked in looking disheveled, wiping sweat from his forehead. He sat opposite them in the conference room.

He took off his baseball cap. "Do you think I'm stupid, Cole? That all this shit you've come up with just came out of that intelligent head of yours? I don't give a shit where you got your blueprint for Rose, but she is light years ahead of anything that has been developed, except for what's in that high-security area, where they have the same damn blueprint."

Cal was usually cool under pressure. They had never seen him so rattled.

Cole just stared at Cal. "What happened on the third floor over there?"

"Not good."

"What's that mean?" Josh asked.

"Not good," he repeated. "The guy she was with could be dead for all I know. He staggered out of the room and collapsed. Let me just think about this, okay?"

"What did Rose say happened?" Cole asked.

"That they were on the bed and she asked him why he kidnapped Paige Turner. I guess the guy didn't like the question, and he took out a knife. She said it reminded her of the thorns on the rose. The thorns are bad and can hurt you. The man with the knife was a bad man. So she responded correctly in self-preservation. She kicked him, and he fell off the bed then she ran to the door. Another successful test flight. Apparently, he fell on the knife when she kicked him off the bed. Karma, right? You live by the sword you die by the sword."

"Unbelievable," Cole muttered.

"If this guy dies, regardless whether he's a bad actor and got what was coming, the Feds are probably going to get involved. The good news is she doesn't exist. No fingerprints and any DNA would lead to Paige Turner, which would confuse the hell out of them. I wore a baseball cap, so hopefully there's no good image of me. If there is a good shot of me, that could be a problem. But I think the police will figure Rose is a hooker, so they won't be looking in the right places. If anything leads here, we would lose our jobs, be blackballed in the industry. Or worse, we might just disappear."

"What do you mean disappear?" Josh asked.

"Whatever they're doing here, they'll protect it any way they can. And we'll be collateral damage. We are in a very difficult position. I don't want to end up like Charlie Nash, and that's where we have to be on the same page. We can't tell anyone about this, not even your buddy, Rick. Nobody. We have to take this to the grave; our lives might just depend on it."

Cole leaned back in his chair. Cal was right; whatever the company was hiding in the secured area would be protected at any cost. As would the upcoming IPO worth billions. It was time to set up a meeting with Chip.

Chapter 25

A fter a good night's sleep in a quiet cabin in Bridgton, Maine, at the first sign of dawn, Joe and Ben carried their fishing rods down a long, narrow stairwell braced by an iron railing to the dock below. They settled into a motorboat, then Joe started the outboard and steered through the morning mist, accelerating out toward the open water. The water was crystal clear, and the propeller blades created a wake of waves.

They found a quiet spot in the midst of lily pads on the other side of the lake. The fish were jumping once the sun had burned off the morning clouds. They cast out their lines, and it wasn't long before they had their first catch of the day. After a couple of hours, the bass piled up in the bucket.

"It looks like we have enough for a good dinner," Ben said.

Joe nodded. "I think this has been our finest hour of fishing ever."

"Damn, we are good. We still got it. I know you kept score."

"No."

"I know you, Joe. Who caught the most fish? Come on."

"Okay, if you need to know, I edged you out by one— four to three."

"But I caught the biggest ones," Ben bragged. "I won based on total weight."

"Is that a new rule now?"

"Hey, a good politician knows when they can't win by the rules, change the rules to fit the narrative."

They both laughed.

"I'm just pulling your leg, Joe. A bet is a bet. So it looks like I'm gutting and cooking the fish tonight." Ben turned serious. "Hey, are you okay? Lately you've seemed to have a lot on your mind. You and Anna doing okay?"

"We're fine, I guess. Other than she thinks I have a drinking problem and every now and then she thinks I'm having an affair."

"She might have a point about the drinking."

"I'm fine, Ben. Really. Have I ever missed a roll call?"

"Well, that's true. And there's not another woman?"

"Did Anna put you up to this?"

"No, I just care. And I've noticed a difference in you lately."

"I'm the same guy I've always been; I look, but I don't touch the merchandise," Joe lied. "Yeah, maybe I drink a little bit more than I should, but it helps me reduce the stress."

"If you ever want to talk, I'm here. We all deal with shit, Joe."

"Yes, we do." The boat had drifted. "Maybe it's time to head for home."

"Okay." Ben pointed. "Hey, look at the bald eagle up there."

"That is an awesome sight." Joe pulled on the cord and started the motor.

"Yeah. Hey, did I ever tell you about the weird thing that happened to me at the dentist years ago?"

"No."

"I had a wisdom tooth extracted, and afterward a man came in and stole the tooth. Pretty weird, huh?"

"You know wisdom teeth have stem cells in them."

"I didn't know that."

"Yeah, so there's probably a clone of you out there now."

Ben cracked a smile. "Well, two of me is better than one."

Ben didn't know how close he was to the truth, Joe thought.

The two senators sat in deck chairs overlooking the lake and spent the afternoon having a few drinks and chatting about their lives and the political theater back in Washington, DC.

"What do you think, time to cook up the fish?" Ben suggested.

"Sure. I'm going to take the boat and get some more beer."

"By the time you get back. The fish will be ready."

"Okay."

Joe took the long walk of shame down the stairs to the dock then hopped into the boat and headed to the other side of the lake to find a package store. He stopped the boat, leaned over the side, and heaved his guts. He didn't feel any better. He felt like a traitor. He had betrayed their friendship, their families, himself, and his country. Joe realized the last ounce of goodness he'd held onto was now gone. He didn't know how he was going to get through this lie.

After buying the beer, Joe went back across the lake to his dock. When he got out carrying the case of beer, he was greeted by a smiling Mal, who held his hand out. Joe shook it, feeling like he had sold his soul to the devil.

"Hey, don't look so grim, Senator. It went without a hitch. Ben is waiting for you with some freshly-cooked bass waiting for you."

"You guys are frigging assholes," Joe said.

"Well, you bought into this a long time ago. So go greet your new Ben, but Luke wants to talk to you first."

Luke emerged from the stairwell with Henry in the shadows.

"I didn't think an old bastard like you could still climb down this many stairs," Joe said.

"I'm full of surprises. Let's take a walk," Luke said, waving off Henry and Mal.

They walked along the shore, which was lined with cabins and summer homes set back in the woods.

"So how're you doing?"

"How do you think I'm doing?" Joe asked.

"I understand this is tough. I do have a heart, you know."

He smirked. "Yeah."

"Look, just be yourself. That's all you have to do. Don't change your routine. And do the same things as you always would with Ben. That is very important. Ben has to feel like you're his best friend."

"You got to be kidding me."

"Do I look like I'm kidding? We've spent hundreds of millions of dollars preparing for this day. The word *fail* is not in this project for all our sakes. If you fuck this up in any way, if you go to the authorities, I'll have Henry wipe out your entire family right in front of you. Do you understand?"

"Yes," Joe said quietly.

"Do you have any more questions?"

"What about the real Ben?"

"He'll be fine and treated well. It will be like living in a five-star hotel—unless you screw this up. Then we'll have no use for him. Your career, your life, your family, and Ben all depend on you."

"I get it."

"Good."

"Go see Ben. He's waiting for you."

Joe marched up the dock stairs; it was the longest walk of his life. He was living a nightmare. There was no way Luke's plan would ultimately work. It was impossible. Someone would figure it out. Hannah would sense it.

He entered the cabin and heard Ben's voice call from the deck. "Hey Joe, is that you?"

He stepped outside. "It's me."

"Where the hell have you been? The fish have been ready for a while."

"Sorry; I had a little boat trouble. Let's check out the fish."

Although he had no appetite, Joe grabbed a plate. He had to play the part in case they were watching. He ate, studying "Ben" in between bites. There had to be a flaw; nobody could create a perfect duplicate of someone.

When he finished eating, Joe couldn't stand the thought of spending more time with this clone.

"Hey, the fish was great, Ben. I'm tired; it's been a long day, and we have a long drive ahead of us tomorrow. I'm going to go to bed early."

"Sure, Joe. That's probably a good idea. I'm tired too."

Joe grabbed a bottle of whiskey then headed to his bedroom and closed the door. He opened the slider to the deck, and plopped down onto a lounge chair, adjusting the back. The moon illuminated the lake, and the stars lit the night sky. Joe drank straight from the bottle and wallowed in self-pity until he fell asleep on the deck lounge chair.

Joe woke up around 8:00 a.m. the next morning, with a splitting headache, his mind trying to calibrate where he was. His first thought was he'd drank too much and had a very bad dream until his reality hit him anew. He stood up, kicking the empty whiskey bottle on his way to the bathroom. When he came out, he could hear Ben in the kitchen and headed that way.

"Hey, Joe, you look like death."

"Yeah, I'm sure. I'm a little hungover this morning." He reached into a cabinet for some Advil.

"There's some eggs and home fries here."

"Thanks. I'm going for coffee and a bagel."

He threw in a K-cup and toasted a bagel. When his breakfast was ready, Joe sat down opposite Ben. He sipped his coffee and picked at the bagel while coming to grips that this wasn't the real Ben. It wasn't a bad dream. He watched the clone, looking for a flaw, something that would stick out, but he couldn't tell. It was like comparing an authentic designer bag with an imitation. Even if you couldn't find a difference initially, but eventually the fake bag would show its flaws. There had to be something that this thing didn't know, and then it hit him.

"Hey Ben, you remember back in high school, the lacrosse team?"

"Of course, we were quite the duo."

"We were. You remember that championship game against St Mary's?"

"Yeah. We won it twelve to eleven."

"Do you remember how we won it?"

"That was a long time ago, Joe."

"I remember. You scored the winning goal."

"That's right, I did."

"We couldn't have won that game without you," Joe said.

There it was. Joe had actually been the one to score the winning goal. So when the clone couldn't find details, it just went along with what was said. What other failed memories would come up in the future?

"Well, you ready to head home?"

"Let's go," Ben said with a smile. "I miss Hannah and the kids."

"I bet you do," Joe muttered.

Chapter 26

Special Agents Wyatt Miller and Cliff Allen were on the scene where a second woman had gone missing in Indiana. The girl's name was Darlene Rich. Her abduction followed a similar pattern to the Paige Turner disappearance—a quick bump and run. The forensic team was searching for any clues.

Wyatt's phone vibrated in his pocket. "Yeah? Okay, we'll be there."

"Who was that?" Cliff asked.

"We might have something on the Paige Turner case that might also be connected to this latest disappearance. We need to head over to the Wilbur Hotel in downtown Indianapolis."

After a two-hour drive, the two FBI agents walked into the Wilbur Hotel and were escorted to the cordoned off third floor where they were greeted by lead detective, Carlos Tanning. He took them over to a body and pulled back the yellow sheet covering it.

"Do you recognize this man?"

"That's Andrew Murphy, our man from the Paige Turner kidnapping video," Wyatt said.

"He also went by the alias Kyle Murray," Tanning said.

"So what happened?"

The detective pursed his lips. "I'll let you come to your own conclusion after viewing the hotel security video, which tells the story."

"Where can we find that?"

"Near the lobby. I'll take you there."

In the surveillance room, the two FBI agents sat in front of the monitor, and Tanning offered commentary as the footage played.

"After the girl with her back toward us sits down at a table, Murphy walks over, makes small talk, then goes back to the bar where he orders drinks and seems to confer with the man leaning against the counter, who then makes a phone call. We don't know who he is. Then Murphy appears to slip something in the girl's drink before walking back to the table. He sits, they exchange some small talk, then they leave together."

When the woman stands and turns to leave, her face is fully visible. Wyatt leaned closer.

"Wait a minute; that looks like Paige Turner, our missing college student."

Tanning said, "Unless she has a twin, that appears to be Paige Turner."

"No, she doesn't have a twin. And this whole scenario makes no sense. Murphy was one of her abductors. Why would she show up on her own to meet up with him? Is it possible she's drugged up?"

"It sure doesn't make sense," Cliff agreed. "Maybe she has amnesia."

"I guess that's as good a theory as any," Wyatt said.

"It gets more interesting," Tanning said. He pressed a button for a different video feed. "After Murphy collapses in the hall, the other man from the bar shows up a couple of minutes later and goes through Murphy's pants to retrieve his phone, then leaves. We're already trying to find who his carrier was."

"Is that it?" Cliff asked.

"No." Tanning brought up another video feed. "Here's

footage of the second man leaving the hotel. A few seconds later this third man there wearing a suit follows him out."

"How do you know he's following him?" Wyatt asked.

Tanning went back to the bar footage. "Look in the back there. That same man is watching Murphy and his friend. We were able to track them for a couple blocks after they left but then lost them."

"What happened to the girl?" Wyatt asked.

"Our theory that she was with her abductors kind of falls apart." Tanning pulls up the third-floor hallway video. "This guy with the baseball cap shows up, and they leave together. Now I'm thinking maybe he's a pimp, and she's a hooker."

Wyatt shook his head. "That really doesn't follow if this is Paige Turner. Maybe there is something to what Cliff said about her having amnesia, and she doesn't know who she is. Can we take the security footage to send to our lab in Virginia? Maybe they can clean up the images."

"Of course," Tanning said. "Seems to me that if you find the guy in the baseball cap, you'll find Paige Turner."

Chapter 27

It was an overcast Sunday morning. Josh was up early, sitting in front of his computer. Cole walked into the kitchen and poured himself a coffee.

"Where's Rick?"

"I think he slept over at his girlfriend's apartment."

"We never see him anymore since he met that girl."

"He's in love. Or he thinks he's in love."

"And we're suspects in a murder. Do you see any news about it?"

"I've been looking. All I've seen is somebody got stabbed at the Wilbur Hotel, but the police are being pretty quiet."

"Maybe that's a good thing."

"We can't worry about this," Josh said. "It will drive us crazy. We weren't even there, and if they can't identify Cal, they'll never know about our involvement. Just another unsolved crime. There's plenty of those in the city."

Cole walked over to the computer and looked over Josh's shoulder at the website of a local news affiliate. He tapped the screen to open a news item then expanded the screen. "I can't believe this."

"You can't believe what?"

"The guy in the photo. That's what the AI I saw in the secured area looked like."

"Senator Johnson?"

"Yes. That's definitely him. I knew he looked familiar."

"It's not possible, Cole. They aren't replacing a senator with an AI copy."

"Maybe that's why Charlie Nash disappeared."

Josh just shrugged. "I think you watch too many science fiction movies."

Later in the day Cole drove home. The farm was serenity, and he needed a breather. This past week had sucked the life out of him. Being an accessory to a murder with an AI clone was enough to assess where your life was heading.

When he got out of his truck, the family dog, Rocky, greeted him with excitement. He made small talk with his brothers and sisters and got a nice hug from his mother with an all-you-can-eat dinner. He drank a beer with his dad but didn't have the heart to tell him the job wasn't all it was cracked up to be, or that if he got a visit from the FBI, he knew nothing.

Cole took a long walk by the lake with Rocky. They stopped at his favorite place, the rock, where he had shared many moments with Paige. He missed her badly; she was his soulmate. A tear rolled down his cheek as he thought about good moments in the past. Cole rubbed Rocky's head, making his tail thump in approval.

The overcast day reflected Cole's mood, dark thoughts consuming him as he stared out at the lake. Paige was never coming back. It was possible the company he worked for was hiding an unethical, immoral, and even an illegal side. Chip had warned him, and now he had seen evidence of a potential diabolical plan. So his life might be in danger, just like Charlie Nash. He had revived an alien technology that was roaming the countryside who knew where. Out of grief he had created a clone of Paige.

He was waiting for his whole world to implode.

Cole took Rocky back to the house, said his goodbyes,

then drove away. He was almost at his apartment when he saw blue lights in his rearview come up behind him.

"Just what I need."

He pulled the car off to the side and watched as a man in a rain overcoat emerged from the unmarked police car and walked slowly to his truck. Feeling uneasy, Cole lowered the window.

The man showed him a badge. "Are you Cole Adams?"

"Yes, sir."

"You were going a few miles an hour over the speed limit. But I'm going to give you a warning." He took out a citation book.

"Thanks, officer."

"Here's the warning."

Cole grabbed it.

"I want you to look at it closely."

The officer waited while Cole read the message. He was to meet Chip the next morning at six o'clock sharp at their special diner.

"Do you understand?"

"Yeah."

"Good. You're all set. Slow down and have a good evening."

The officer got back in his car and sped off.

Chapter 28

Ross Cullen, a retired military veteran turned private investigator, parked his car in a rundown neighborhood on the east side of Indianapolis. He had tracked the man from the Wilbur Hotel to a two-story house up the street. Murphy was dead, but his partner was a possible link to Paige Turner's disappearance. Ross had observed the two men at the Wilbur, but he could not have imagined the chaos that would ensue. The girl at the hotel looked strikingly like Paige Turner, which added to the confusion.

A man with curly, black hair opened Ross's passenger side door and slid in holding two coffees in one hand and an egg sandwich in the other. He handed Ross one of the cups.

"No sugar, Fred, right?"

"No sugar. You tell me that every time, Ross."

"Did you send all the photos to Chip?"

"All set. Any movement?"

Ross sipped his coffee and nibbled at the egg sandwich. "Nothing. No phone calls either. It's too damn quiet if you ask me."

"Why don't we go in and shake the guy down and get him to talk?"

"You just want to put a bullet in the guy's head."

Fred shrugged. "You're right. He's no different than the slime I dealt with overseas. After I'm through with him, he'll give us everything he knows. Trust me; he'll wish he was dead."

"We're not overseas. You'll have to be a little patient. Somebody is going to show up. And then they'll lead us to the hornet's nest."

"How do you know that?"

"I've been doing this for a long time. A guy gets killed, these guys scurry to their partners in crime to cover their tracks, and they do it pretty quick."

An hour later a car rolled up and parked in front of the house. Three men got out, walked up the driveway, and went into the house.

"You were right," Fred said.

"Criminals are pretty predictable. While you're doing nothing, how about putting a tracking device on that car."

Inside the house, a large, casually dressed man with a belly hanging over his belt, stood by the door as two strong-armed men, dressed in black with shiny tattoos on their arms, sauntered into the kitchen.

"So Jerry," the heavier man said, "what happened at the Wilbur Hotel?"

"Andy saw this girl that looked a lot like that Paige Turner."

"You were going to bring her to us."

"We remembered how much Roy got for her."

"You remembered that? Who told you that?"

"I forget."

"You forget," he repeated, looking at his partner. Then his eyes narrowed, and he slugged Jerry with a clenched fist on the side of the face. He hit the floor. "What the hell were you thinking? We paid you well to keep a low profile."

Jerry got up slowly. "I'm sorry. We just thought you could get a lot of money for her."

"You thought? You were going to bring her from a hotel with surveillance cameras everywhere and deliver her right to the farm?"

"We thought Roy would like it."

"Jerry, let me tell you something. We don't pay you to think. Now what happened at the Wilbur Hotel?"

"Andy took this hot girl back to his room."

The two men laughed. "So he was going to have a little fun with her."

"Yeah. I told him it was a bad idea. Let's just drug her and get on our way."

"I guess you were the smart one."

"Yeah. I was waiting downstairs. It was taking too long. I went up there and found him on the floor with a stab wound. I took his phone. Nobody will know who he is. He had an alias. We're good."

"The girl stabbed him."

"I guess."

"Good for her. Good for us. It worked out for everyone. Andy was an idiot."

"Yeah," Jerry agreed.

"I like you, Jerry. Your mistake was hanging around Andy. People like him just get you in trouble. You're better off without him. What we do only works if we do the jobs right. You pick your spots. What Andy did the other day was really stupid, and Roy wasn't too happy, especially the timing. You know what I mean?"

"Yeah."

"We don't like to use the same people for this reason. People get sloppy, the Feds catch on, and the next thing you know, everybody is in prison. We created a market for our merchandise. It's very profitable if you don't get greedy. Ours is a niche market, and our customers are very specific in what they are looking for."

"I get it, Willie."

"I know you do, Jerry."

"I'll do anything you want me to do."

"I know you will."

He pulled out a white envelope. "I have here a one-way ticket out of the country."

"Okay. I'm out of here, Willie. You won't see me again."

"I know, Jerry. Where's Andy's phone?"

"It's on the counter over there. The blue one is mine."

"Good. You got something to drink here?"

"I got a beer."

"It's a little early. I was thinking maybe a glass of juice."

"Sure, I have orange juice." He turned and opened the refrigerator.

Willie's partner pulled a knife, wrapped his arm around Jerry's head, and in an instant, Jerry was lying on the floor in a pool of blood.

They picked up the phones and calmly walked out.

Ross observed the three men coming out of the house. He snapped off a few photos. "Three men enter, three men leave. What are the odds that our target is still alive?"

"You think they killed him?" Fred asked.

"I don't know. I think it's more than 50–50. Two well-dressed guys and one grunt for any heavy lifting."

"How do you know that?"

"I've seen this movie before. These power guys like to see men sweat in front of them before they pull the curtain. They're just covering up all the loose ends."

"Why don't we put a wager on it?"

"Okay. How about ten bucks?"

"How about twenty?"

"Fine with me; it's your money. Fred, do you see their trilateration on the screen?"

"Yeah. I'm following their location now."

"Good. Let's go in and see who won the bet."

The two walked up the driveway and pulled out their guns prior to opening the unlocked side door and entered cautiously. They held their nine millimeters with both hands at the ready as they moved through the first two rooms to the kitchen.

Fred just shook his head, standing over the lifeless body. Fred pulled out a twenty-dollar bill and held it out.

Ross smiled. "Thanks. Now let's see where this next lead takes us."

Chapter 29

At 5:45 a.m. Cole drove his pickup to exit 146 off I-65 to Rosebud Diner in Thorntown. He was in deep. There was no turning back. He didn't like his job anymore. He knew what was coming. They would take Rose away and turn her into something that was diabolical by human standards—whatever that was. But there was more that scared him. The sight of a cloned senator reflected dark intentions of a company.

He walked into the diner at 6:10 a.m. and saw Chip at a corner table. He was dressed in a gray suit with his gray hair slicked back and a white beard that hid his face. He waved Cole over.

He smiled. "How're you doing?"

"You know how I'm doing. You did a bait-and-switch to get me to do your dirty work, knowing the magic word that would pull me into this mess. How are we doing in finding Paige? I'm starting to think that maybe she's never coming back."

"I need something from you, and you need something from me. But this isn't going to work unless you start telling me the truth. I've been pretty honest with you from the beginning. I understand your reluctance. But there's more here than you're telling me. Am I right?"

The waitress came over. "Are you ready to order?"

"Bring us two coffees then give us fifteen minutes."

The waitress left.

"I really have no idea who you are," Cole said.

Chip leaned forward with his hands folded. "This isn't about you and me. I know you understand that. I'm sorry you got pulled into this. When the time is right, we need to expose the bad guys. And I need you to do that."

Cole sat back in the booth. "Why do I feel like the closer I get to the truth, the more my life could be in danger?"

"As they say, the truth will set you free. You need to tell me everything, or this isn't going to work. And you're right; it could get you killed. These people didn't murder a bunch of scientists for the hell of it. There's a plan. So, do you have anything you want to tell me?"

Cole shook his head.

"Maybe this will break the ice."

Chip pulled out a manila folder from a briefcase and pushed it across the table. Cole opened the folder. Inside were photos. On top was a picture of Rose. Another photo was of Cal and Rose together.

Cole exhaled like a balloon losing its air. "What do you want to know?"

"Last time we met I told you I had a private investigator working to find Paige. That led to one confusing situation at the Wilbur Hotel. It was a big surprise to realize the Paige he found really wasn't Paige at all. And it all leads to Round Robotics. Who's the guy with her?"

Cole hesitated then said, "Cal Jensen. I work with him."

"And the Paige look-alike?"

"It's an AI clone of Paige."

"I'm guessing you know exactly what happened at the Wilbur Hotel, am I right?"

"I wouldn't use the word exactly. But if you're talking about Paige's abductor getting killed, yeah, I know that. I don't know for sure how he died. And I know he had an accomplice."

"Isn't this much better, Cole? You are in deep. An accomplice to a murder. Sure, the guy was a bad apple, but the idea of a genetically engineered AI clone killing someone really changes the game. How do you think Round Robotics is going to react if they find out? Or worse, if someone figures out clone Paige isn't exactly real."

"They're not."

The waitress brought their coffee. Chip opened a packet of sugar and slowly sprinkled it into the cup.

"That's the best answer you got?"

"What do you want me to say?" Cole asked, anxiety running through his body.

"Well, you better hope the authorities don't figure it out or come snooping around Round Robotics. You just made our job harder."

"It is what it is."

"You're right. I'll give you some good news. We have the second guy who was at the Wilbur Hotel under surveillance. If we're lucky, he'll lead us to the human trafficking ring responsible for Paige's abduction. They just struck again a few days ago down in Fulton County."

"How do you know that?"

"It's been in the news. Same type of abduction as what happened to Paige. It's definitely the same crew. Let's order, and then I have some more questions."

He called the waitress over, and they placed their orders. Chip flirted. When she left he smiled at Cole.

"Ah, if I were young again. She likes you. A pretty girl, but with a little baggage. She has a kid, lives at home with her mother. Taking night courses at a local college. Working hard to get out of her hole. A smart person is someone who won't make the same mistake twice. That's what I call a good catch."

"How do you know all that about her?"

"I talk to people. It's amazing how much people will tell you if you appear interested. If you listen, you can tell what makes people tick. Back of your mind, you're leery of me. What are his true motives, you wonder? I've told you the truth from day one. Now, it's time you start telling me the truth. My first question: how did you create the AI in college? Sid told me he had never seen anything like it. You're good, but you didn't build it. You found one of these things on your farm from the ship that was found there years ago, right?"

Cole paused, conflicted, then told him. "Yes, I pulled one out of the lake. I dried it out and woke it up using a defibrillator."

"Amazing," Chip said, meaning it.

"I worked on it, and eventually it restored itself."

"Not only can they put themselves in a hibernation state, which is probably for deep-space travel, they have the ability to regenerate parts, systems—cells as well. We have the same genetic code to regenerate; we just don't know yet how to turn it on. Evolution eventually solves that problem, I guess."

"This alien machine—or whatever you want to call it—got up and walked away one day."

Chip's expression was somber. "You're telling me we have one of these things roaming the countryside now?"

"Yeah."

"Did you ever consider these things could be dangerous to mankind? That it could cause a lot of damage if it decided to? They have the ability to hack into anything. They understand mathematical equations at levels we can't even imagine. They might want to shut down the grid or cause a nuclear war; the list is endless."

"Okay, I get it. But I kind of look at him as friendly."

"Can you say that with certainty?"

Cole looked away and shook his head. "No."

"I'll need resources to track this thing down. I'll need an image of it."

"I don't know if I have one."

"Find one."

"I'll try. He also left me instructions for how to build one of them."

"Let me guess—AI Paige."

The waitress delivered their plates of food, placing then carefully on the table. When she left, Cole leaned forward.

"There's one other thing."

"It wouldn't be from the full security clearance you received, would it?"

"How do you know that?"

"How do you think you got it?"

"From you?"

"No, Sid gave it to you. It was deliberate. We figured you would get curious. It was a shot in the dark. You found something, didn't you?"

"Sid was behind that?"

"Yeah. He wants to know what's behind the secure area that Bill runs with an iron fist, especially since Charlie Nash disappeared."

"Does Sid believe that Nash was murdered?"

"I don't know; you'd have to ask him. It's too bad he's dealing with an illness. Makes my job a lot harder. So what did you find?"

"Well, first they're building machines with buried code. And they've made a clone of Senator Ben Johnson."

Chip didn't say anything at first, digesting what Cole had just told him.

"How do you know this?"

Cole related the story of how he ended up hiding in the lab and saw technicians and a suit going over the AI. Chip listened then finished his food.

"You've done well, Cole."

"That's it? You don't seem very concerned."

"Oh, I'm concerned, just not surprised. I know what these people can do."

"So what's their plan?"

"Their plan?" He tilted his head in thought. "Johnson is an excellent candidate for president. He could win. A nice guy who will turn bad once in office, all with a touch of a keystroke."

"What does this mean?"

"Well, the bad news is these people will kill you. There is no good news."

"What are we going to do about it? You can stop it, right?"

"We aren't going to stop it, not yet anyway. You ever play poker?"

Cole shook his head.

"Well, when you have a crappy hand, you try to get the most chips from the other players without showing your hand. That's what we are going to do."

"We're just going to let them kidnap the senator? What if they kill him?"

"There's risk in everything. If we pull the plug on them too early, they'll just scatter and try something else. We need to expose the players and take them all down."

"We know the players. You know the players, starting with Luke Richards and Bill McDonald."

Chip gave Cole a patronizing smile. "Those aren't the real players. It's the people behind them controlling the strings. Yeah, Richards is a greedy and soulless bastard, and Bill is just waist-deep in shit. He's well-paid to do their bidding and probably worried about losing his life. But there are other players we need to flush out."

"What is their real purpose?"

"Remember that spaceship you found in your dad's cornfield?"

"Yeah."

"Well, just to give you a little sample of the technology," Chip looked straight at him. "You've seen those stealth fighters. Do those jets look like they're from our world?"

"Wow!"

"The real purpose, you ask?" He sipped his coffee and put it down. "They have a way off this planet. All from that spaceship found in your father's cornfield. A new beginning for the privileged. What was found on that ship's database were the directions to thirteen Earth-like planets, which have the same atmospheric conditions and the same chemicals that are found on this planet. It's amazing. They are quietly building these ships to transport human life to the nearest Earth-like planet—the beginning of colonization for mankind. Except they need at least $2 trillion or more to finance their endeavor. They need to raise the money quietly without tipping off the world. This planet, regardless of what anyone says, is dying. Nobody will ever admit it. The scientists know it. There's only so many people the planet can hold. We are running out of resources and the Earth's magnetic field is getting significantly weaker. And these people will do whatever they need to do for a ticket to a new planet. I can't be more honest than that. In one way this ship was a gift; in another way it will bring out the worst in mankind. Having AI technology that will build a new world is a beautiful dream. All the mistakes on this planet will be erased by the new utopia. A better Earth." He chuckled. "Humans will always repeat their flaws. History never changes."

"What do you want me to do in the meantime?"

"Just do what you normally do. And don't tell anybody about the senator."

"I already told my friend."

Chip shook his head. "You can't tell anybody about this. You got that? You tell your friend to keep his mouth shut. These people will kill you."

"I understand."

"Good. That's all I got, Cole. You pretty much know everything now."

Cole finished his breakfast. He felt queasy. He knew too much.

30

Senator Ben Johnson's eyes popped open. He was lying on a bed wearing shorts and a T-shirt. His head hurt, and his throat was dry. The last thing he remembered was drinking a beer at Joe Brock's cabin cooking fish. Then it all went dark. He sat up, confused. He didn't recognize the room he was in. He stood up, a little wobbly, and opened the door to a large living room with an adjacent kitchen. The sun slipped through cracks in the drawn curtains. He saw a side door and opened it, the sunlight momentarily blinding. He focused and looked out on a large open area with a pattern of brick pavers surrounded by manicured green grass, with a table shaded by an overhead umbrella. It was a nice backyard, but in the background was a high wall topped with barbed wire. The setup now seemed more prison than vacation home.

He stepped outside, studying his unfamiliar surroundings, wondering where Joe was. He had a very bad feeling about this. He walked the forty yards to the wall and stared up at it.

Where the hell am I? What the hell was going on?

Behind him three men stepped out onto the patio.

"Senator Johnson, how're you feeling?" one of them called out.

Ben turned and went back to the patio. "Who the hell are you? And where am I?"

"Looks like you're feeling better. That's good. I'm Mal.

I'm here to make your stay as comfortable as possible. Let's take a seat over here on the patio, and I'll try to explain the situation." He waved off the other two guys. "Do you want anything to drink or eat?"

"No. The only thing I want is an explanation," Ben said, annoyed.

"First, I hope you like your accommodations. We put a lot of effort into making you as comfortable as possible."

"What the hell are you talking about?"

"You are not going anywhere, Senator. So just calm down and sit. Enjoy yourself. You don't have to do much but be good. We have plenty of reading material. We have cable television. Anything you want to eat is at your service. If I were you, I'd look at this as a vacation at a five-star hotel."

"Did you kidnap me? Is this what this is all about? You'll never get away with this. They'll be looking everywhere for me. What did you do with Senator Brock?"

"A lot of questions. I know this is going to be hard to understand, Senator. Someone has to be the bad guy here. The word *kidnapping* is a little harsh. It's like global warming is now climate change, and an illegal alien is now undocumented. They all mean the same, but do nicer words really change the cold hard facts? I would say it's more like a sabbatical. It sounds better, don't you think? But technically I guess you could call it a kidnapping. If you make this hard, it could go in a very bad direction, and we don't want that."

Ben shook his head. "They'll find me."

"Well, let's hope they don't, for your sake." Mal pointed. "You've noticed the twenty-foot high wall with barbed wire at the top. I wouldn't try anything stupid. And if you're wondering, the area is monitored 24/7. There are cameras everywhere. It's futile to think about escaping. We spent a lot of time making this compound fully secure and comfortable."

"So I should just curl up and read a book or something!"

"Excellent idea. I'm sure you haven't had time to binge-watch a series. Well, you do now," Mal said with a smile, then his face got tight. "Just don't cause me any trouble."

"What did you do with Senator Brock?" he repeated.

"I like your concern for him. It just shows we picked the right guy. But he's doing just fine. He actually helped us. I'm sorry he's not quite the friend you thought."

"He was in on this?"

"Unfortunately."

"I don't believe that."

"He played a big role."

"No."

"Whose idea was it to come out to the cabin? Then think about how Brock conveniently left the cabin. It doesn't matter what you believe, Senator. You're here and he's not."

"How much is the ransom?"

"There is no ransom."

"Then what the hell do you want with me?"

Mal laughed. "Nothing, really."

His phone buzzed. Mal answered and walked a few feet away. When the call finished he came back.

Holding out his phone, Mal said, "Let me show you something. I think you'll have a much better understanding of why you are here. Images are much better than words. That looks like you, right?"

Ben stared into the phone and looked as if he'd seen a ghost. It was impossible. He was watching a doppelganger explain his legislation on job training in a live news report. Whoever it was had the exact same voice pattern and mannerisms.

"Who the hell is that, and what the hell is going on?"

"What, you don't like watching yourself?"

"That's not me."

"Oh, but it is, Senator. That is a genetically engineered AI clone of you from head to toe. Remember how somebody stole your wisdom tooth? We needed a few stem cells to help us produce a carbon copy of you. Pretty amazing, huh? You'll accept it eventually. It's hard at first."

"You'll never get away with this. My wife will figure this out."

"I don't think so. She is going to like the new you, if you know what I mean."

"Go to hell, you bastards."

Mal just smiled. "The new you isn't going to get tired, and he's not going to get stressed out. No, I think your wife is going to like the new you. He's a great listener."

"What's the purpose of all this?"

"You don't know? You're a smart guy, Senator. You'll figure it out."

He shook his head. "You want this thing to run for president."

"I knew you were a smart guy. You're the perfect candidate. The kitchen is fully stocked. I'm sure you can figure out what to eat. Other than that, I would relax because there is nothing you can do. It's out of your control."

Ben dropped into a patio chair, staring at his new confines. He prayed this was a bad dream and he would wake up any time, telling Hannah what an awful nightmare he'd had. But this was no dream. His mind was trying to comprehend how this could have happened. Where did this technology come from? He had been on enough Senate committees and never heard of anything like it.

Most horrifying was they wouldn't even know he was missing. And Ben knew that at some point, there would be no reason to keep him around. He had to find a way out. His life depended on it.

Chapter 31

The clouds hung low over a field in Hancock County, Kentucky. Ross Cullen lay in the weeds looking through his binoculars. Fred scuttled up next to him as if he was on a special ops mission.

"What do you see?" Fred asked.

Ross set the binoculars down. "There are at least seven of them in the farmhouse, maybe more. I saw the kidnapped girl, Darlene Rich. They're getting ready to take her somewhere. Let's take care of business. Did you get the GPS on the small airplane out in the field?"

"Yeah, all set."

"And Ned, Jay, and Bob are in place?"

"Yeah."

They waited until the sun began to dip behind the trees. Then Ross and Fred sprang into action and snuck up to the farmhouse in a crouched position. They drew their guns, adrenaline soaring. The small plane started up its engine. Three men came out onto the porch and escorted the girl to the plane. She hesitated and tried to hold her ground, wailing in despair, but it was futile.

Ross said into his headpiece, "Take them out when you get a clear shot."

Almost immediately the crack of sniper shots echoed, and the three men were down. The girl shrieked and hit the ground. The plane began its ascent without them. Two men came running out of the farmhouse. Ross and Fred took them out, then maneuvered onto the porch. When Fred signaled he had him covered, Ross pushed open the front door, and semi-automatic bullets began ripping up everything in his direction. Ross hit the floor. Fred took a bullet to the shoulder and yelled in pain as he fell backward. Ned extracted the girl from the field as Jay and Ed advanced to the farmhouse.

Ross maneuvered inside under a hail of bullets that didn't stop and yelled commands through his headset.

"They're heading out the back door!"

The team swung around to the back of the house, where they encountered two more of the kidnapping crew and exchanged gunfire. Ross sprung up firing and shot one square in the chest as he was reloading. The second kidnapper put down his weapon and raised his hands. Jay and Ed emerged from the back door with the girl. It was over.

Ross checked on Fred. "You okay?"

"I think I'll live."

Ross went up to the girl. "You're going home." Then he looked over at the last kidnapper. "It's your lucky day, or it's your last day. Your choice."

"I don't know anything. I want a lawyer."

The other men laughed.

Ross smiled wide. "You think we're law enforcement? That's pretty funny."

Ross nodded toward Fred, who walked up, clutching his shoulder in pain. "That's Special Agent Fred Walsh."

They all laughed except Fred.

"I'm in pain here, Ross. I don't have time for your humor. Let me put a bullet in this guy's head and be done with it."

"Hey, Ned, can you take the girl someplace while we talk to our friend here?"

"Sure, boss," he said, gently leading the girl away.

Ross walked up to their prisoner. "What's your name?"

"I'm not telling you anything until I see a lawyer."

Ross grinned. "I was just kidding about the Special

Agent thing. I don't have a problem putting a bullet in your head. We have our own rules."

On Ross's nod, they took the prisoner to the kitchen. Jay tied the man to a chair while Ed filled an empty water bucket.

"What are you doing? I want a lawyer!" the panicked kidnapper shouted.

Ross straddled his chair. "You ever hear of waterboarding? It's a pretty effective incentive for getting information."

The man's face turned a pale white. "You can't do that to me!"

"You know, it really pisses me off that the bad guys today get to do what they want in this country now. That's why I like what I do. I eliminate shit like you. That's my job, and I'm really good at it. You are going to wish you were dead if you don't tell me what I want to know. So, let's begin with the first question. Where's Paige Turner?"

"I don't know who she is."

"Okay, you want to make this hard?"

Jay and Ed draped a cloth over the man's face then tilted the chair back. Ross picked up the bucket and slowly poured water over the cloth. The man started choking and gasping for air. They set the chair back upright.

"Not pleasant, huh? Don't try my patience. Let's try this again, Where's Paige Turner?"

Still choking and coughing, the man rasped, "Okay, I'll tell you."

"I'm waiting. I don't have all day."

"They'll kill me."

"I'll kill you sooner." He lifted the bucket

"They auctioned her off. That's what they do. They kidnap select girls and auction them off for big money."

Ross shook his head in disgust. "That was easy. Now where is Paige?"

The man hesitated.

Ross nodded. The men began to tilt his chair.

"Okay, okay. I heard Peru."

"Peru. And who has her?"

"I heard he's a wealthy industrialist in Peru. That's all I know. His bid was the highest."

Ross crouched down like a catcher. "What's your name?"

"Larry."

"Larry, you did good. One more question: who sets these auctions up or creates the logistics to bring in all the buyers into the world of human trafficking?"

"A man from Texas."

"And who would that be?"

"I don't know."

"I was hoping for a better answer."

Ross nodded. Jay and Ed began to tilt him again.

"Wait! There's a guy we deal with by the name of Roy Small. He left on the plane. I don't know anything else, I really don't know," he pleaded, broken.

"I believe you, Larry."

"Are you going to let me go now? I gave you everything I know."

"You did. But you're a scumbag. You never thought about those girls that you auctioned off. You took them away from their families to be abused by monsters. No, I don't give a shit about you or your friends. In fact, I feel like it's my job to get rid of people like you."

"But you said—"

"I know what I said." Ross leaned in and stared intently, saying softly, "You now know what these girls felt. It's not a very good feeling, is it? You're an animal, and I'm just sorry I have to waste a bullet on you."

He raised his gun.

"No—"

Ross pulled the trigger then grabbed Larry's phone and walked away.

Chapter 32

Special Agents Wyatt Miller and Cliff Allen had surveyed the murder scene on the eastside of Indianapolis. Detective Carlos Tanning had called them in.

"It looks like a hit," Wyatt said. "Our suspect from the hotel is now a deadend. No pun intended."

"What do you think?" Cliff asked. "Was it the guy who was following him?"

"I don't know," Wyatt said. "But it does appear from the way his throat was slit he never saw it coming. His guard was down. Maybe he was a liability."

"We talked to some neighbors," Carlos said. "A young kid said he saw three guys go into the house. He couldn't offer anything other than that."

"If it's our human trafficking ring, they're covering their tracks," Wyatt said. His phone buzzed. "Yeah? … We'll be there as soon as we can."

"What's going on?" Cliff asked.

"They found Darlene Rich. Alive."

"That's great news," Cliff said. "Did they say how they found her?"

"They found her alive along with eight bodies, whatever that means."

The car rolled down a dirt road to a farm in Hancock County, Kentucky, surrounded by squad cars. Wyatt and Cliff emerged from the car wearing trench coats, their shoes squishing in the muck as they walked. As they approached the farmhouse, they were greeted by the lead detective. A forensic team was already on site studying the crime scene.

Yellow tape and body bags littered the area around the farmhouse.

After introductions, Wyatt asked, "What do we have here? It looks like a war zone. If they hadn't found the girl, I would have said it was a drug deal gone bad."

"I'll give you an overview," the lead detective said. "The three bodies out in the field appear to be clean sniper shots."

"Military experience, my guess," Cliff stated as they walked back toward the farmhouse.

"Yeah."

"What happened?" Wyatt asked.

"From the girl's account, she was being dragged to a waiting plane when those men got picked off one by one. The plane took off without her."

"Did she know where she was going?" Wyatt asked.

"She didn't. She doesn't know much other than the guys that saved her appeared on a mission. She said there was a gunfight and one kidnapper survived. The lead guy ordered one of the men to take her out in front, and then a few minutes later she heard a gunshot. That's about all she knows."

"How many good guys?" Cliff asked.

"I wouldn't exactly call them good guys," the detective said. "She saw at least five."

"They weren't here for Darlene Rich," Wyatt observed.

"How do you know that?" the detective asked.

"We had two men who were possible suspects in the disappearance of Paige Turner and who we believed were part of this human trafficking ring. One died at a hotel in Indianapolis, and the other guy died at a house on the eastside. Our guess is that the second murder was done by this human trafficking group covering their tracks. What they didn't know, somebody was tracking them and took the law into their own hands."

"Who are they?"

"Your guess is as good as mine. But I think they're looking for Paige Turner. She was kidnapped a year ago."

"You think the family hired someone, Wyatt?" Cliff asked.

"I don't see a connection. I met the Turners. They are a very nice Midwestern family. And these aren't your average private investigators. These guys are cold-blooded."

They walked past two more bodies lying in front of the porch. They entered the farmhouse and saw a dead body lying on the floor. They moved on to the kitchen where a man was slumped over in a chair, with his hands tied to the arms. A bucket half-full of water was nearby.

Wyatt observed the scene and rubbed his chin. "Former military," he muttered.

"Why?" Cliff said.

"Waterboarding, a very effective method for extracting information. They're not done. They're just following the trail until it leads them to Paige Turner."

Wyatt tried to understand the crime scene. None of it made sense. Just like at the Wilbur Hotel with the Paige Turner look-alike, and yet they didn't follow that path. Why?

"Who do you think is paying these guys?" Cliff asked.

"That's a good question," Wyatt said. "Why are they looking for Paige Turner. These people don't even care what they leave behind. They're surely not worried about us. To them this is just another job, and they are quite good at what they do. We're just cleaning up their mess."

The detective said, "I guess you'll be taking over from here."

"Yeah. We'll take it from here, but thanks for all your help," Wyatt said. "I'm thinking the people behind this human trafficking ring might be a little paranoid. They must know by now that somebody is coming after them—unless we get there first."

Chapter 33

Senator Joe Brock sat at the bar of a popular politician lunch spot outside the Capitol. He waved the bartender over and ordered a whiskey sour. He stared at the TV until the bartender placed the drink in front of him. He took a couple of sips, then swished it around like it was his last while waiting for AI Ben Johnson. He hadn't talked to him other than a few texts since the switch.

He wondered how the whole plot was going. He figured it was time to check in and see if there were any dents in the armor. His job was to play the part. If there had been a problem, he surely would have heard about it. So he had to imagine everything was going as planned. He wondered how the real Ben Johnson was doing. Did he know he'd been betrayed by his life-long friend? The shock probably hadn't worn off that an AI clone was taking over his life.

Joe sucked the whiskey dry then ordered another. He was curious what Anna would say about her lunch date with Hannah today. There was always the gossip, the untold story. If there were any cracks, Hannah would be the first to sound the alarm. While the game was being played, it would give him time to figure out a way to expose this diabolical plan and the people behind it without anybody getting hurt. He sipped his whiskey, but it didn't dull the pain.

Senator Johnson walked in, and Joe waved him over.

"I'm sorry I'm late," Ben said. "The damn finance committee ran late. I thought I would find you at the bar."

"I see you haven't lost your sense of humor."

"You are pretty predictable. Every time I see you, you have a drink in your hand."

"Funny. I've got a lot on my mind."

"Alcohol only masks the real issues, Joe."

"Wow, you sound like Anna."

"Well, maybe she has point."

"Maybe. We've been friends since childhood, and if anybody knows me, it's you, Ben."

"That's true."

It was hard talking to a fake Ben. Hell, he didn't know what he was talking to or how he should approach any subject. It was a fake conversation, like fake news. None of it even mattered. This Ben was real without a soul. It didn't feel. It didn't love. It just said the right things and acted as designed. It reacted perfectly to each situation. The facial expressions were perfectly timed. It was as if it was an actor who knew all their lines and could project the right emotions on cue. Over time it would fail.

"Hey, I wanted you to be the first to know," Ben said.

"What's that?"

"I'm giving running for president deep consideration."

"What a surprise," he said sarcastically. "That's great, Ben. I think you can win."

"I think I could. I might need a good running mate."

Joe played his part and acted surprised. "You're thinking of me as your wingman?"

"No, vice president."

Not quite perfect, Joe thought. *Didn't get the analogy of the wingman.* "You need a drink?"

"I'm all set, Joe."

"Not during work hours, I get that. I think I'll have one more before I get a bite of lunch."

Hannah and Anna entered a cozy, upscale restaurant in the Greenport section of the Hamptons. They got comfortable in their seats at a wooden table next to a window. The waitress brought over menus and asked what they wanted to drink. They both ordered iced coffees, and the waitress walked off.

They were quiet at first. Focused on the menu, neither offered up a subject for conversation until they figured out what to order, then the words flowed, talking about the kids and their issues, the daily grind, some house projects, even the dogs. They saved the best for last—their husbands.

"How you two doing?" Hannah asked.

"I don't know. He seems to be drinking a lot more. He's distant. We'll be having a conversation, and he's not even in the room. You know what I mean."

"Oh, yeah."

"I'll ask him what I said, and then he turns it back on me like it's my fault or something. I sometimes think he's having an affair. He doesn't care about sex, and he's never home. There's always some sort of urgent project or crises that only he can figure out. I think it's all bullshit. I don't even know what he's doing half the time. I'm here, and he's in Washington. He could have another family, and I would never know. I've seen that on a show; their husbands have two families, and you say to yourself: *How could that ever happen without the wives knowing?* But I can see how it could happen."

"Maybe you're letting your emotions get the best of you. Your mind can make up crazy stuff sometimes."

"I don't know. When I do see him, he sits out in the backyard like he's in another world. And he sometimes snaps for no reason. I've even thought about hiring a private investigator to find out if he's cheating on me. Do you think that's a little too much?"

"Maybe. Why don't you just ask him?"

"Ask him if he's cheating on me? You really think he would give me an honest answer, Hannah? Remember that woman he had an affair with years ago, Terry? That almost destroyed our marriage. I thought about the kids and forgave him, but in the back of my mind, I always wonder if he's cheating on me again."

"I can see your point. But you can't just assume every time he's away that he might be cheating. You have to work on trust, or you have nothing."

"I know," she said, frowning. "So, do you think he's cheating?"

"I don't know. I could ask Ben if he knows anything or to keep an eye on him."

"That's an idea. You think Ben would do that?"

"Yeah, I guess. And what if Joe is cheating? Would you leave him?"

"I don't know."

"You need to answer that question first. Maybe if you confront him about your fears, he'll come clean, and then you can give him an ultimatum. It's her or you, or you throw him out. Marriage counseling might help. Do you think he has a drinking problem? That might be the heart of the problem."

"I've always looked the other way about his drinking, told myself it was part of his job when dealing with people. I never told anybody that I really think he's a functional alcoholic. His father was. It was the main reason his parents got divorced when he was a teenager. He can charm anybody; you know that. I could see him charming some young naïve intern and having an affair."

"You need to talk to him. I would think seriously about counseling."

"I think you're right. Thanks for listening."

Hannah smiled gently. "You can tell me anything. I'm always here for you."

"You're lucky Ben is so good. You guys are a great couple."

She made a face. "I don't know about that."

"You're not having problems, are you?"

"Well, I don't know."

"What, he didn't like what you cooked one night?" Anna chuckled.

Hannah smiled uneasily. "He's just been different. I can't really explain it. Ever since he came back from the fishing trip with Joe, he just seems different."

"In what way?"

"Well, don't laugh, but he's always in a good mood, agreeable with everything, he brings me flowers, and he's a machine in the bedroom."

Anna started laughing. "You're rubbing it in that you have the perfect guy. I think every woman would love to have your problems."

"He's different in a way that makes me think he's seeing someone."

"Ben's not like that, Hannah."

"I'm serious. He's different in the bedroom."

"What? He has some new moves?"

"Yeah. I mean, he's like a machine. He just doesn't stop."

"And you think that's a problem?"

"I'm thinking he's been with someone else. I don't know; maybe I'm just over-thinking this. I guess I should be happy."

"Yeah, you should be. It's better than being like me, ignored with nothing happening in the bedroom."

Hannah half-smiled. "You're probably right."

Back in the Hamptons on a summer evening, Joe Brock plopped down on a patio chair as the sun began to set with streaks of orange outlining the sky. His tie hung low, his collar was unbuttoned, and his suit jacket was opened wide. He looked disheveled. He took some sips of beer and leaned back, staring out into the abyss. He had always sworn he would never be like his father, yet when he looked in the mirror, that's who he saw. The stress of cyborg Ben and the kidnapping was taking an emotional toll. It was tearing him apart from the inside, but the more he drank, the less it dulled the pain.

Anna walked out to the patio, unhappy. Her red hair looked like an inferno. Her eyes piercing. She crossed her arms and stared at him with a woman's scorn.

"I know that look," he said. "I'm not in the mood for a fight, okay? Whatever I did wrong, you win." He grabbed the white towel next to him and waved it. "I surrender."

"Did you even say hello to the kids?"

"I did. I worked all week in Washington. It's no picnic in today's political arena, and when I come home you want to take my head off. I'm just not fighting. Nope. I'm watching the sunset, and I'm enjoying this beer, okay?"

"Since when have you gotten into sunsets? Is that your new pastime?"

He nodded, taking a slow sip. "As a matter of fact, it is. I've come to appreciate sunsets. It's kind of closure. Some days you don't want to end, and in others, you can't wait for the next day."

"How many drinks did you have today?"

"I had a whiskey sour with Ben at lunch," he lied. "I had a beer at the airport, and now I'm enjoying another beer. This is how I relieve stress, Anna."

"I know you've had more than that today, but it doesn't matter. You once told me that you were never going to be a drunk like your father."

"Here you go. What do you want me to do? Get some help?"

"Yeah, for our marriage's sake because I can't do this much longer."

"You want me to get help with my drinking? Okay, I'll do it for you."

"Don't do it for me. Do it for yourself and our family."

"You're right, Anna. You're a good woman, and I don't deserve you. I know that."

"Don't go down this self-pity path with me."

"You're right. I'm not here to fight. I just want to relax. I know what you're thinking. That maybe I'm cheating on you. I'm not." He held his hand out. "Why don't you join me? Grab a glass of wine, and let's talk without arguing. That would be a start. It's a lot better than you taking my head off."

She agreed and poured herself a glass of pinot noir and walked back out onto the terrace, sitting down opposite Joe.

"You see, isn't this much better?"

"It doesn't fix anything, Joe. I think we need to see a marriage counselor."

"Okay, if you think it's needed. Let's do it."

"We need it."

"Okay. Arrange it and I'll be there."

"Why are you being so agreeable?"

"Because you're right. I've been absent around here. You've never forgiven me for the affair or my womanizing ways. I get it."

"So you'll do this?"

"Yes. I said I would. I'll do it for both of us."

Anna forged a slight smile. "Have you been drinking the same Kool-Aid as Ben?"

"What do you mean?"

"I had lunch with Hannah today?"

"I remember you telling me that. How was it?"

"She was complaining about Ben."

He perked up. "Why, what's going on?"

She shook her head. "Imagine complaining about how awesome your husband has been lately."

"What do you mean?"

"Well, the way she was describing it, something seemed different since you guys got back from your fishing trip."

"How so?"

"He's more agreeable about everything. He goes out of his way to bring her flowers, and get this; he's now a machine in the bedroom."

Joe chuckled. *He's a machine alright.* Hannah didn't

know how close she was to the truth. "So, Hannah is complaining that he's too nice lately?"

"Yeah."

"That makes a lot of sense actually. You see, even when a guy is nice, you women think there's a reason. Maybe he's having an affair. Maybe he wants something, usually sex, right? Why can't a guy just be nice?"

"Because we know men."

"Yeah," he said, grinning.

"Is there any truth to that?"

"Truth to what?"

"He's having an affair."

Joe thought how an affair was a whole lot better than the reality. "Ben having an affair? Come on. He blushes at the sight of a woman. A guy can't do nothing right. Either he should be in the mood to perform on the push of a button, or if he isn't chasing you around the house, he must be seeing another woman. Women."

She laughed. "Yeah, that's about right."

Joe took one last look at the setting sun. There was a weakness in that thing, and Hannah was slowly figuring it out. It was just a matter of time. Then a dark thought seeped into his mind of what might they do to her or Ben if she figured out the truth.

Chapter 34

At the FBI's Indianapolis office, Wyatt sat in a high-backed chair at his desk, looking over the Paige Turner case. The plane that had taken off from the farm in Kentucky that was part of the human trafficking ring had disappeared into thin air. Another dead-end. The assassins were ghosts. The FBI was just following the trail of dead bodies. The men shot at the farm were two-bit criminals that had yet to lead to any significant break in the case. It was almost by design.

The frustration of the case was getting to him, knowing that just maybe Paige was still out there alive. Every now and then he would hear from Paige's mother asking if they were any closer. It's was heartbreaking to tell her they didn't have anything new but were relentlessly working on the case. Hollow words.

Wyatt ran his hand through his hair and got up from his desk to look out the window. His phone vibrated in his pocket. He answered, listened, and then put the phone back in his pocket.

The case was about to take a sharp turn he never saw coming.

Cliff drove the unmarked sedan with Wyatt at shotgun through a quiet suburb outside of Indianapolis. The car rolled to a stop on a street lined with manicured lawns, a half-dozen police cruisers, and a crowd of curious neighbors.

Wyatt and Cliff were greeted by Detective Carlos Tanning. "My friends from the FBI, we meet again. Follow me."

Detective Tanning led the way into the house and to a large living room. Hanging from a wooden beam running along the center of the ceiling was a young man with a noose around his neck. Wyatt knew he had been doing this work for far too long—it hardly fazed him seeing a body dangling in the air.

"I didn't want to disturb the scene until you got here. Just in case you saw something we might have missed."

"I appreciate that, Detective Tanning," Wyatt said, studying the room as if he was looking for buried treasure.

"Why did you call us in?" Cliff asked.

"Look closely," Detective Tanning said.

As Wyatt walked closer to the body, it hit him. "Detective Tanning, I guess you don't forget a face. This is the guy who was with the Paige Turner look-alike at the Wilbur Hotel."

"Exactly. His girlfriend was the one to notify us. She's pretty distraught at the moment, and the guy's family isn't doing too well. We asked her what state of mind the deceased was in. She said he had no reason to kill himself. He had plenty of friends, a really good job, and was about to make a ton of money on his company's IPO, and they were newly engaged."

"When you deal with depression, sometimes people hide it well," Cliff said. "What's the deceased's name?"

"Cal Jensen. He was twenty-nine years old. We did find some Xanax in the medicine cabinet."

"We all have anxiety from time to time," Cliff added. "Of course, if you're an accessory to a murder and living a double life, you might need some Xanax a lot more than the rest of us."

"Did you show her the photo of Paige Turner with Cal at the hotel?" Wyatt asked.

"Not yet. I will though."

"We can wait another day," Wyatt said. "Where did the kid work?"

"Round Robotics," Detective Tanning said. At Wyatt's reaction, he asked, "Does that mean something to you?"

"It does. I remember Cole Adams, Paige's fiancée, telling me he got a job there. Odd."

"I don't get it," Cliff said.

"It's probably a coincidence that Cole Adams and Cal Jensen worked there together, and a Paige Turner look-a-like shows up with Cal Jensen at the Wilbur Hotel."

"What are you getting at, Wyatt? That they made a robotic clone of Paige Turner?" he asked, chuckling.

"You all done laughing, Cliff? We need to pay a visit to Round Robotics."

"And what do you think we'll find there?"

"I have no idea what I'm looking for, to tell you the truth," Wyatt said. "Maybe Pandora's box. But this is not your average suicide even though all the evidence appears that Cal Jensen took his own life."

"There is something else," Detective Tanning added. "A little over a year ago, a young man named Charlie Nash, who was also coincidently employed at Round Robotics, went missing after a night of drinking."

"Foul play?" Wyatt asked.

"I don't know. We never found a body."

"Maybe it's all just a big coincidence, or maybe there's more here than meets the eye," Wyatt said. "Let's get the body down and have the forensic team do their work."

"I think we'll have a better idea when we get the toxicology report back."

"Yeah. One other thing, Detective Tanning?"

"Anything."

"For the record, until further notice, let's rule out any suggestions of foul play. Cal Jensen committed suicide."

"I'm good with that," Tanning replied.

They showed their badges at the front gate of Round Robotics and were allowed to pass. They parked in the front of the building.

"What do you think we are going to find, Wyatt?"

"I really don't know, Cliff. But don't you find it a bit strange that a Paige Turner look-alike is connected to a guy who committed suicide and the fiancé of Paige Turner works at the same company?"

"First, we are speculating that the person we saw in the video footage is not Paige Turner."

"That couldn't have been Paige Turner."

"Wyatt, you can't say that with certainty, and if it's not her, do you think this company is creating them?"

"I don't know," he exhaled. "I'm just following my gut, okay? Let's go in and see where it goes."

They were greeted by Carol, who escorted them to the office of William McDonald. She opened the door and gestured they go in.

Bill stood and walked over to them.

"I'm Special Agent Wyatt Miller, and this is my partner Special Agent Cliff Allen."

"I'm William McDonald, chief scientist. You can call me Bill."

They shook hands, and then Bill pointed to some chairs. "Take a seat. Can I get you agents anything?"

"No, we're all set, thanks," Wyatt said.

"So, what brings you here?"

"I'm not sure if you've been notified, but one of your employees, Cal Jensen, committed suicide."

"Actually, I was just told a little while ago. I feel horrible about it. He was a good employee, very talented. He seemed like a happy kid, but sometimes there are pressures in life, and everybody handles them differently. We'll make sure his family is taken care of. Everybody is family here. We will miss Cal. Anyway, how can I help you?"

"I have a photo here of Cal Jensen with a missing person that we've been trying to locate, and maybe you could tell us if this person was an employee of the company."

He handed the picture to Bill, who stared at it, frowning. "I'm sorry; I can't help you." Struggling to keep his composure together, he handed the photo back to Wyatt. "Anything else I can do for you gentlemen?"

"I'm curious. What do you guys do here, exactly?" Wyatt asked.

"I like to say we are building for the future. A world where people let AI do all the work."

"Robots," Cliff said.

"Yeah. You start off with simple tasks now, and then someday an AI will be able to fly a spacecraft."

"Interesting. Can we see some of this stuff in action?" Wyatt asked.

"Well, today's kind of a bad day. Perhaps if you come back some other day, I'd be more than happy to show you around. But you've already seen one of our prototypes in action."

"Where?" Wyatt said. He glanced at Cliff, who shrugged.

"The secretary that greeted you."

"What?" Cliff said. "That was no robot."

"Yeah, she is. Carol does basic tasks—gets coffee, escorts people in, has a small vocabulary—nothing too involved."

"That's amazing," Cliff said.

"Not really. We understand the human psyche, so when it comes to men, you put a hot-looking woman in front of them, and they become stupid. They're too busy looking to notice anything. I'll call her in. Now that you know she's AI, you'll notice her personality."

Carol came back in, and Bill asked, "Carol, where did you get your great looks?"

Carol stared, trying to compute. "I don't know."

"Do you need a ride home tonight?" Bill asked.

Carol stared. "I don't know."

"Can you get me a cup of coffee?"

"What type would you like?"

"Regular with a teaspoon of sugar."

"Okay. I'll be right back."

"Thank you." When she left, Bill said, "She can only respond to certain commands, like taking coffee orders. The default, if you want her to stop bugging you, just say *I don't know*, and she'll say *I'll surprise you* with a touch of flirtation."

"Wow, I wouldn't have noticed," Wyatt said. "I guess we are all set after the demonstration."

"Good. If there's nothing else, I have work to do."

"We would like to talk to Cole Adams."

"Why, if you don't mind me asking?"

"He knows Cal, right?"

"Everybody knew Cal. Just follow me."

They all got up, and Bill led them out of the office and into a long corridor. They passed the high-security area as they were walking.

"What's in there?" Wyatt asked.

"That's our high-security lab. We do a lot of business with the DOD."

Cole sat upright when Bill walked into Cole's office along with the two FBI agents. He almost threw up. They were on to them.

"Cole, this is Special Agent Miller and Allen from the FBI."

Cole nodded. "We've met before."

"It was nice meeting you," Bill said to the agents then left.

"Have you made any progress finding Paige?"

"Interesting you ask. Maybe you can help us."

"How?"

"Have you been told yet about Cal?"

"What about him?"

"Unfortunately he was found dead this morning. He hung himself."

Cole turned a pale white, his heart pounded, and his mind went to a thousand places. *Did Cal really hang himself, or was he murdered? And am I next?* Fighting panic, he snatched his water bottle and drank the contents, yet his mouth was still dry.

"I take it you didn't know," Wyatt said.

Cole's voice cracked. "No."

"Week and a half or so ago, there was an incident at the Wilbur Hotel where a man appeared to be killed by a Paige Turner doppelganger. She was a spitting image. The strange thing about it, the man killed was one of Paige's abductors. So when we saw this, it was very confusing. Was it Paige or somebody who looked like her? We went with the latter scenario. The hotel had surveillance footage." He took a picture out from his pocket and slid it across Cole's desk. "You know anything about this?"

Cole looked down. There as clear as a cloudless day was Cal with Rose. Chip had warned him. And now Cal was dead, and the Feds were involved, which would make someone at Round Robotics very nervous.

"I can't explain it," he said, swallowing hard.

"I'll give you a little advice, Cole," Wyatt said sternly. "Officially, Cal Jensen's death is listed as a suicide. But you know what I believe? Cal Jensen was murdered, and whoever did it made it look like a suicide. Now, if you know something here, whoever took care of Cal, might find you a liability too, you know what I mean? Cal worked here, and somehow there's a carbon copy of Paige Turner running around at a robotics company. I don't think that's a coincidence, do you?"

"Do I need a lawyer?"

"You might, if you're an accessory to a murder. So

for your sake you should work with us. It's in your best interest."

"Maybe you should focus on finding the real Paige," Cole said defiantly.

"We are trying to find Paige, but there's something going on here that doesn't add up. And I think you're holding back on me. I'm going to tell you something; I would be careful who your friends are. That human trafficking ring we discussed over a year ago? Well, somebody decided to join the fun and killed eight of them. They took care of business and saved a girl in the process, but before you say hurray, they weren't there for the girl. You have any ideas?"

Cole didn't know what to say. Miller didn't have all the pieces, but he was going in the right direction. He played coming clean in his head. *You want the truth? Here you go. Yeah, Rose is a self- sufficient human-engineered organic clone that happened to be part of a murder. And while you're at it, there's a carbon copy of Senator Johnson out there. Oh, and by the way, there's some DOD guy that has assassins working for him and downstairs in the lobby take a hard look at the security guy with the crazy eyes and no soul; I'm sure he's got a list of dead people to his name.*

Cole sat tall. "I don't know."

"You don't know what?"

He shrugged. "I don't know anything. I think you should leave now and focus on finding Paige."

"Is that it?" Wyatt said in a raised voice. "I hope I don't get a call and have to tell your folks that you won't be showing up for dinner."

Wyatt walked out in a huff.

"I'm sorry, kid," Cliff said. "But if you know something, it would be to your benefit to tell us, okay? Think about it. Here's my card."

Cliff walked out and caught up with Wyatt. "What the hell? You were really tough on that kid. I've never seen you like that."

"That kid is hiding something. He knows more than

he's telling us, and he's scared. Did you see McDonald's face when we showed him that Paige look-alike photo? He knew something too."

"Okay, I'll give you that. But I think you've been watching too many sci-fi movies, Wyatt.

"When I walked into Round Robotics, my gut was telling me there's something amiss. A kid goes missing last year and now a suicide. You can think they are just coincidences, but they're not. They all go together, and I'm going to find the connection. If that Cole kid isn't careful, he's going to end up like Cal Jensen."

"He'll come around."

"I hope so. You tell me, Cliff. If they can do that with a secretary, what stops them from creating a Paige Turner look-alike?"

Chapter 35

S enator Brock couldn't sleep. He tossed and turned and then stared up at the ceiling. He could now feel the tremendous weight of the decision made years ago tearing him apart. He didn't know how long he could hold it together. He had nowhere to turn. He started thinking that maybe he was expendable. There was never a guarantee that they would keep him around. He knew too much.

He quietly walked downstairs and brewed a K-cup. Lately, he noticed the landscape more than he ever had. He caught himself remembering his painful past of lies and conquests and had finally gotten to a place with no return. He had done the unthinkable by betraying Ben. He realized at that moment he wasn't part of the end game. How could he be? He was a liability. He was just the setup guy with a time limit. One day, it would be over. He had connived through tough spots in life. He had to have a plan B.

He looked at the time; it was five a.m. He took out the laptop and scanned the internet, picking up the latest news. Round Robotics' IPO was happening today. The sad part was he didn't care. He—along with the heavyweights of Washington—were going to make millions from the stock. He thought of how DC had abandoned the people. He was part of the problem, drawn to all the power and perks that went with it. The politicians resembled entertainers, and actors pretended to be politicians now. There was no truth in Washington.

He viewed an old press conference from two years ago in upstate New York. A special agent by the name of Wyatt Miller led the charge. He seemed like an honest, ethical guy. A straight shooter. Someone who looked like he could be trusted.

Joe wrote some notes down and did another search on the internet. He had his man: a Special Agent from New York. He wasn't sure how he would approach him. He would have to do it secretly. The question was how to get ahold of this agent. He took a long drive, looking for a telephone booth. He found one. He called one of his trusted aides and told him to find Special Agent Wyatt Miller's cell number discreetly and to call him back at the phone booth's number. The aide called him back with all the information. Joe wrote it down and made another request of the aide.

"Get me a flight to Indianapolis. Tell Anna I have an important meeting in Washington, and I will call her later."

Senator Joe Brock landed in Indianapolis aboard a private plane around 10 o'clock. He rented a car and drove to Avon, Indiana. The car rolled into the parking lot of Corner Stones, a small restaurant that served lunch and breakfast. He walked in and found a corner table that faced the door and was close to the bar. He ordered a whiskey sour and leaned back, watching the stock ticker go across the TV screen. The talk of the day was the Round Robotics' IPO. A $40 opening and the price was approaching $100. What should have been an exciting day just made his gut churn. He ordered another whiskey sour as Agent Wyatt Miller walked in. Joe waved him over, and he looked exactly as he had in the press conference: tall and sturdy with a hardened look. The perfect agent to carry the torch at the news of his demise.

Joe got up as Wyatt approached. "You do look like a special agent," he said. They shook hands. "I appreciate you could talk to me on such short notice."

Wyatt grinned as he sat. "I'm just down the street. You're the one who had the long travel, Senator."

"Not a big deal. Hey, let me get you a drink."

"Um, I'm good."

"Okay. It's good for the nerves. Anyway, you are probably wondering why I wanted to meet with you." A waiter dropped a whiskey sour in front of Joe.

"Yeah, I'm curious."

Joe swirled around his glass and leaned back in his chair. "I saw you in a press conference in upstate New York. I think it had to do with some serial kidnapping. How'd that go?"

"It's still ongoing. I'm getting closer though. But I'm sure that's not why you flew out here to see me, Senator."

"True. I know people, and you look like an honest and ethical guy who'll do the right thing."

"I'm probably not the proper channel to be going through. So I'm not sure you should be talking to me."

"No, you're the right guy. I can feel it."

"I've got a lot on my plate right now, and I don't see what I could do for you, Senator."

"See, that's the beauty of this; nobody will have an idea about you. Going through proper protocol could be a problem."

"Death threats? Maybe you should be talking to the Secret Service."

He laughed. "Special Agent Miller, I wish I had that problem."

"Let's get to the point then."

Joe pointed toward the TV. "Look at Round Robotics' stock price. It's over $100. Some of the big fish politicians are making a bundle on that. That's how they all get wealthy. I'll make a few bucks myself on it. It's a local company right here in Indiana. Have you ever heard of Round Robotics?"

Wyatt immediately took notice. That Senator Brock talking about the IPO of that company couldn't be another coincidence. "I actually have."

"You should buy some stock in it. They tell me its technology is going to revolutionize the AI industry."

"I've heard that. I don't want to cut you short, but I have some other obligations today."

"I'm sorry. There's a lot at stake here, and I can't exactly tell you what sort of mess I'm in."

"Why?"

"Because people's lives are at stake. No, this has to be done quietly and in a way that doesn't tip off anybody."

Wyatt exhaled. "Senator, you are not making any sense. How can I help you if you don't tell me?"

"I know I'm making this hard. Do you have a family, Agent Wyatt Miller?"

"Yeah. A wife and two kids."

"I have a wife and four kids. What I want to tell you is, if something happens to me, and I believe it will, I need you to investigate it."

"So you're telling me beforehand the future, yet you've told me nothing. What are you involved in?"

"I wish I could tell you. This isn't the time or place, and you would never believe it."

"Try me. You'd be surprised."

"Nice try. You care about your family, right?"

"Of course."

"That by itself is a reason to hold back."

"Then why bring me in?"

"You're the right guy for the job on the news of my passing."

"What do you mean? Someone is going to kill you?"

"That's why you're here," he said, staring at Wyatt intensely. He leaned in. "When it happens, it's probably going to look like a suicide. I'm telling you right now, I'm not committing suicide, okay? Whatever happens it will be obvious yet not what it appears to be."

"If you know this, I don't understand why you can't stop it."

"I can't. Just remember, Agent Wyatt Miller; if I die, it's not the end. It's just the beginning."

Wyatt shook his head and got up. "I wish I could help you, Senator."

"You already have." Joe stared at the TV screen. "Agent Wyatt Miller, do you believe in cyborgs?"

Wyatt's eyes followed his gaze to the TV. "The funny thing is, Senator, I do."

"Well, that's a start."

As Wyatt strolled out of the restaurant, he had a bad feeling about this. And once again Round Robotics seemed to be at the center of it.

Wyatt got in his car and opened the glove box where he'd stashed a pack of cigarettes. He lit one and leaned back in the seat. He exhaled a cloud of smoke, staring at the road ahead. His eyes closed, and his finger felt the scar from a bullet that had pierced his shoulder. He was told he was one lucky guy; one more millimeter to the right, and he would have been a dead man. He grimaced at that thought.

He reflected back on that assignment from a few years back. He'd been part of a unit investigating a violent gang that was terrorizing the Long Island area. The surveillance was night and day. He had taken a break and gone to get a cup of coffee at a local convenience store. As he got out of his car, he noticed a person who appeared to be in distress in the back seat of a car. Walking into the store, he passed two men that were troubled souls. His instincts kicked in, and he stopped in his tracks. He couldn't let it go. He followed the men out and could tell they were gang members just by the tattoos covering their arms. He placed himself in front of the store.

"FBI!" he shouted, then instructed the men to put up their hands.

A shot rang out, and he fell back. In shock at first, he then reacted purely on instincts, pulling the trigger time after time. It was a blur, but after it was over four gang members lay dead. He leaned on the car hood, blood oozing down his arm, sirens in the distance. Then he noticed a young kid weeping in the back seat with his hands tied. The boy would have been heading to his death if he hadn't stepped in. Wyatt wondered if the kid's redemption had set him on the right path. After a month of office duty, an investigation declared that his actions had been warranted.

His phone buzzed. The caller's number was blocked.

"Special Agent Wyatt Miller. Who's this?"

The man on the other end said, "I have information on who is responsible for the missing girls."

"How did you get this number?"

"Nathan Ogden, he's your ringleader. He's the son of billionaire Ed Ogden."

Wyatt changed his tone. "Who are you? How do you know this?

"Keep following the path of dead bodies."

"What do you mean?"

"You know what I mean, Agent Miller. The dead bodies on the farm in Kentucky. There were eight of them. We squeezed enough information out of one."

"Ah, you're with the group tracking them down."

"Yeah. I want you to arrest Nathan Ogden for running a sex trafficking ring. But his father, Ed Ogden, is a powerful person who is well-connected in Washington. So, I'll give you five days to bring him in."

"I need evidence."

"You want evidence? I'll give you evidence. We have an associate of Nathan's right here. He's been a good chap and has given us all the information we need. He needed a little persuasion."

Wyatt heard a bang in the background. "What was that?"

"Another dead body for you to follow, Agent Miller. You got a pen?"

"Yeah." He wrote down the information.

"Remember five days—and that's being generous."

"I'll need more time."

"I'm sorry, Agent Miller, but you have five days."

"And if I don't take him in?"

"We'll take care of it ourselves. The old-fashioned way."

"Wait; who are you?"

"One last thing, Agent Miller. He told us that they were planning another kidnapping tonight for a businessman overseas. Well, it won't happen."

"You can't take the law into your own hands."

"Criminals tend to respond very well to our tactics; you guys are soft. My guess is you won't be getting much sleep tonight."

"Who are you?" he repeated.

"To these thugs I'm their executioner. Good luck, Agent Miller."

The phone went dead.

Wyatt looked at the information the caller had given him, then punched in a number on his phone.

"Cliff? Pack. We're going to Kansas City."

36

In downtown Maryville, Missouri, as the band played in the background, Suzy sat on a stool at the bar nursing a vodka and lemonade, or so it appeared. With long, blonde hair, a perfect smile, and blue eyes, she played the role of a college kid looking for fun many times on campuses and in downtown bars, nights she couldn't remember. She played an easy target for kidnappers looking for a pretty, blue-eyed blonde. Tonight, she would be the bait.

It didn't take her long to be noticed by the traffickers. They homed in on her like a cat to tuna. A man wearing a baseball cap sat on the barstool next to her. He ordered a beer and glanced over at her from time to time. She ordered another "vodka" and lemonade, but it was just water. She played the part of a girl under the influence and flashed a smile at the man next to her. That was his opening.

"My name is Tim."

"Nice to meet you, Tim. I'm Suzy. You come here often?"

"Sometimes. How about yourself?"

"I come here every now and then. I go to school here. So what do you do?"

"I work as an accountant."

"Accountant, huh?"

"I'm majoring in political science." Suzy said.

"You're going to be a lawyer?"

"Yeah. I want to lock up the bad guys."

"Nobody locks up the bad guys anymore. Hell, petty crime is a career."

"Is that so?" she said with a warm smile. "You sound like a criminal, Tim. For an accountant, you sure have an opinion on crime."

"My brother is a lawyer. He says this stuff all the time."

"Let me guess. He's the good brother; you're the black sheep of the family," she said with a grin.

"Maybe. Where are your friends?" he asked, trying to figure out his next move.

"Oh, they're around here somewhere."

"I love your blue eyes."

She smiled. The joke was on him. They weren't blue eyes; they were killer eyes. She had to put up a charade. She was no shy, sweet, naive girl, and if this was one of the kidnappers, he would show his hand.

He leaned back confidently and nodded his cap at a guy in the background, as she took a sip of her drink. It was on. But little did he know they were being stalked. In a jungle, sometimes you're so focused on the kill you forget about the other predators on the prowl.

She got off the stool and swayed. "Whoa."

"You okay to drive?"

"I'm fine. I'm only up the street. My girlfriends have a ride. It was nice to meet you, Tim. Maybe I'll see you around here sometime."

"You're going already?"

"It's getting late. I got to get up early tomorrow."

"You sure you can drive? I can give you a ride."

She grinned. "I'm sure you're a nice guy, Tim, but a girl can't be too careful nowadays," she said with a chuckle. "You never know what nut you might bump into."

"So you think I'm one of those guys."

"Of course not, Tim," she said, patting his cheek and pretending she was tipsy.

He watched as she strolled to the door. She was perfect. It should be an easy snatch. He followed. The plan was in play. His wingman had identified her car and hopped into a waiting van. There were two guys in front. He rode in the back. They pulled up to the front of the bar, and Tim got in the back.

They followed her car, waiting for their opportunity. She rode through downtown Maryville and took Highway 46. They followed in the shadows. She turned onto a side road and drove along farmland with no cars in sight. They pounced.

Suzy felt her car being banged from behind. The next jolt caused her to lose control and spinout off the road. She was in a gully. She was dazed at first, then gathered her composure in the nick of time. When two men approached, the doors were locked. They immediately smashed the driver's side window.

Tim reached in and unlocked the car and forced open the door and grabbed her with both hands. "Suzy, you remember me. I'm sorry. You can make this hard or easy, but you are coming with us."

She cocked the hammer with one hand and pulled the gun close. "I'm sorry, Tim, you picked on the wrong girl."

She fired off two shots, striking him. He fell back with a stunned look. The second man reached for a gun but was too late. Suzy fired two more shots hitting the man squarely in the chest. He fell. A third man who'd been leaning against the passenger side door of the van sprang forward, hopped into the van, and sped off. Suzy emptied her magazine, hitting the back tire. She reloaded as a second car raced behind the van.

She went to look over her handy work. Tim was moments from death, his eyes wide. She looked down at him, wondering what he was thinking. She felt no remorse. He got what he deserved.

Meanwhile, Ross was in the car with his partners as they chased down the van, which spun out when it failed to negotiate a curve and landed in the woods. The two men in the van scrambled to get out and exchanged gunfire. Ross's men finished off the third kidnapper and tracked down the fourth, dragging him out of the woods on his knees.

"Well, well, well," Ross said, looking down, "I'm not sure what to do with you."

The man acted defiant. "You guys have no idea who you are fucking with."

"Oh, I think we do. I actually like getting rid of scum like you. Taking these young girls without caring about all the misery, pain, and suffering you cause everyone. No. I enjoy this, actually. You got anything to say?"

"Fuck you."

"Ah. Should I call Roy? He's been pretty hard to get ahold of lately. You want to know why? Because he's dead. We're our own legal system. It's very effective."

The man looked beaten.

"Your ties to the cartels aren't going to help you. I've taken this kind of personally. I have a daughter, and I told her when she was little there weren't any monsters in the world. I fibbed. Anyway, you have nothing to offer me. I hate chaos; listen to how quiet it is right now. That's peace. We have to be going, and the cops are probably on their way."

There was a gunshot, and then Ross walked away.

Suzy's car rolled to a stop as Ross and his crew were finishing up. She said through her shattered car window. "I guess you didn't need my help after all."

"It looks like you didn't need us, but thanks for helping us out on short notice."

"My pleasure. Here you go."

"What am I going to do with a blonde wig?"

"Try it on," she said, with a sly grin.

Chapter 37

Senator Ben Johnson stared out into the small quad surrounded by the wall topped with barbed wire. The green grass and the patio gave it a luxurious look, yet, it was the devil's den. He exercised in it every day, taking half-hour walks around the perimeter. He tried to figure if there was a way out, but it was sealed tight. He wondered how his family was doing and didn't want to think about the imposter that had taken up residency, a horror that chilled his bones.

He was dressed like he was on vacation, in shorts and a T-shirt. He now had a beard with no interest to shave. It was like he was on a deserted island waiting for a ship to rescue him. He ate a breakfast of oatmeal and a banana. He loaded up a K-cup and watched the coffee flow into the mug and walked out to the terrace and stared at the high wall with the bright sun in the background.

He did his usual stroll, walking along the perimeter of the wall, when a voice called out from the other side. "Hey, Senator, how're you doing?"

Ben stopped and moved toward the voice on the other side of the wall. "Who are you?" he whispered.

"I work here. My name is Charlie. I keep the place running."

"What do you mean?"

"It's not what you think. The people that serve you aren't real."

"What are you talking about?"

"They're advanced AI. It's a test facility. I keep them working. That's how I stay alive. They can hear everything in this place except this dead spot."

"What about security?"

"Security here is very real. I'm working on a plan to get us both out of here."

"Is there a way out?"

"Possibly. It might take some time, but I think there is a way out."

"Good. Who the hell is behind this?"

"I don't want to say too much right now. I'm a prisoner like you, except I have job duties with a little more freedom. I just do what they say."

"Why me?"

"You are just a conduit for a bigger plan. That's all I really know."

"Can they actually make a carbon copy of me that no one would know the difference?"

"Afraid the answer is yes, Senator. I got to go. We'll talk another time, okay?"

"Yeah."

There was hope.

Chapter 38

C ole walked into the facility, walked down the long corridor, and paused as the eye scanner unlocked the lab door. He wondered if Cal had really committed suicide. It seemed too coincidental. He had this bad feeling they knew about the incident at the Wilbur Hotel, and having Special Agent Wyatt Miller asking questions put a target on their back.

He saw Josh leaning back in a chair.

"What the hell are you doing, Josh?"

"Waiting for you."

Cole looked around. "Where's Rose?"

Josh shrugged. "They took her."

Cole's heart dropped. "What the hell?"

"With Cal's death and the FBI snooping around, hell, we don't need them. We've made a killing on the IPO. If we leave, we can sell our shares. We don't have to wait six months. I don't need this shit, Cole. We can get a job anywhere with our résumés."

Cole was quiet, trying to comprehend his future. He sat down next to Josh.

"I was afraid of this day. Cal is gone. What the hell are they going to do with us?"

"Well, they aren't going to keep paying us to sit in an empty lab."

"No shit. I got a bad feeling about all this."

The lab phone rang. Josh went over and picked it up. He listened, said, "Okay," and hung up.

"What?" Cole asked.

"McDonald wants to see us."

"Great."

"Yeah. At least it isn't crazy eyes. Yet."

They both marched down the long corridor until they came to the reception area on the lower level and took the escalator to the second floor. They went past Sid's office and came to McDonald's, where their favorite AI Carol greeted them.

"This feels a little like déjà vu," Josh said. "I feel like Dean Benson is getting ready to call us in."

"Yeah."

The door opened. Bill stood tall. "Come on in," he said, not smiling. "Take a seat."

Bill sat at his desk, hands clasped, leaning forward. "A lot has happened in the past month. I've been distracted. Sid has been on leave. Cal took his life. The IPO. We are negotiating the final details of a big defense contract. I just didn't have the time to focus on your project. Now you are probably wondering what's going on and what happened to your AI, Rose. She told us her name. It's amazing what you guys accomplished basically unsupervised. Sid told me you were a savant, Cole. He wasn't too far off the mark. You created a genetically engineered AI out of thin air. I mean Rose ..." He shook his head. "You couldn't distinguish the difference between her and a human. It's frigging amazing." He smiled. "You guys thought I was going to fire you, didn't you?"

They both nodded.

"I'm actually promoting you guys. You are moving up to level two. You guys will work with Mitch for the time being. You'll both get a nice ten percent pay raise. Meanwhile,

while the paperwork goes through and you get updated security clearance, you have the rest of the day off. A little token from me for a job well done." He leaned back and smiled. "Well, what do you think?"

They both felt a sense of relief.

"That's great, Mr. McDonald. Thanks for the raise," Josh said.

Cole tried to put on a happy face; he had just gotten a raise and a promotion. It just all seemed too convenient. Maybe he was being too cynical, but he sensed there was something more to all this. He just stared at Bill, blocking out Josh's conversation, and he saw the devil.

"Cole, what do you think?"

"It's great, Mr. McDonald. Thank you."

"That's not all. Luke Richards is having a small gathering with officers of the company at his house this evening to celebrate the IPO and the direction the company is heading. Mr. Richards is expecting you both."

"We look forward to it," Josh said excitedly.

"Good. Seven o'clock. Bring your appetite. It's casual attire."

Chapter 39

"We are going to meet Luke Richards," Josh said on their way to their CEO's house. "He's been on the cover of *Forbes*. I wonder who else got invited."

Cole drove in silence, deep in thought while Josh rambled on.

"Richards probably thinks we're awesome. We're getting a raise, a promotion into Level 2. We are millionaires, just look at the stock price; it goes up every day. It's unbelievable. And now we're invited to the CEO's house, and you act like all doom and gloom. Snap out of it."

"This is about Rose."

"So what?"

"They know."

"They know about the incident at the Wilbur Hotel?"

"Yeah."

"We just got a promotion and a raise; they can't be too pissed. You know, you have to get over Paige. She's probably never coming back. You've been a mess since then. Where's the old Cole, the swivel head and all? I just get gloom and doom. You can't live like this."

"I was going to marry her for God's sake, Josh. I loved that girl the first day I saw her in kindergarten. I didn't go to Stanford because of her. You're right though. I shouldn't have built Rose in Paige's likeness. I got carried away. I fucked up, okay."

"Hey, I'm sorry. I miss her too."

"It's okay, Josh." Cole stared straight ahead, his eyes welling up. "Maybe you're right about tonight."

"Forget about it."

"Let me ask you a question."

"Sure."

"Do you think Cal committed suicide?"

"I don't know. He was engaged. Maybe the engagement wasn't going well, and he just ended it. I don't know."

"You know what I think? It has something to do with the Wilbur Hotel or Rose. Then there's the Senator clone and Charlie Nash's disappearance. I don't know; I just have a bad feeling. They take Rose, they give us a promotion and raise, and here we are driving to the CEO's house. Maybe I'm just paranoid. But there is a lot about this company we know nothing about."

"Just relax, Cole. We're good. They know Rose is amazing. They aren't going to fire us."

"That's what I'm not worried about."

The pickup rolled to a stop at the gate, and they were let through by security. The truck arrived at the mansion as an attendant directed them to stop and took the truck.

They walked through the large front doors and were greeted by a smiling Bill. "Hey, you guys look like you could use a drink. First, follow me into the den."

The room was large with oval windows and a partition for either a small discussion with couches and leather chairs or a boardroom meeting. A makeshift bar was set up in the corner of the room. Bill introduced them to the few attendees in the room. They mingled and made some small talk while Bill went to get them some drinks. He came back with a couple of beers.

"Here you go, guys."

They sipped their beers and talked between themselves. It was uncomfortable being there. It felt like all eyes were on them.

Cole nudged Josh. "Look who just walked in."

Luke Richards entered the room wearing a gray suit that matched his hair. The conversation stopped. He shook hands with everyone and saved Cole and Josh for last, walking over to them slowly.

Bill interrupted his path. "Luke, these are the two associates, Cole and Josh, who worked with Cal Jensen creating the AI I was talking to you about."

They both shook his hand nervously. They didn't know what to say. It was like a joke waiting for the punchline.

"So you're the guys who created that unbelievable AI," he said. "I must say it was a job well done. That's as human as you get. She seems to know her name. Even has an attitude. Bill here tells me he had no idea how advanced your skill-set is with this stuff. I like smart people, especially the ones on my team. Well, get something to eat, and I want to talk to both of you later."

They helped themselves to some food, made small talk with the other guests, sat by the pool bar drinking beer. After two hours, Cole suggested they leave.

"This is pretty boring."

"Didn't Luke Richards say he wanted to talk to us later?"

"Yeah. Maybe he's forgotten. I don't think he gives a shit about us."

The grounds surrounding the pool were quiet. "Are we the only ones here now?"

"Just us and Crazy Eyes," Cole said nervously.

Bill walked out to the pool bar. "There you two are. Mr. Richards is ready to talk to you."

They followed Bill into the den, which felt eerily empty. Luke stirred a drink, took a slow sip, and turned to face Cole and Josh.

"Make yourself comfortable. I'm sorry I didn't get a chance to talk to you earlier."

They sat down on the couch. He sat opposite them.

"Quite a place you got here, Mr. Richards," Josh said.

"Yeah, it's not bad. What do you think about Round Robotics?"

"Great company," Cole said. "We like it."

"That IPO was sweet, huh?"

"Yeah," Josh said.

Luke stood up. "They tell me you two created an amazing AI in college. It got chewed up on a farm or something like that. And then Sid puts you on a project to create an AI from scratch. It's sad that Sid is dying from cancer. A good employee, loyal. But that's life. Bill here failed to monitor what the hell you guys had been doing for the past year. Right, Bill?" Luke said, staring at him intensely. "Now, Rose is a technology marvel. Our best scientists couldn't duplicate what the both of you did. Not to mention it was done in a year's time—quite the feat. I'm curious how you were able to create a DNA-based, genetically engineered AI that is as close to human as you can get. Help me out. But before you do, let's bring her out. I like clear images of what you created."

Rose stepped out from the shadows and stood next to Luke.

"Just simply amazing. Images are more powerful than words. While the rest of the industry is busy trying to advance techniques such as model-based reinforcement learning to enable robots to teach themselves through trial and error using direct input from sensors, you've jumped all those hoops into an area very few have gone. Just look at her intelligence, mobility, the beauty, the ability to reason, etc., etc." He walked around her rubbing her shoulders. "And you created all this from scratch. Now, let me in on your little secret."

Josh felt the room get smaller. The accolades he was expecting now seemed to be going in the wrong direction.

Cole gulped hard and sat stone-faced. He didn't know what to say. He had no answer. Josh just looked at Cole as if he had the perfect answer. "I was born to do this. I've been creating things since I was little kid. It was just another step. I don't know. It just came to me. I can't explain it."

"It just came to you, Cole? You are probably right about that. Rose has been a delight. We are not quite sure what to do with her yet. And the more I looked into you, the more interesting you've become. A girlfriend—or was it a fiancée?—got kidnapped over a year ago. I'm sorry to hear that, but Rose here was a good substitute. So much so she told us how much she looked like her. Rose doesn't look like her; she's a damn carbon copy. I guess you really miss her. But there's more."

Cole and Josh could feel the perspiration wetting their shirts. They continuously sipped their beer, hoping it would quench their dry throats.

"Now, the incident in the Wilbur Hotel. You don't need to explain it to me. Revenge, maybe. I have no problem with that. That's a human trait. You wanted to kill the man who kidnapped your girlfriend, and rightly so."

"That's not true," Cole blurted. "We were just testing Rose in a social setting to see how she reacted. That was it."

"And Paige Turner's kidnapper just happened to be there."

"That's right. It was a big coincidence."

"Okay. Let's say I believe you. But allowing Rose to go to a secluded hotel room. What was that?"

"I don't know."

"Deep down you wanted Rose to do your dirty work."

"No, I didn't."

Luke smiled. "We've all done bad things in this room." He glanced at the remaining participants—Bill, Henry, and Mal—who stood in the back of the room. "I don't fault you at all, Cole. You did what you needed to do. I admire that. And Josh, you're no angel; back in college you liked seeing sorority girls naked without their consent."

Josh's smile disappeared.

Luke's smile turned to anger. "Your little caper has put this company in a bad spot. The FBI is nosing around. Everything we've built here could be erased just by the stupidity of a few. I'm not done. Back to Rose, you want me to believe you created her based on your intelligence? Is that what you are saying?"

"I guess."

"You guess? Let me give you a few facts, Cole. When you were a little kid, they found an alien spaceship on your father's farm. Am I right?"

"They found something."

He shook his head. "From what I gathered, a bunch of little kids saw something, which the government denied of course, and they called it some new jet fighter they were testing, but you were there. You saw it, and you know what you saw—aliens that crashed their ship. Let me jump ahead. You found one of these things on your farm and put Humpty Dumpty back together again. Am I close, Cole?"

Cole didn't answer.

"You don't need to lie to me. You somehow copied this technology and applied it to Rose. I'm well aware of what was on that ship, and you've duplicated it. It's like having all of the answers to a test. You have a blueprint, and you executed better than most, which is a skill in itself. Now the question is, are you two assets or liabilities?"

"You know Rose knows the difference between evil and good," Cole said. "You know why I call her Rose, Mr. Richards?"

Rose on cue left the room as if she had been prompted, but Richards was locked in on Cole. He shrugged.

"Because we live in a world of roses and thorns. You just have to know to stay away from the thorns as attracted as you are to the rose."

"Metaphors are nice, but sadly they are only words."

"Words with meaning, Mr. Richards. I quit."

He smiled, looking around the room. "I'm sorry to say, Cole, you can't quit."

"I can quit."

"No, you really can't," Richards said, shaking his head.

"I don't need any more liabilities. Henry and Mal are going to escort you out. I'm sorry that it had to end this way. It's hard to find talent like you two, especially you, Cole. You would have been an asset and become very wealthy, but you just couldn't keep your nose clean."

"You won't get away with this," Cole said, not sure what was going to happen next.

Mal led the way, and Josh and Cole followed with Crazy Eyes Henry in the rear.

They walked down a dimly lit hallway and turned down a stairway. Cole could hear his heart. Josh looked pale. Getting fired would be a piece of cake compared to his dark thoughts. As they got closer to an outside door, another man was waiting. Maybe he was the cleaner, the guy that disposes of the bodies, and nobody finds them again. He wasn't going to go down without a fight if that was their intention.

He heard a commotion behind him. Henry dropped like a bag of weights. Mal turned and was hit by a direct shot from a Taser. He flopped like a fish out of water.

A voice said: "Run!"

Cole and Josh took off like rampaging bulls, knocking down the man by the door. Once outside they didn't stop, the fresh air hitting their lungs giving them a boost. They jumped over a row of small bushes onto an acre of manicured grass. With a half-moon hanging over their heads, they sprinted across the freshly-cut lawn like track stars. They then scrambled through a field of high-grass and maneuvered through dark woods. After an eternity of running, they finally stopped to take a break. Both of them bent over, trying to catch their breath.

"I've never run that fast or for that long in my life," Josh said, wincing and holding his side. "This is a nightmare. Do you think they were really going to kill us? It sure seemed that way."

"I don't know, but I wasn't staying around to find out. We've got to keep going, Josh. They could be on our trail."

Josh leaned against a tree. "Where are we going?"

"I don't know. I don't think we can go to the police. We definitely can't go back to our apartment or to our parents' houses."

"Then where?"

His breathing almost back to normal, Cole leaned against the tree next to Josh. "There's something I've got to tell you. I've been working with this guy from the Department of Defense to uncover the dark side of Round Robotics."

"And you're only telling me this now?"

"I couldn't tell you. These people are killers, and they have an agenda. And the less you knew, the better. I was just protecting you. We can argue about this later. We need to go to Sid's house and find my contact."

"Is Sid in on this?"

"I guess. I don't know much, Josh. But one thing I do know is we got to keep moving."

Mal hurriedly jogged back to the den, where Luke was sitting in a chair holding a small glass of scotch.

"Luke, we have a problem."

"Do we?"

"They escaped. We'll track them down."

"And how did that happen, Mal?"

"Rose hit us with a Taser."

"You hear that, Bill? Rose! Loyal to her creators. We are learning so much about these things, aren't we?"

"What do you want me to do with Rose?"

"Nothing, for now. I like Rose; she has spunk. We can learn a lot from her, Bill."

"We'll find them," Mal chimed in.

"For now, let them go. It will work out better this way."

"What do you mean?" Mal asked, confused.

Luke got up and stared out at the pool. "They're not going to the police. They were accomplices in a murder at the Wilbur Hotel, but that exposes our business, and the last thing we need is legislation into the AI business now. Then we have Cal Jensen's death as a fallback option, a little misunderstanding, and Cole and Josh took care of business. Right, Mal?"

"There's something I got to tell you."

"I don't like the sound of that. What?"

"We got Adams on a surveillance camera snooping around the restricted area in one of the labs."

Luke's face turned cold. "You didn't think it was important to tell me that, Mal?"

"I don't think he saw anything."

"You don't think. What lab was it?"

"Lab 5."

"The lab that our AI senator was in?"

"Yeah, but it was hidden below."

"Do you know for sure he didn't see anything?"

"No," he said in a low voice.

"I'll bet he knows. And how did he get access to the area?"

"Sid."

"Good old Sid. I was going to give you the night off, but now find them. Fucking find them now! Where the hell you going, Bill?"

"I'm not needed here."

"Well, maybe if you had kept a better eye on your employees and had your billion-dollar security systems worked, I wouldn't have to put out these fires."

"There was a lot going on with Sid being out and making sure your senator worked properly."

"Is the pressure getting to you, Bill?" Luke asked quietly. "I pulled you from that dead-end job. You knew what you signed up for, and there is no turning back now. You like the good life, the fancy cars, the hot women, and the big money. Don't screw up again, or you'll end up six feet under. We are all expendable, Bill. Unfortunately, this stunt by Sid is going to cost him his life, and it's on you. We're doing him a favor, and he's no use to us anyway."

"We don't need to do that, Luke." Bill pleaded. "The guy's got cancer for God's sake."

"He's a liability and no use to us now."

"You're such a cold bastard."

"No, the people behind me are the cold bastards. I have to answer to them. You don't want a visit from them. Tomorrow Mal will sprinkle a little DNA around, and it will be case closed for Cole and Josh. That's the great thing about science today. Don't forget our objective and the big picture; you got that?"

Bill nodded. "Yeah."

"Good."

Chapter 40

W yatt and Cliff landed in Kansas City and took a car to the address communicated to him by the man responsible for the dead bodies that were piling up. The car rolled to a stop in a quiet, somewhat run-down neighborhood of small homes. A place where people minded their own business.

They got out of their car and walked up broken brick steps. The front door was unlocked. They drew their guns and entered the home, making their way to the kitchen. There, just as the man on the phone had said, was a dead man tied to a chair.

Wyatt saw the man's phone, put a glove on, and looked through his calls. "Dead men have a hard time answering calls," he joked. "I'm sure these calls might link all this together. Cliff, why don't you call this in while I look around."

Wyatt walked through the run-down house. The faucets dripped. The refrigerator stored only beer. The floors were stained. The ceiling paint was peeling, and the walls had holes. He rubbed his chin, unsure how this player tied into the international trafficking ring.

"They're on their way, Wyatt."

"Good."

"Who the hell are these people?"

"I wish I knew, but they're doing a lot better than us. We're just following their trail of dead bodies with no results."

"Well, eventually they'll run out of bodies."

"You would think so. I'd just like to know what's in it for them."

"They like it."

"Yeah, they do. I also think they're having fun taunting us."

"Look at this place," Cliff said. "It's a shit-hole. This isn't any sophisticated trafficking ring."

"Looks can be deceiving. Let's find out who this guy is and his connections. That will give us a clearer picture."

Wyatt's phone buzzed, the caller unknown.

"You remember me, Agent Miller?"

"How could I forget?"

"I told you, it's a waste of time tracking my phone. My IP address is well masked, and none of your specialists have the talent to break it."

"Why're you calling?"

"I figured you'd have arrived. You've assessed the situation and are no further along than you were before. I'm going to save you some time. The phone calls will lead you to right where I just finished up. The man in the kitchen is Roy Small, not a real nice guy. The world won't miss him. Taxpayers won't be paying his bills in prison. It's a win for all of us. A punk who started off with petty crime, Roy worked his way up to larceny and graduated to racketeering, drug trafficking, and now human trafficking. Served time in prison and made more contacts as he honed his skills. Great system we have."

"The system doesn't need a self-proclaimed, judge, jury, and executioner."

"You're mocking my methods, Miller. You would still be scratching your head back in the office with nothing to show for it. And without expediting information out of Roy, we wouldn't have been able to stop their next kidnapping that happened tonight."

"Where?"

"In Maryville, Missouri, about ninety-five miles from where you are. Four dead bodies for you."

"You're efficient."

"I don't want you to miss anything. There are two bodies about a mile up from the car accident. Good luck. And don't forget you have four days before we take things into our own hands with Nathan."

"I need more time."

"Everybody needs more time, Agent Miller. Once I wrap up this assignment, I'm hearing the next job is going to be quite interesting. I don't want to spoil it, but I have a feeling we're going to be working together indirectly."

"Is that so? Who the hell do you work for?"

"All in due time, Agent Miller. But I'm going to give you a little hint; it has to do with a senator."

"Wait—"

The phone went dead. Wyatt replayed the weird conversation he'd had with Senator Brock and felt a queasiness turning his stomach. But for now he needed to focus on the case in hand. He saw a pair of police officers and a forensic team enter the house.

"Come on, Cliff; we're going to Maryville, Missouri."

After a ninety-minute drive, they found the crime scene in the early morning hours. There was a line of cruisers lining the empty road. They flashed their FBI badges to a sergeant at the scene.

"We didn't call the FBI," the officer said. "How the hell did you guys get here so quickly?"

"We're good," Cliff said.

The sergeant smiled. "Right."

"There's a dead body in Sheffield that's tied to these guys," Wyatt added.

"Wow. It looks like a drug deal gone bad or that these guys owed someone money. Then they just executed that guy on the ground. You might have a different idea."

"Well, it wasn't a drug deal," Wyatt said, looking down at the dead body.

"We're analyzing the tire tracks, shell casings, who these people are."

"They're expendable, low-level criminals who are part of a ring trafficking young women," Wyatt said. "You won't find much here. The people who killed them are highly professional."

"How can you tell that?"

"I've been tracking this ring for two years now, starting in New York, except somebody now is tracking them down and taking the law into their own hands."

"Makes your job easier," the sergeant said, grinning.

"That's a nice way to put it," Cliff said. "But it opens up another can of worms."

"A mile up the road, you'll find two more bodies," Wyatt said.

"How do you know that?"

"I'm good," Wyatt quipped. "Check the nearest bars and see if they have any surveillance footage of these guys."

"Okay. I'll send my officers up the road."

"Thanks."

Chapter 41

Sid heard a loud and relentless pounding on the door. He looked at the clock; it was 6:00 a.m. He dragged his tired body off the bed and slowly shuffled to the door as if he had lead in his feet.

"Hold on, I'm coming," he barked in a hoarse voice. "Who the hell is it?"

"It's Cole Adams and Josh Finnigan."

Sid slid the door bolt to the side and opened the door, dressed in a T-shirt and sweatpants, his hair long gone.

"I should be surprised, but I kind of expected it. Come on in." He stuck his head out and peeked out at the neighborhood before closing the door. "Sit down. You want some coffee or something to eat? You guys look like hell. What's going on?"

Cole and Josh looked at each other.

"How're you feeling?" Cole asked.

"Look how thin I am, and it's not diet pills," he quipped. "Seriously, I got six months or so. The cancer has metastasized. All that smoking when I was young, I guess. Nobody is going to miss me, though. Sad to hear what happened to Cal."

"You heard he committed suicide?"

"He didn't commit suicide. No way. He told me about your little test drive with Rose."

"He did?" Josh asked, surprised.

"Cal would come over here in the evening from time

226

to time and give me an update of what was happening at work." Sid coughed, deep and wet. "Hold on a minute while I get this crap up."

When he came back from the bathroom after a series of wracking coughs, Cole asked, "You okay, Sid?"

"Oh, I'm fine. I'm used to the coughing fits and spitting up crap and blood. At least I still got my mind. Anyway, I know all about you creating a genetically engineered AI in a year's time. Cal told me it broke all the laws of physics, but he just went with it. It was amazing watching Rose develop. I knew your college project AI was from the same technology that Round had in its possession. I never worked with it, I'll admit. Part of me didn't want to hire you, and the other part wanted to see how far you would go."

"You know what's going on there, right?" Cole asked.

"I do and I don't. It's dangerous if you know too much, as I suspect you are finding out. I'm sorry I put both of you in harm's way. But seeing what you saw was well worth the risk. The senator, pretty damn diabolical."

"They can't pull that off, can they?"

"I don't know. It does seem crazy. But it doesn't really matter to me. I'm not going to be around."

"We have to stop them."

"That's Chip's job. The world is going to hell in a handbasket. According to Chip the planet is dying anyway."

"What do you mean the planet is dying?" Josh asked, concerned.

"I wouldn't worry about it, Josh. You have some time. I just mean based on natural disasters, a pandemic, nuclear war, asteroids, and over-population, all good things come to an end."

"Just as I become rich, now you tell me it's going to end sooner than later?"

Sid shrugged. "Hey, you never know when it's your time. But maybe you'll be one of the lucky ones and get off the planet in time."

At Josh's look of utter confusion, Sid looked at Cole. "You never told him?"

"I couldn't. Chip told me to be quiet."

"Who's Chip?" Josh asked.

"The DOD guy I just told you about in the woods," Cole said.

"Well, you can explain it to him on the way," Sid said.

"On the way where?"

"Nobody pounds on my door at six in the morning unless they're in trouble. And looking at your disheveled states, I would say you need to get out of Dodge."

"I thought Chip could help us," Cole said.

"Oh, he's going to help but not here. You're going to take a train to Cheyenne, Wyoming. Chip will have someone pick you up there."

"Won't people wonder what happened to us?" Josh asked.

"Well, you have two choices: you can either end up like Cal and Charlie Nash—which I don't have time to explain—or you can disappear for a while."

"I already know about Charlie Nash," Cole told him.

"Good. Then you know what you have to do."

"What about you?"

"What about me? Do I look like I'm in any shape to travel? And does it really matter? I'll be just fine here. So you saw Luke's dark side?"

"Yeah. I think he was going to kill us."

Sid smirked. "This is just the beginning for you two. It's going to get a lot harder than you know if they actually think you can foul up their plans. Going forward shut off your phones and no calls, no internet. You two are going dark if you care about your lives." Sid got up and escorted them to the door and handed Cole a key fob. "Take my car to Jackson Station and leave the key under the mat. Good luck."

"Thanks, Sid," Cole said. "I wish we'd have met under better circumstances."

"Yeah. But you guys have a higher calling."

Later that morning Sid sat down with a bottle of water and a mound of pills, his daily routine. It was getting old. He was losing his strength a bit more each day. He got up and wobbled to the kitchen and stared out the window, watching a hawk soaring above. For most of his life, he'd never taken the time to notice such things or even cared. The one thing this slow death was giving him was the opportunity to see the world for what it was. The smallest things now grabbed his attention. And all those times he thought he'd had problems—those were never really problems.

His thoughts and reverie admiring the hawk were interrupted by a knock on the back door. He was a popular guy this morning.

"Who is it?"

There was no answer. Then a moment later Mal pushed the door open and walked in followed by Henry.

"Sid Martin, how're you doing?"

Sid shuffled backward, almost losing his balance. "What a surprise."

"Do you know where Adams and Finnigan are?"

"Why would I know that?"

"It doesn't matter, Sid."

"Luke sent you, huh? He afraid a dying man might rat out his little Orwellian plan?"

"No. You are going to serve a nice purpose," Mal said with a sly grin. "Henry's got a little DNA to throw around. You see where we are going?"

"This is looking like a frame job. You guys are good at that, like with Cal Jensen's suicide. So how are you going to take me out? I'm not fond of hanging. Pills are an easier way out. Look at all the insurance costs I'll be saving."

"You're right, Sid. Cole and Josh are about to be wanted men at your expense. So just consider it taking one for the team. I'm sure Luke will repay your good deed by sending a nice bouquet of flowers to your funeral."

"Well, you'll have to thank him for me."

Sid grimaced and shrieked in pain as a knife pierced his back, dropping him like a rock. Henry stood emotionless over Sid until he passed his last breath.

Chapter 42

C liff turned their rental car onto a tree-lined street with manicured lawns in the affluent town of Highland Park, Texas.

"Nice neighborhood," he said. "You'd never guess this was command central for a human trafficking ring."

"Once they know we're on to them, they'll just move the operation somewhere else and we'll never get the big fish," Wyatt said, his voice glum.

"Isn't that always the case? The big fish more times than not get away."

"I'm torn over telling this guy that he's on a termination list."

"Maybe we should just stake it out to see who these guys are that are hunting them down," Cliff suggested.

"No, we'll tell him and see what happens."

"Do these vigilantes know who his father is?"

"They don't care, Cliff. They're hell-bent on finding Paige and taking out whoever is in their way."

"But if they know now where Paige is, why waste their time finishing off this guy?"

"Good question. Maybe it's personal."

The car rolled to a stop in front of a modest house. "You would never know that the son of Ed Ogden would be living so modestly," Cliff said.

"Maybe it's a good front."

They got out of the car and walked up to a charming cottage, knocking on the door.

"Who is it?"

"FBI."

The door opened slowly. "You have badges?"

"Sure." They held up their ID. "Are you Nathan Ogden?"

"No."

"Can you get him?"

"I'm Nathan. What do you want?"

"Do you know a Roy Small?"

"I've met a lot of people in my lifetime."

"Well, let me jog your memory." Wyatt pulled out a picture. "Is that you and Roy."

"Yeah. He's an acquaintance. So what?"

"Well, he's dead, and he had a long criminal history and is associated with some of the nastier people in the world."

"What do you want from me?"

"Roy Small is, or should I say was, connected to a human trafficking ring. Actually, it's a worldwide ring, and your name happened to come up in conversation."

"I have nothing to say. What's your name?"

"Did I forget to introduce myself? I'm Special Agent Wyatt Miller."

"Do you know who my father is?"

"We have a good idea."

"Good. You know if I make one phone call to my father, you won't have a job. So if you want to talk to me again, you'll have to go through my lawyer."

"That's fine, but we're here to give you a heads-up. We have intel that these men who killed Roy Small are looking for you."

"I'm a big boy. I think I can handle myself."

He shut the door.

"That went well," Cliff said.

"Yeah. He thinks because he's Ed Ogden's son that he's untouchable."

Wyatt was back in his Indianapolis office. His desk was a mess, piled with computer printouts. He fiddled with the computer, putting together a timeline and going over the forensic evidence. He studied videos and snapshots of the dead players. The original crime spree had started as a perceived serial killer, which transformed into a human trafficking ring then morphed into the bizarre: a vigilante hit team tracking down the kidnappers.

He was in the process of requesting a search warrant for Nathan Ogden's residence, but it was a 50-50 shot that the judge would grant it based just on his association with Roy Small. The mystery caller that taunted him with the body-count updates was the one holding the key information, but he had his own agenda.

The phone buzzed from an unknown caller. The FBI had failed to track the number, saying it was untraceable at the moment. He stared at his phone, afraid to answer it. He already knew the update.

He picked up the phone, "Agent Wyatt Miller."

"So formal."

"What is it today?"

"You already know."

"You took down Nathan Ogden."

"Yeah. I warned you. I expected the Bureau's slow response; somebody's got to clean up the mess."

"Why do you keep calling me?"

"I like you, Wyatt. Like I said, I have a new assignment, but I got one more item on the current list before I'm done. So I won't be calling you for a while. I'm going out of the country."

"Are you bringing Paige Turner home?"

"Maybe. You have your hands full. When I get back, we'll talk."

"Who the hell do you work for?"

"Well, if you do your homework, Agent Miller, you just might figure it all out someday. Good luck." The phone went dead.

Wyatt got up and peered out his window. He straightened his tie. A voice shattered his thoughts.

"Wyatt," Cliff said. "I just got a call from Detective Carlos Tanning."

"Yeah, what did he want?"

"He said a guy who just happened to be an employee of Round Robotics was found dead in his home this morning. He was stabbed in the back."

"A coincidence I'm sure. Well, at least this time it's a straight murder."

"There's more. A witness, a paperboy, saw two guys go into his house early yesterday morning."

"And?"

"Detective Tanning identified those two guys as employees of Round Robotics."

"Let me guess, Cole Adams and Josh Finnigan."

"Yeah."

"They're not killers."

"Well, they were reported missing yesterday evening."

Wyatt smirked. "Let's go see our favorite detective."

He grabbed his windbreaker, and a thought crossed his mind; this was all tied to Senator Brock's fears that his life was in peril, and the repeated calls from the mystery caller who knew something that he had yet to reveal.

Chapter 43

A black limousine drove down a paved road surrounded by beautiful wine vineyards in Napa Valley. It came to a stop in front of a large mansion with an old-fashioned porch supported by large white, round pillars.

A small man wearing a tailored suit and fancy sunglasses emerged from the sedan. He carried a suitcase and marched up five steps to the main porch and was greeted by Ed Ogden, a bald, broad-shouldered man with a rugged complexion who controlled a wine and real estate empire. He had powerful friends in Washington who he influenced when favors were needed. He sat in a low-backed chair, sipping a coffee and staring out at his vast landholdings.

He exhaled. "It's been a tough day, Stan. Let's go for a walk."

The two men walked along a worn path. "The vineyard comes to life on beautiful days. I walk this path when I have a lot on my mind; it seems to energize me," Ed says. "I appreciate that you could get over here on short notice. You're a loyal friend. In this day and age, loyalty doesn't mean much, but to me it means everything. The politicians, they don't even know what loyalty is. They change like the wind. Very few have any convictions to anything. I might not agree with you, but at least you stand for something, I can at least respect that."

"How's your wife doing?"

"She's distraught. Planning a funeral is not an easy task, especially when it's your son. The kid never listened. He wasn't like his brothers and sisters. He was always looking for the shortcut. It didn't matter what I said. He was the black sheep of the family. He used our name when he needed it. I can't count all the times I bailed him out. He just ran out of lives. I can't say I'm surprised it happened. I figure it was just a matter of time. I told him to stay away from the cartels, the drugs, the slick people who acted like your best friend. But he didn't listen and here we are. I'm not sure I want to hear this, but what was he into? Any ideas who might have done this?"

Stan removed his glasses. "From what I've found out, Nathan was managing a human trafficking ring."

"What do you mean?"

"It looks like he was kidnapping young women and selling them."

"You've got to be kidding? I didn't raise him to do shit like that. I thought the drugs were bad. You know the kid was never right. He hated me, except when it suited him to bail him out. A frigging human trafficking ring? That's all I need is for this to get out in the media."

"I already took care of it. We scrubbed his computers. The Feds were already snooping around; it was only a matter of time before they'd figured it out. An associate of his was killed a few days earlier. He had quite the rap sheet."

Ed shook his head. "You know I can't let this go unanswered. You know that. As much as he probably had it coming to him, he's blood."

"Yeah."

"Any ideas who was behind this?"

"It appears that somebody is looking for one of the missing girls and is hell-bent on finding her. And they are a fearless bunch. From what I been told, there is a long line of bodies from Indiana to Texas."

"So a parent of one of these kids hired this crew. Hell, I would do the same to find my kid, and I wouldn't spare anyone," Ed admitted. "They just shouldn't have picked on my kid."

"Most of these kids came from low or middle income. I doubt it was one of the parents funding this. They would have needed some serious money to hire these guys. My guess they are ex-military, and somebody connected has a reason why they got involved. Usually nobody gives a shit."

"You think you can find the source?"

"I think so."

"Are you going to use Tucker for this? He's never let us down."

"He's on the top of my list."

"Good. Take care of it, Stan. It sends a message to those out there who want to fuck with me."

"I understand."

"Do this discreetly as possible."

"Don't worry. I'll take care of this."

"I know you will."

They shook hands.

The black limousine traveled down a bumpy dirt road until it came to a farmhouse in the backroads of Texas. Stan emerged from the sedan with a folder in his hand. He walked around the house toward the sound of gunshots echoing off the hills.

Tucker pulled back his long, black hair. He wore jeans and a T-shirt that fit his lanky frame. In a crouch position, he fired a nine-millimeter continuously at targets placed at different ranges. He reloaded then turned to see Stan standing behind him.

He removed his earmuffs. "Stan the man. Even with earmuffs I knew someone was behind me. But don't ever sneak up behind me again; you might end up with a bullet in your head. Come on in. I need a beer."

The two men walked inside. Tucker reached into the refrigerator and pulled out a beer. "You want one?"

"No."

Tucker smirked. "Stan, I like fast cars, that's why I have a vintage GTO sitting out front. I like fast women. I like hang gliding and parachuting. I like living on the edge, defying death. You, on the other hand, work in the shadows, sitting in front of a computer plotting people's demise, and yet you always believe that the shit will never come upstream. How many hits have you ordered? The guy who looks like a librarian that everyone can trust. I know who you are; you're cold as ice. And the funny thing is, if someone paid me to take you out Stan, I wouldn't hesitate. Now that I got that off my chest, sit down." Tucker put his feet up on the table and leaned back in the chair. "What do you have for me?"

Stan took out a folder from his briefcase and slid it across the table.

Tucker opened it and slowly scanned the contents. "It's too bad about Ogden's kid, but he was garbage and got what he deserved. As we all eventually do. So the old man wants me to take care of the people who took out his pathetic son." He took another swig of beer.

"Will it be a problem?"

"No."

"I don't know the source yet, but when I do, I'll let you know. This needs to be done discreetly."

"How discreetly, Stan? I mean, aren't they all done discreetly?"

"Yeah."

Tucker went through the photos. "Quite a group. I'm curious why an elite group like this would be involved with this piece of shit."

"That's not for you to worry about."

"Stan, everything matters," he said. "You wonder why I've lasted so long in this business? It's because I need to know what makes my targets tick. What did the kid do to get their attention? Drugs? What? You want me to do the job or not, Stan?"

"The kid was into human trafficking."

Tucker took another swig of beer and shook his head. "Our business is always about revenge. It's a never-ending cycle, never solves anything. You ever read history? It's all wars and bloodshed and the masters of society who always think they have control, but in reality they really never do. I make my money off people like Ogden who think they are in control." Tucker belched out a laugh.

"The same terms apply. I'll wire the first installment."

Tucker looked at Stan, brows furrowed. "I got to tell you something. I don't want you to panic, but whatever you do, don't get off that seat."

"Why?" Stan asked, concerned.

"Well, I wasn't expecting company today, and earlier I was practicing and placed a pressure-sensitive IED device under your seat. Forgot all about it. So don't move."

"Do something!"

"Stan, do you ever smile? Where's your sense of humor? You work in a business where someday you are going to piss off someone, somewhere, and you might or might not see it coming. So loosen up."

Stan sat as still as possible.

"Now where's my cutters? I have to find them. You'll have to hold on."

"You are not going to leave me here!"

"Wait; my cutters are right here, but you know what? I think I'm going to take a ride in my car."

"You can't leave."

"Okay. Then I need an extra $50,000 for this job."

"Forget about it."

"Did you say forget about it?" he grabbed his keys. "I hope you got some stamina, Stan."

"Okay, okay, $50,000 more."

Tucker stood over him like a grizzly bear. "Let me remind you in case you've forgotten. You are the only one that can connect me to the world. Nobody knows I exist except you. My alias Tucker was your invention. So just to be clear: if the day comes that somebody figures out what you are and you give me up, if they don't kill you, I will."

He found the cutters, exhaled, and squatted down next to the chair. He reached underneath, and Stan heard the sound of the clippers cutting.

"That was simple. You can get up now, Stan. And thanks for the extra 50k."

"You are a sick bastard."

"I was just playing with you; there was no IED." He broke into laughter. "If you could only see your face. I had removed it earlier. I thought I would have a little fun with you, and I got another $50,000 out of the deal. But you telling me I'm a sick bastard, I kind of take that personally. You're the frigging cold-blooded mastermind behind the desk, making all the decisions."

"Don't fail, Tucker."

"There you go again. Have I ever failed you before?"

"No, but these men are well-trained."

"I'm going to give you a little tip. If the hunted don't know they are being hunted, it doesn't matter how trained, smart, or how good they are with a gun."

"I'll be in touch," Stan said, and then walked away, still shaken.

"Don't forget what I said," Tucker shouted.

Chapter

44

Victor Diaz sat in front of a computer in an office located in the heart of Lima, Peru. The high-rise building overlooked the Pacific Ocean.

His associate Juan walked in. "Rafael is on line one. He's not too happy."

Well-dressed and unflappable, Victor picked up the receiver. "Hey Rafael, what's the problem?"

"What do you mean what's the problem? I don't see the funds for the latest shipment."

"I wired it yesterday; it should already be in your account."

"Well, it isn't. And you know how I feel about money. I warned you in the beginning: you fuck me, you die."

"Come on, Rafael. We've been doing business for a few years now. Have I ever been late or stiffed you?"

"No. that's why I'm giving you until tomorrow to get me my money. Or you won't have to worry about the next day."

"Hey, I'm sure it's just a bank glitch. I'll have my people straighten it out. Don't worry."

"I'm not worried. It's you who should be worried."

"I'll get you your money." The phone went dead. Victor looked at Juan. "Where's Rafael's money?"

"I sent it last night. He should have it."

"Check with the bank—now."

A few minutes later Juan came back into Victor's office. "There's no money, Victor."

"What do you mean there's no money? I have over $800 million in various accounts. This isn't funny."

"I'm not kidding. Look for yourself."

Victor logged into his bank accounts, staring incredulously at the screen. One account after another all had a zero balance.

"Where is all my fucking money?" he said, pale with panic. "Call every bank, Juan!"

"I have. They said you authorized the transfers."

"What?! I never did that. Somebody's hacked into my accounts."

"What do we do?"

Victor pulled on his beard and covered his face with his hands. "Without that money I'm a dead man."

His secretary opened the door. "Mr. Diaz, there is a man on line one who says he knows where your money is and wants to talk to you."

Victor grabbed the receiver. "Hello. This is Victor Diaz. Who's this?"

"Does it matter who I am?"

"A name would help.

"Well, a friend of mine called me Robby."

"Okay, Robby. Do you know where my money is?"

"I do."

"I want it back."

"In this world people want a lot of things. But you're in luck; I can put all your money back with a push of a keystroke."

"What do you want?"

"I don't want much. But how you answer the next question is going to mean life or death for you. I don't need your dirty money, but I want Paige Turner."

"Could I just put you on hold for a moment?"

"Sure."

Victor looked at Juan. "Tell me this Paige Turner girl is alive and well."

"She's the American girl you paid for over a year ago. She's okay."

"You're sure?"

"Yes."

Victor pressed the blinking light on his desk phone. "Yes, we have her. She's fine."

"Good. I want her home ASAP. You don't get your money until the girl is safely home."

"How do we know you'll act in good faith?"

"Humans are so funny. Always trying to manipulate the situation. You don't. I'm in control here, Victor. You are just going to have to trust me."

"How do I know you actually have control of my money?"

"I have a soft side. Look at your Interbank account. I just put $500,000 back into the account. So get the girl home."

Victor logged into the account, and there was the money. "Why is the girl so important to you?"

"I'm doing this for a good friend. So get her on a flight to San Antonio then a connecting flight to Indianapolis. The sooner you do this, the sooner you get your money back."

Paige sat in a first-class seat on a Delta airline flight. She was almost back in the United States. Her captives had let her go for no apparent reason. They hustled her out as if frightened of something. Then just like that her one-year ordeal was over. All she wanted was to be back in Indiana with her family. She was blocking out the past year and was looking ahead.

When the plane touched down on the tarmac at San Antonio International Airport, relief flooded over her. She felt safe now but still looked around the terminal with caution, watching everybody and anyone. She was tempted to call her mom, but she just wanted to get to Indiana before she made that call. She sat down in a café and ordered a coffee while waiting for her connection. She noticed a man looking at her from a distance. He looked familiar. As she stared he started walking slowly toward her. She froze when it hit her; it was the AI man from Cole's shed.

He came up to her table. "You remember me, Paige?"

She didn't flinch. "I can't believe this. You were in Cole's shed. You're a machine."

"Funny the way you say that. I'm more than a machine, Paige. I'm human without the baggage. Anyway, you're here because of me."

"You got me out! How did you find me?"

"A little persuasion goes a long way. I have special skills in this world, and I owed Cole for what he did for me. I would still be in a dark place in the bottom of that lake, maybe forever. I felt his loss when you disappeared. A human emotion. Can I sit down?"

"Sure."

"Are you okay?"

"I'm okay. Now."

"You live in a barbaric world. You're safe now, Paige. Do you want to call your folks and let them know you're coming home?"

"I want to surprise them."

"Very well."

"I can't believe I'm having a conversation with you."

"You can never predict the future, too many mathematical calculations."

"Did Cole send you to find me?"

"I left about a year ago. I have my own plans, Paige. I can't stay here."

"Here in San Antonio?"

"Here on Earth."

"How will you leave?"

"Let's just say an opportunity has come to my attention."

"How's Cole?"

"That's a good question. He works for an AI company that doesn't have good intentions for mankind."

"What do you mean?"

"Paige, just get your life together. Forget the past. Find Cole. His heart has been broken since you left. Cole has a good heart, and he loves you."

A tear slowly rolled down her cheek.

"This is what is so unique about humans; they have the ability to love and in the same breath to self-destruct and destroy everything around them. Well, Paige, it was good to see you. I must be going. You be careful."

He stuck out his hand. Paige shook it, watching a tear slowly roll down his cheek.

Mrs. Turner heard a loud knock on the front door. She looked through the peephole and let out a shriek of joy that bounced off the walls of the house when she saw Paige standing on the porch. The screams brought the other family members rushing to find Mrs. Turner's arms were wrapped tightly around her daughter, both weeping. Paige's father and brothers watched in amazement with dazed smiles and free-flowing tears.

Paige was home.

The unbelievable had happened. The lost was found. Their daughter and sister were home. The uncomfortable questions would come later, but at that moment, emotion beamed with hugs, smiles, and kisses because prayers had been answered. They circled her like a pride of lions protecting a lost cub.

Then she asked, "How's Cole?"

The room got quiet. Her voice shook. "What's happened?"

Her father broke the silence. "He's missing, along with Josh."

"What do you mean?"

"I don't know the details. All I know is that Josh and he are missing, and the police are involved."

It made no sense in Paige's mind. She had come home, and now Cole was the one missing after an artificial man had saved her from her tormentors. It was a nightmare that wouldn't end.

Chapter 45

Wyatt sat at his desk, contemplating his next moves. He was at the crossroad, and thought about paying a visit to Ed Ogden, but wasn't sure what that would accomplish. Then Detective Tanner had called to say arrest warrants had been issued for Cole Adams and Josh Finnigan in the death of Sid Martin. And there was Senator Brock, with a mystery the politician wouldn't detail, but that Wyatt's mystery man seemed to know something about.

Cliff walked in his office. "Did you hear the news?"

"What news?"

"Paige Turner's home."

"What? How?"

"She's not talking yet. The family had no comment, and they wanted to be left alone for now."

The mystery man did it, Wyatt thought. *He got her back working outside the system.* "Well, the kid has been put through an ordeal, I'm sure. Makes sense she just wants her space, but I would sure like to know how she got home and where she's been."

"What do you think about the arrest warrants for those two guys at Round?"

"I think Adams and Finnigan were framed."

"By whom?"

"You really want me to tell you?"

"Yeah. What's your big theory?"

"It leads back to Round."

"I thought you would say that. What's their motive?"

"I don't know. Maybe they're accomplices to the crime at the Wilbur Hotel, and Sid Martin knew too much."

"I doubt it," Cliff said. "The evidence strongly points to them. You can't deny that. The paperboy saw them around the time of Martin's death, and their DNA is all over Martin."

"It's just too damn perfect."

After a day and a half, the train rolled into the Cheyenne, Wyoming, station. Cole and Josh disembarked and dodged through the crowd to reach the pick-up area. The late afternoon sun was breaking through the clouds as they tried to blend in with the other tourists waiting for an Uber.

A dark sedan pulled up near where they stood. The passenger side car window slid down, revealing a grinning man with shades.

"You guys Cole and Josh?"

They nodded.

"Hop in."

They nervously climbed into the back seat. The man in the passenger seat removed his sunglasses. "My name is Ross. We have a change in plans."

Cole exchanged worried glances with Josh. "Where's Chip?"

"He's tied up, Cole. It's no longer safe, especially for you two. He sent us to pick you up."

"What are you saying?" Josh asked as the car pulled away from the train station.

"That we're aiding and abetting two fugitives," Ross said. He and the driver looked at each other and started laughing.

Cole frowned. "What's so funny?"

"Sorry. Here are your passports with your new identities. We're going to British Columbia."

"What about Wyoming?" Cole asked, feeling numb.

"It's too dangerous right now. The bad news is you are wanted in the death of Sid Martin."

"Sid's dead?" Cole shook his head in disbelief.

"We just saw him," Josh said.

"Exactly. I'm sure they set you up pretty good. Now for the good news; Cole, your girlfriend, Paige, has come home."

"What? She's home! She's okay?"

"Sounds like it."

"I can't believe it. Paige is alive!" he shouted out loud. Nothing else mattered at that moment. He settled down, his eyes watered, his mind preoccupied with thoughts of Paige. His life had turned 360 degrees and now he just wanted to run to Paige, but he couldn't. Then he blurted, "Did Chip have something to do with it?"

"It's not like we didn't try, but no. She's home; that's all that matters."

Cole gazed out the window. He still couldn't believe it, Paige was home, and now he was on the run.

"How long do we have to stay in Canada?" Josh asked.

"Well, that all depends," Ross said with a grin. "The bad boys are going to be looking under every nook and crevice for you. And if you turn yourself in, they'll be able to get to you in any jail or prison. So it might be a while before you get your life back. When Chip gets a chance, he'll fill you in on the next plan of action."

"I told him I felt like a character in a novel."

Ross chuckled. "Let's hope we have a good ending."

The sun was still strong in the late afternoon as Senator Brock sat on a patio chair under an umbrella sipping on a whiskey sour. He found himself constantly looking over his shoulder, wondering when the nightmare would end. He felt like he was on borrowed time. He was in over his head and could feel the pressure of the evil decision he made many years ago.

He kept to himself more even with four kids bouncing from sporting event to sporting event. His heart wasn't into it, and it was easier to grab a drink and let Anna do all the transporting. Joe knew it was straining their marriage, but his vices were all catching up to him. He wondered how Ben was doing. It had been eight weeks since the beginning of the nightmare, and the question that haunted him was whether Ben was still alive. It was an unforgivable act.

Anna walked onto the patio. "You don't have time to see your kids play a soccer game or even ask them how they are doing in school, but you have frigging time to sit out here and have a drink. You know, I've looked the other way for a long time, thinking maybe you would change or see what you were doing to yourself. But I realize that was just wishful thinking."

"Did you come out here to argue with me? I'm sorry. I have a lot on my mind that you could never imagine. Between the Hamptons and here in Washington's most desirable suburb, you live a pretty good life. But that's not enough for you."

"I'd rather have my husband participating in our lives instead of some distant dad who doesn't give a fuck."

"That's a little harsh, Anna. What do you do during the week when the kids are at school? Go to the tennis club, get lessons from the young studs over there. Have a nice lunch with your well-to-do friends, talking about how your kids are all awesome. Same old conversations with all the stay-at-home moms. I never heard you once say: *Thank you, Joe, for making my life so easy.*"

"It figures you would think that. I do everything around here, but you wouldn't notice because you're never home."

"I'm here now. And you do look nice in that dress. How's that?"

"You are such an asshole."

"I'm not going to argue with you on that. Today, I'm going to agree with you. Anything else?"

"Yeah. Hannah's coming over, and she wants to talk to you."

"About what? Is Ben coming over?"

"No, she wants to talk to you alone, and it's about Ben."

"What about?"

"She thinks he might have a brain tumor. She says ever since you guys came back from your fishing trip earlier in the summer, he's not been the same. I guess she wants to know if you've seen anything peculiar."

"Okay, I'll talk to her. I understand her concern. She loves the guy."

"What does that mean?"

"Nothing at all."

He leaned back in his chair and finished his drink as Anna walked away in a huff.

Brock's phone buzzed. It was a number he didn't want to answer but had to.

"Hi, Mal. I had a feeling you guys would be calling me."

"You need to put out a fire."

"We have a problem?"

"We might."

"What can I do?"

"Hannah is getting a little suspicious."

"Can't say I blame her. Ben was never perfect," Joe chuckled.

"It's not funny. She's headed over to your house now. And we're sure she's going to ask you about Ben."

"What do you want me to say?"

"Let me put it to you this way. If you don't persuade her that Ben is just feeling the pressure of working through some issues in Washington, we might have a serious problem."

"I'm thinking you've never been married, Mal. You have no idea what it's like in balancing a family. I think this is something you guys kind of overlooked."

"You make this right, or you might never see the real Ben."

"You don't have to threaten me, Mal. If we have a problem, it's because you guys fucked up, thinking an artificial machine could somehow replace a human being. But I'll see if I can solve your problem."

"Just keep in mind that we'll be watching, Senator."

A little while later Hannah arrived. Joe knew Hannah was a good judge of character. The one who had gotten away, she had seen through his charm and facade a long time ago. She had seen Ben's good heart and had made the right decision. Now she was dealing with an illusion due to Joe's deception.

When Hannah and Anna walked out to the patio, Joe was into his second drink. The girl of his dreams that

Ben had snatched up was now asking questions about an AI look-alike that was pretending to be her husband. *You couldn't make this shit up*, he thought.

He stood to greet her. "Hannah, how you been? That's a nice dress. With those almost identical sundresses, you guys almost look like sisters. You want something to drink, Hannah? We have a good selection of wine."

Anna rolled her eyes. His charming ways were getting old.

Hannah half-smiled. "I'll take a glass of wine. I've been under a lot of stress lately."

Joe took a seat on the outdoor couch next to Hannah as Anna went to get a bottle of wine.

"Anna was telling me you are a little concerned about Ben."

"I'm hoping you can help me out because you know Ben better than anyone. He just seems different."

"How so?"

"I don't know. It's really hard to explain. Maybe it's his emotions. He never gets upset about anything. He's overly agreeable. And it's like he's missing his sense of humor sometimes. To be honest, he just doesn't seem like the same guy. On the surface, he looks the same, he talks the same, but there's something missing, and I can't put my finger on it. You might think I'm crazy, but I actually think he might have a brain tumor."

"That's what Anna was telling me. He might be going through a mid-life crisis, he might just be feeling the pressure of being on some of those committees, or maybe he's thinking about his political future. If he's thinking about running for president, that might cause him to seem distant."

"No, that's not it. Have you noticed anything different about him?"

"When I see him, he seems fine to me, but you live with him."

"Can you talk to him?"

"Sure."

Anna came out with a bottle of wine and two glasses.

"And could you do me a favor and get him to see his doctor?"

"I'll try. You know he can be a stubborn bastard at times, and he hates doctors."

"But he might listen to you. especially after I've been bugging him about it."

"I'll talk to him."

"I appreciate it, Joe. I'm just worried about him, you know?"

"I understand. We'll figure it out, Hannah. It will be okay."

He put his arm around her consolingly, but it was all a big lie. All his life, Joe had been good at saying what was needed regardless of the truth. Hell, he was a politician; he was good at selling a lie. Now, it was such a burden trying to maintain the lie. Hannah couldn't comprehend the true magnitude of her situation. Imagine Ben getting a brain scan—the horror. The doctor calling her in and telling Hannah her husband was not really her husband, just your everyday cyborg. Joe couldn't even imagine what Hannah's reaction would be, nor could he fathom the chain of events that would follow.

Chapter 47

Cole and Josh stared out the car windows at the Canadian countryside as the vehicle turned off Highway 97 at Cache Creek and traveled north through the Bonaparte Valley. The car turned onto a dirt road that led to a lakeside cabin. Finally, after thirty hours of nonstop driving, they had reached their destination in British Columbia.

The four men exited and stretched their cramped legs and backs. Josh and Cole gazed at their surroundings as the sun crept through the trees and burned the mist off the calm lake below.

"Wow, this is really nice," Josh said.

"This ain't a vacation," Cole snapped.

"I don't know. I think I'm going to be doing some fishing, Cole. Where the hell are we going? I think you forgot we're wanted men. Nobody is going to find us here."

"Josh has a point, Cole," Ross said. "You guys aren't going anywhere for the time being. Let's go in."

The men entered the cabin and were greeted by a small pug that barked momentarily then walked abruptly away.

"What's wrong with the dog?" Josh asked.

"I turned the dog off," Chip said.

He sat in the shadows of the screened back porch, which overlooked the lake, sipping coffee in between puffing on his tobacco.

"An AI dog, why not?" Josh muttered.

255

"Man's best friend, especially when you don't have to feed them," Chip quipped as they entered the screened porch. "Well, well, well, you guys made it. I don't even know why they call them borders. Nobody checks anything. So you must be Josh."

They shook hands.

"Welcome to the wanted men's club. This is not my first rodeo. Someday I'll tell you some stories, but we can't stay. A lot is going on with the next phase of the operation. I hear Paige is home, Cole. Great news."

"They told me you guys didn't bring her home."

"They did? Ross, you could have at least given us a little credit. We left a lot of dead bodies along the way that Cole knows nothing about, and we probably made a few enemies, all for Paige. I hope you appreciate what we've done, Cole."

"Sure. I'm sitting here in British Columbia a wanted man, there are people looking to kill us, my family has no idea where I am, Paige is home, but now I can't go home, and I don't even have a job. Great future."

"So you're blaming me for all this? You're both here because of your own actions. But you've got a point about your job. If we find a way to stop Round Robotics, your pot of gold may be worthless. Oh, the irony."

"Wait a minute," Josh said. "I'm counting on that investment. What's going to happen to Round?"

"I don't know what to think," Cole said.

"Well, I do," Chip said. "My theory, for what it's worth, is that your alien AI got her home."

"How could he do that?"

"Well, for starters there's nothing in this world they can't hack into. They're mathematical wizards. They can sabotage a grid. The list is endless. This world is a toy to them. They see what's behind an image, where we see just the image. But that thing is not your buddy. It's alien technology. What are its intentions? Its mission? Is it good or evil? Who the hell knows? But if he is behind this, he's most likely been monitoring us. He knew where to go."

"If it was him and he got Paige home, that's all that matters."

Chip stood, looked out at the calm lake, and took a sip of coffee. "Morning is the best time of the day," he said. "A new day, a new opportunity. Life looks better on a sunny morning." He turned around to face Josh and Cole. "They killed Sid. He was a good guy. As we discussed before, Cole, these people will do whatever it takes to reach their destination. We no longer have anybody on the inside. Now we need to find out if our AI senator is in play and who is pulling the strings."

"How are you going do that?" Cole asked.

"We have our ways. We are about to enter a dangerous phase in this game."

"What about us?"

"Ross and I have to head back to the states. You guys relax. There's a boat at the dock below. The shelves are stocked with food. There's plenty of booze. Just stay out of the way and stay off the internet and your phones. You should be safe up here."

"How long?" Josh asked.

"I don't know. Could be a while. I guess we'll have to see how it all plays out. Both of you are liabilities to these people. Cole, you know what happens to liabilities at Round. They seem to have accidents."

"So we're just going to hang out here?"

"Why, do you have a better idea?" There was silence. "I didn't think so." He gestured to Ross. "We need to get going."

As Chip headed out of the cabin with Ross, he said, "We'll be in touch. If something comes up, I'll call you on the landline."

"So that's it?" Cole asked, irritated.

"You got Paige back, right? Be happy with that, and that you're still breathing. Seems like a win-win to me."

Chapter 48

Senator Brock and AI Senator Johnson sat at the bar of their favorite lunch spot near the Capitol. The glasses hung from the racks, and the liquor bottles were lined up on top of hardwood cabinets underneath the flat-screen TVs in the center of a circular bar.

It was Friday afternoon of what had been a long week. The pressure was building. Joe sat gazing at the TV, but his mind was elsewhere. He was in a tough spot. Hannah was beginning to suspect that her husband wasn't right, and it was his job to right the ship. He had to put his acting hat on; the software program was flawed, and the more you updated it, the more things got screwed up. What was he going to say: *Hey, Ben, stop acting perfect; a little more human would do. It's okay to get upset at a little spilled milk.*

Joe downed a shot and tried to reason with something that basically couldn't reason in a human way.

"So, Ben, how're things with Hannah?"

"They're fine."

He hated this whole farce, and there was no way out. "Anna told me that Hannah has been a little concerned with your health."

"I'm fine. She thinks I have a brain tumor or something and wants me to get it checked out. Crazy, huh?"

"Yeah. Crazy."

"Maybe we need a little bro time."

Joe couldn't help but chuckle at that line. "Bro time?"

"You like that? I got that from my son."

"Oh. Yeah, we need some bro time," Joe said. "Maybe we should get back out to the lake sometime."

"Yeah, that's a good idea."

Joe agreed. It would give him some time to figure things out. Maybe the programmers could figure a program that could respond to Ben's shortcomings. But he didn't think it was possible to design a program that could understand a woman. If Hannah was hell-bent on him getting a CAT scan, it would implode the whole gig, and in the process, doom her husband.

Ross walked into the crowded lunch spot wearing a base-ball cap and timed his entrance for when a seat opened up next to Senator Brock. He had observed that the senators were being watched, which meant he had to be careful and avoid getting identified.

He sat next to Joe, ordered a drink, and then pretended to be a fan. "Are you Senator Brock?"

"Yeah."

"I voted for you in the last election. You're doing a great job."

"Well, thanks," Joe said, not wanting to engage or be bothered.

Ross looked at the soccer game on the TV. He pointed at the screen. "You a fan?"

"No," Brock said, waving the bartender over.

"It's on me," Ross said.

"It's okay, sir. Really."

"You sure?"

"Yeah." Brock turned his back to Ross. He didn't need a fan today.

Ross sat there sipping his beer, observing the exchange between the two senators. He studied Senator Johnson as best he could. There wasn't a chance in hell the senator was a living, breathing copy of the real senator. It was all too natural.

Chip, who Ross considered a savant in AI, had instructed him how to use the device in his pocket. It would cause any AI connections to hiccup for a few seconds, almost like a small seizure. Ross wasn't expecting much to happen. He took a large sip of beer and closed his eyes for a second then pressed the red button. He heard a low hissing sound as an ultrasonic sound wave was emitted from the device. Senator Johnson shook and dropped his glass, which bounced off the wooden countertop. The glass didn't break, but his drink spilled in his lap.

"Damn." He stood up, wiping his pants. "I'll be back."

Ross couldn't believe the device had actually worked just like Chip had predicted. The biggest surprise was the senator was not the senator. He couldn't believe it. Chip had told him this technology in the wrong hands would change the world. He wasn't kidding.

"You're being watched, Senator Brock," Ross said, staring straight ahead. "Don't look at me. We know what's going on. You keep playing your role."

"Who are you?"

"You don't need to know."

"You did something."

"Maybe." Pretending to be a fan, Ross raised his hands up as one of the teams on TV scored a goal. "We'll be in touch when the time is right, Senator."

Ross finished his drink and left.

Joe leaned back in the stool and wondered who that man was. What did he know? Who did he work for? What was his agenda?

Maybe there was hope after all.

Ross and his team celebrated the end of their last assignment at an upscale restaurant on the outskirts of Washington DC that had a view of the Potomac River. The six former military men bantered back and forth about family, past military exploits, and their future endeavors. They laughed, joked, and drank. For a group that had spent years on the frontlines, the mistake their adversaries usually made was not being prepared for the unexpected. It had been drilled into them, never let your guard down—never.

Tonight, the hunters would become the hunted. A lapse in judgment was all it would take. This popular restaurant was crowded with the beautiful people. It was a place where the rich and famous could be found. It was a tough reservation to get, but Ross had pulled some strings and got a nice quiet room for the group. It was private, separated by a glass enclosure but with a nice wide view of the Potomac River.

Ross knew this would be the last celebration for a while. Chip had reviewed the next assignment with him, and it would be the toughest one yet. There would be no safe places. They were not sure of all the players. Chip knew where the technology was being used, but he didn't have the whole picture, and now with Senator Johnson being replaced with an actual AI look-alike, the other side had too much to lose. But it would be his job to follow the path to the masterminds behind the scene.

The waiter came in, and after ordering his meal Ross headed to the men's room. Another round of drinks was ordered. Tucker and two others watched from a distance. It was time. They were dressed in waiter's outfits: a nice white shirt with black slacks and a bow tie. Tucker grinned and cracked his neck as he straightened his bow tie. He'd always had a fascination with gangster movies. The art of the surprise was the difference between a good hit and a bad hit. The excitement of pulling off the execution that went according to plan was exhilarating to the soul. He lived for these moments. The aftermath and chaos that followed and slipping through the crowd and driving off while the blue lights zoomed by you. There was no feeling like it. He was ready to go.

Tucker and his partner each grabbed a tray and put a few drinks on it. They hid semi-automatic weapons under their trays. Tucker motioned to a third partner to head to the bathroom and take care of that straggler. Tucker and his partner strolled through a maze of tables and people approaching the targets' private dining room.

The third man walked quietly down a corridor and screwed the silencer onto the muzzle of the pistol. He entered the bathroom. It was quiet. He looked under the three stalls and saw two pairs of shoes. In the background he heard a round of bullets being shot. The man stepped in front of the first stall and kicked the door in. The man in the stall looked shocked as the gunman fired two shots into his chest.

But the hitman had picked the wrong door. Ross's ears were keen to gunshots. He stood on the toilet too late to stop the gunman's first act of terror but hit the assassin with several shots. Twenty seconds later, a second gunman fired into the bathroom, Ross dove for cover as low as he could go. Plaster and pieces of bathroom fixtures splintered around him. When the gunfire stopped he gathered his composure and cautiously approached the bathroom door. He held his gun with two hands and pushed open the door. The restaurant was in chaos. People were screaming and crying. He could hear sirens in the distance. He moved near the private dining room and knew his men were gone. They had been ambushed as if they were walking the streets of Afghanistan. The glass enclosure was smeared with blood. It was a gruesome scene. His heart sank as he saw their slumped, lifeless bodies still in their chairs.

He moved forward ducking and covering as if he was in a battle zone. All his instincts kicked in, and he made his way out of the restaurant amid the chaos. He didn't know where the enemy was or the identity of the brazen hitmen. He got to his car just as three police cruisers entered the parking lot. Ross sped off. He would regroup and assess the damage, proceeding as if his cover was blown using the same skills needed on a special ops mission.

Chip had been notified of the carnage that took place in Washington DC the night before, dealing his team a big blow. Somebody was onto them. It wasn't safe. He needed to leave his home in Wyoming and immediately head to the cabin. Cole and Josh might be at risk in British Columbia. They were all now the hunted. It was time to take the gloves off, but they needed to regroup and put together a plan. This was a war now. A quiet one.

He looked out at the mountains as the sun rose in the eastern sky and puffed out a few smoke rings. He was nervous. What did they know, and who had been broken?

Chip hurriedly put together a suitcase and then walked out and got into his Honda Odyssey and pushed the start button. The loud explosion that tore through the car rocked the neighborhood and could be heard blocks away. Flames engulfed the vehicle, and by the time the fire department got there, it was a charred metal mess.

Chapter 49

Ross had landed at Vancouver International Airport around two o'clock in the morning local time. He had taken the first flight out of Washington DC and didn't sleep during the seven-hour flight. His adrenaline was still pumping. He regarded every passenger as a hitman. The safest place was the cabin at Loon Creek until he could gather a response to the threat.

He rented a car and headed east. He had called Chip but got no answer. He was angry and was going to exact his revenge on the perpetrators. It would be just a matter of time. The first thought that crossed his mind was that Ed Ogden was behind this, a businessman with a vast fortune flexing his power, no different than a Mafia kingpin. Even though his son was a pathetic dirtball, blood always mattered, even if the deceased brought it on himself.

Now he was involved in something that hit at the core of power—artificial intelligence. It had been weaponized like a Trojan Horse. By the time the public got the news, the damage would already be done. This war was personal, and Ross would finish it his way or die trying.

As he drove along Highway BC1, his phone buzzed. He grabbed the phone and answered. It was a short call. He put the phone down, and then his emotions got the better of him. He slammed his fist on the steering wheel, then he did it again. Chip was dead, blown up in his vehicle. This was now more than revenge.

How had they found out about Chip? he wondered.

The network was compromised. Somebody had broken. Chip had infiltrated quietly into the players of power and had played it well. Until today.

It was a game of chess; you make a move, they make a bigger move, and on and on it goes. War was like that; you push your will on the other side until they break.

As he drove along the open highway, a thought crossed Ross's mind. He needed someone on the inside. Agent Wyatt Miller was perfect. He had been feeding him information along the way on the human trafficking ring. Now it was time to extract information from him. The idea of a senator being replaced by an AI look-alike, real in every way, was a news-shattering event, but it would need to be massaged along until the players behind the plot were exposed.

He picked up his phone and punched in the number.

It was Saturday, so the office was quiet. Wyatt's phone buzzed on his desk. He glanced at the number. It was unknown. After a brief hesitation he answered.

"Special Agent Miller."

"Hello, Wyatt. It's me."

"I know. I was afraid to answer it."

"Why?"

"Because every time you call there are more dead bodies. What do you want?"

"I might need your help."

Wyatt laughed. "You are talking to the wrong guy."

"You don't know it yet, but we're on the same team."

He chuckled again. "I don't see that. In fact, you probably should be arrested."

"For what? You have no evidence that I personally did anything wrong. But I didn't call you to talk about the past."

"Before I forget, I want to congratulate you on getting Paige Turner home."

"We had nothing to do with it."

"I don't believe you."

"Well, you can believe what you want, Wyatt. But I called for a reason. There was an incident."

"What type of incident?"

"It happened at the Woodstove Restaurant outside of Washington DC yesterday evening."

"I heard about that. A bloody mess. You know something about that?"

"I was the target along with my buddies who weren't so lucky."

"I told you more dead bodies. I'm sorry for your loss. I'm sure you didn't see that coming."

"I guess not. But I'll find the people behind it and take care of it my way."

"I know your way."

"Yeah, you do."

"Why're you telling me all this?"

"I guess you need to get your butt over to the crime scene since the victims were the people responsible for all the dead bodies you've been tracking down for the last few months. Of course, you won't be any closer than before, but it will impress your bosses that you're tracking down these lawless gunmen who have been taking the law into their own hands."

"There's a reason you're telling me this."

"Sure. The logical suspect behind this is Ed Ogden. He's a philanthropist and well-connected. Dig deep, Agent Miller, and you'll find a lot of secrets. He's well-protected by a horde of corrupt politicians for a reason."

"Well, thanks for the tip. By the way, do you have a name?"

"It's Ross. I didn't call you to talk about what happened at the Woodstove. That's the past," he said coldly.

"They were your buddies, and you've already moved on?" Wyatt asked, surprised. "That tells me something about you."

"It tells you nothing about me. I've seen a lot, Agent Miller. It's always been survival of the fittest. In my business you don't get too close to anybody. You, on the other hand, will never be able to find the truth. You have too much to lose. I have nothing to lose, and I'm going to help you find the truth. You guys only lock up who the political establishment deems a true threat to real power. It just emboldens the bad guys."

"And you're the good guy."

"I never said I was."

"So why are you calling me?"

"Here's another tip. The two Round Robotics guys you're looking for are safe at the moment."

"You know where they are?"

"Use your imagination, Agent Miller."

"So you are now aiding and abetting fugitives."

"You know they didn't kill anybody, which leads me to the real reason I called you. It's a political bombshell—or better yet an evil conspiracy. It has to do with a senator."

Wyatt leaned back in his chair. The words stirred in his head as if he had bitten into a cold popsicle with a bad tooth. It registered with a bang from the strange conversation he had with Senator Brock. "Tell me more."

"What I tell you, it's just between you and I."

"You trust me to keep it quiet?"

"Who else can I trust?"

"I find that hard to believe. You might be setting me up."

"I'm not that type of guy, Agent Miller. When you hear what I have knowledge of, you'll appreciate my candid information."

"Okay. What do you have?" He figured it couldn't hurt to hear what this Ross had to say.

"A man in Gillette, Wyoming, was killed this morning by a car bomb. His name was Chip Butler. He worked for the DOD as a consultant. His expertise was artificial intelligence and interplanetary travel."

Wyatt wrote down the name. "A car bomb sounds like a hit."

"You're catching on, Agent Miller. He was one of the good guys. Look at his expertise; that's a big hint. One other hint: Cole Adams had an event on his farm about fifteen years ago. That should get you started."

"I don't need riddles."

"You're an investigator, Agent Miller. You'll figure it out. You are just going to have to work for it for now."

It all kept going back to artificial intelligence, but he was still in the dark. Nobody wanted to let him in on the punch line.

"Why're you telling me this?"

"I'm just preparing you, Agent Miller. When the time is right, we'll meet, and I'll let you in on the dirt. But there is a major storm coming, and you are going to be right in the middle. And just maybe with my help, you'll get through it intact. I'll be in touch."

The mystery man was gone.

Wyatt knew Ross—if that was really his name—was telling the truth just by his own interaction with Senator Brock. It was time to set up another meeting with the senator.

Chapter 50

Cole stood on the deck, looking out at the lake, cooking two T-bone steaks on the grill. His mind wandered into the abyss, worrying about his future. They couldn't live here forever.

Josh stepped out onto the deck and nudged Cole with a beer. "Here you go, buddy. A beautiful day, huh?"

"It's a frigging paradise," Cole said, being sarcastic.

"We might as well make the best of it. We got a fridge full of beer. Cabinets full of food. We get to fish every day on an awesome lake. It could be a lot worse."

"A regular Club Med, Josh. I guess you're right, though; it could be a lot worse."

"Damn right. We're cooking T-bone steaks and drinking beer. It will work out for us, Cole; it always does."

"We've just been lucky. Have you taken the time to think about our situation?"

Josh sat in a deck chair with his feet stretched out, taking swigs of his beer. "I don't want to think about it. That guy Chip, he seems smart; he'll figure it out for us."

"You don't even know the guy."

"Cole, you worry too much. It will work out somehow."

"Let's see; we can't turn ourselves in because we are wanted for murder. I always dreamed of being a fugitive. Then we have the people at Round Robotics, who most likely have a bunch of henchmen looking for us. And if they figure out what we know, we'll never be able to go back home. Then there's the miracle of Paige's return, and I can't go home to see her. Oh, and what about our families, Josh? What the hell do you think they're thinking? I can't believe you are not worried."

"That's why we've been partners in crime since birth. You always worry, and I coast in and save the day."

They both smiled.

"Like the time we got lost during that camping trip."

"That was your fault, Cole."

"What do you mean?"

"You're the one who went off the beaten path. If it wasn't for me, they would have never found us."

"Yeah, right. If I recall, a couple of hunters found us."

"Yeah, but who had the granola bars to get us through and the flashlight?"

Cole shook his head. "Just like at Pale State when we almost got expelled because of your crazy idea of checking out the girl's sorority."

"Cole, we didn't get expelled, and I got to see Mandy's great rack. I think it worked out just fine."

"I hear she's available."

"What?"

"Yeah, she's available, and with your newfound wealth, you should have a real shot. But wait a minute; it might be a little hard being a fugitive and looking over your shoulder for Crazy Eyes."

"You're a real killjoy, Cole."

"Cheer up; after we get out of prison, Mandy might be ending her third marriage."

Ross pulled the car off to the side of the road and killed the engine. He stretched his legs, then stared up at the clear blue sky to see if there was a trace of any drones following his every move. He then walked around the car, bending to look under the chassis for any tracking devices. He had become paranoid. He was accustomed to being the hunter, not the hunted. He didn't like the feeling.

He sat in the driver's side with the door open. Chip had been the glue that held the network together. Everybody knew their specific roles, and that was it. He had no idea how the network worked or would operate going forward. Chip had set up a number to call in the case of his demise, but Ross ignored it.

He peered at his phone and wondered if it was still secure. He got up from the driver's seat, removed the storage card from the phone, and then slammed his phone to the ground. He stomped on it until it was in little tiny pieces.

Ross arrived at the cabin in the late afternoon. He knocked hard then turned the handle and pushed in the door

Cole and Josh jumped to attention. Their conversation stopped. The beers dropped. They weren't expecting company. They whispered back and forth until they realized it was Ross.

"You scared the shit out of us," Josh said.

"Sorry about that. I haven't slept in a day or so. We have a problem. Chip is dead."

"What?" Cole felt as if the air in the room had been sucked out. "What happened?"

"A car bomb."

"What do we do now?" Josh asked, his hopes of Chip finding a quick solution to their problem suddenly out the window.

"That's a good question. I don't know what's compromised. Chip gave out assignments; you were just one piece of the puzzle. He's not the only one that got rubbed out. My team for the most part is gone."

"Like dead?" Josh asked.

"Yeah, like dead." Ross glanced around as if looking for something.

"Do you know who did it?" Cole asked.

"I have an idea, but right now I'm worried that they know about this place, which means we are all in harm's way."

"Great."

Cole couldn't believe how his life had become a roller coaster. He never imagined he would be hiding out in British Columbia, with his life on the line, a wanted man on the run not only from the law but from killers in the shadows. It wasn't what he and Paige had drawn up. They should have already been married, maybe living in a house with a white picket fence. That dream seemed a distant memory.

"So what now?" Cole asked.

"I'm waiting for a buddy to show up, and then I'll make a phone call. Until then we wait."

Chapter
51

Special Agent Wyatt Miller parked their car down the street from the Woodstove Restaurant. They walked along a line of dark sedans, police cars, and specially fitted vans then maneuvered around the yellow tape. The crime scene had an array of specialists analyzing the massacre. The coroner had already taken the bodies to the morgue. A group of forensic experts were busy collecting evidence. They wore special suits to avoid contaminating the scene.

They were greeted by the crime scene manager, who directed operations. "Hey, how're you doing?"

"We came in from Indianapolis. I'm Special Agent Wyatt Miller, and this is my partner, Special Agent Cliff Allen."

"News travels fast," the manager said. "It looks like a Mafia hit. A lot of blood and a lot of bullets. Not a good mixture if you are on the receiving end."

Wyatt look around, imagining the upscale restaurant filled with beautiful people eating.

"Pretty brazen."

"I would say so."

"How did it go down?" Cliff asked.

"According to some of the witnesses we interviewed, two men dressed as waiters walked over to the private dining area, dropped their trays, and started firing. The victims never had a chance even though they all had firearms.

It was a complete ambush. Then a third perp went to the men's room. He must have drawn the short straw, and it looks like he made a bad choice in the bathroom."

"What do you mean?" Wyatt asked.

"Well, there were two guys inside taking a dump in different stalls at the same time. The hitman picked the wrong door. He put two slugs into the guy in the first stall, which gave the guy in the second stall time to react, and he took care of business."

They followed the crime scene manager to the bathroom and peered inside.

"A lot of bullet holes," Cliff said.

"I would say one guy was lucky he had to take a dump when he did. So one of the group survived."

"How do you know it went down that way?" Wyatt asked.

"The bullets found in the dead man's body were Winchester PDX1, which were a different caliber of bullet than those found in the private dining room victims and walls. And we got some DNA help in the second stall. You can see how somebody might forget to flush."

"You sure it was the intended target?" Wyatt said with a chuckle.

"I'm no expert on shit, but I know there's usually toilet paper left behind, and people always wipe their ass."

"You guys are good," Cliff quipped.

The manager chuckled. "Yeah. I'll take DNA any way I can get it."

Wyatt left Cliff at the crime scene and went to the Quantico Lab in Virginia, on a mission to find the pieces to the puzzle. He went through an array of security checks until he finally got to his destination. He was greeted by a smiling young man.

"How can I help you, Special Agent Wyatt Miller?"

"I'm looking for some fifteen-year-old news reports from Green River, Indiana."

"Any particular date or month?"

"I wish I knew that."

"Well, you're going to have to do it the old-fashioned way—microfiche."

"I haven't used that in a long time."

"Just follow me."

They entered a small, windowless room with a line of microfiche machines against the wall. The man went in the back room and came out a few minutes later with a box.

"Here you go, knock yourself out. If you need anything, just holler. I'll be up the hall."

"Thanks."

He began his chore. He wasn't sure what he was looking for, popping in one cartridge after another. Finally he hit the jackpot: an article about an experimental jet crashing in Green River on Mike Adams's farm. According to the article, the townspeople were convinced it was an alien spacecraft. A government spokesman from the DOD, Chip Butler, asserted it was just a top-secret experimental test flight and that the rumors of an alien spaceship were overactive imaginations.

Eight kids were tested for radiation. The government spent three days there under tight security. Nobody got close after the government became involved. They eventually wheeled out the object in the dead of night when the media was asleep, and the story eventually died like a passing, violent thunderstorm.

Wyatt leaned back in the chair, his mind working overtime. He couldn't believe the Chip Butler connection. Another piece of the puzzle, yet it did nothing to get him closer to solving the puzzle since Butler had just been executed. Wyatt thought: This is what conspiracies and the cover-ups to follow are made of—witnesses disappear. He couldn't help but think that this had something to do with Senator Brock. A preview of something bigger to come.

Agent Wyatt Miller continued his investigation by him-self. He caught a flight that afternoon from Ronald Reagan Washington National Airport to Indianapolis where a car was waiting. At seven o'clock that evening, his car rumbled down a dirt road, the sky still illuminated by the light radiating from the sinking sun. He slowed to a stop in front of the Adams's family farmhouse. He was back in Green River and where it all began fifteen years earlier.

Mike Adams looked out the door and saw a man with a suit making his way to the front porch. Mary put her hand to her mouth, fearing the worst. Scotty watched from the open living room window. Mike stepped out onto the porch, assuming a protective stance.

"Can I help you?" he asked in a stern voice.

"I'm Agent Miller with the FBI," Wyatt said, waving his badge. "Is this a good time to talk?"

"Well, that all depends. My son is being framed. He would never kill anyone. I know that for a fact. I really don't know what's going on. So unless you've got some news, I think you should leave."

"I believe Cole is innocent as well. I came by to tell you both Cole and Josh are okay at the moment."

"Thank God. Do you have him in custody?"

"No."

"Then how would you know that? Did he call you?"

"I have a reliable source."

"Thanks for coming by and letting us know. We've been worried sick. Nobody has told us anything."

"Can I come up to the porch? I would like to talk to you about what happened here fifteen years ago."

"Why do you want to know that?"

"I'm just trying to figure out a case that might have something to do with that event, or maybe it has nothing to do with it, to tell you the truth."

"Come on up. You're the first one that's ever asked about what happened. But there really isn't much to tell. It wasn't an experimental aircraft, which the government passed off to the media. It was an alien spacecraft; I'd bet my life on that. I believed my sons when they said they saw something that appeared human, maybe half human, half machine through the window of the spacecraft. I saw the metallic object. It wasn't from this world; that I know. There's not much more I can tell you. It was the talk of the town back then, now nobody ever talks about it, as if it never happened. I don't even think about it to tell you the truth."

"So Cole saw what was in it?"

"Yeah. I think he was only nine at the time. He said it was human-like but scary."

"Hmmm."

Cole's mom came out to the porch and stood by Mike, who said, "This is my wife, Mary."

"Did you hear anything about Cole?" Mary asked.

"I hear he's okay," Wyatt said.

"There's been stuff in the news. You don't think he'll be arrested if he turns himself in, do you?" she asked.

"If he comes in, they'll arrest him and most likely charge him and Josh with murder."

"Oh my God," Mary said, stifling tears. "He's a good kid. He would never do that."

"I agree. I don't have any control over it. I met your son while working on the Paige Turner case. I can't believe she's home. Great news though."

"The whole town is ecstatic," Mary said. "It's a miracle. A true miracle. Cole and Paige are engaged."

"Well, let's hope this is just a bump in the road for the two of them and all works out for everyone."

"Can I get you something to drink, Agent Miller?"

"Yes, thanks. Then I guess I'll be going."

When Mary went inside, Mike asked, "What made you bring up the crashed spaceship, if you don't mind saying?"

278 J. P. Farrell

"I'm just working on a hunch," Wyatt said. "It might mean nothing. My partner thinks I'm nuts."

Scotty came outside. Mike look sternly at his son.

"Why don't you go back inside, Scott?"

"I just need to tell Agent Miller something. Um, Cole found one of them in the lake."

Mike frowned. "What do you mean, Scotty?"

"He found an intact alien in the lake and brought it back to the shed."

"Is it there now?"

"No. It left."

Mike looked confused. "What do you mean it left?"

"It walked away."

"How?" Wyatt asked.

"Cole brought it back to life. It looked human, but it wasn't. It was a humanoid, I guess."

"Why didn't you tell me?" Mike asked. "Why didn't Cole tell me?"

"He tried to show it to you one day, but it was gone."

"You mean one of these things is out there running around somewhere?" Wyatt asked.

Scotty shrugged. "I guess. Cole also had some stuff on his laptop. I'll be right back."

Scotty went inside and a few moments later returned to the porch with a laptop. He booted it up and opened a file that showed the ship and the AI humanoids being hit by a tornado. Mike and Wyatt watched the short video intently.

When it was over, Wyatt just shook his head. He had safeguarded one of these strange looking heads down in his cellar. He remembered showing this dismembered head to Cole. And the tornado made sense now, after what he had found twenty miles away.

Scott opened another file, this one showing the location of thirteen habitable, Earth-like exoplanets. Wyatt stared, remembering Ross had said that Chip Butler was an expert in artificial intelligence and interplanetary travel. He wondered about the contents of that alien ship and would bet anything that Round Robotics was using this technology. And maybe they had cracked the code for space travel. He had heard of people reporting weird sightings around Area 51, Nevada. It was all getting clearer.

Scotty clicked on another file and showed it to everyone.

"What's this?' Wyatt asked.

"Robby left Cole the instructions for how to build one of the humanoids."

"Robby? This thing had a name?" Wyatt asked.

Mary came out to the porch with a bottle of water. "Here you go, sir."

"Thank you. I need to be going. Please keep that laptop secure until I figure out what we can do with it."

"I'll make sure of that," Mike said.

"I'll be in touch if I hear anything on Cole and Josh. Can you let Josh's parents know that he's okay?"

"We sure will."

Wyatt headed down the stairs toward his car, thinking that Ross knew a lot more than he was telling. All the little bits and pieces pointed to something big going on. Wyatt couldn't help but think that Senator Brock had a key to an ongoing conspiracy but was too scared to let him in on the dark secret. Then another thought crossed his mind: just how many of these AIs could be running around out there?

Chapter 52

Senator Ben Johnson looked out at the evening sun and the spectacular orange hue that lit the sky. He calculated that he'd been held captive for almost two months. He had no idea what was going on in the outside world. He couldn't believe whoever was behind this could keep up the façade with a clone taking his place. It was damn impossible and downright evil.

He had more than ample time to play with his thoughts. When he wasn't thinking about his family, he was thinking about escaping with Charlie's help.

He was fed like a pig waiting for slaughter. The bed was made every day as if he was at a five-star hotel. The meals were served as if prepared by a world-renowned chef. They made it as comfortable as possible, ensuring their captive would have no incentive to leave. The ever-polite AI help went about their business as if he was invisible and on a retreat. He'd had no human communication with his captors except for the first day of his captivity when they explained nobody would be looking for him. Charlie was the voice he occasionally heard from the other side of the wall who explained the setup.

Ben was isolated, a far different life than the hustle and bustle of Washington. He was watched 24/7. Cameras were mounted throughout the compound. He had spent many sleepless nights just staring at the ceiling or sitting outside gazing up at the stars. He also prayed a lot. His biggest worry was that one day they would kill him, and nobody would ever know. He worried how a replica could interact with his family. It wasn't possible; Hannah would figure it out. It was so diabolical; these people had no soul. If he ever got back to the outside world, he would exact his revenge on the people behind this. But before that, he had to figure a way out.

Charlie was working on an escape plan and waiting for the right time to spring it. Charlie knew the holes in their security systems. He was the guy that kept the AI in good order. Ben couldn't believe it when Charlie told him the facility was made up of genetically modified AI machines that appeared human in every way. But the security outside was completely human. They made sure nothing got in and nothing left. Every now and then Charlie was allowed to go into town for odds and ends. Charlie told Ben he was living in an old refurbished mansion in Maine. Charlie also admitted he was just a pawn; they'd threatened to kill his family if he didn't cooperate. He was afraid to defy them.

Ben took his evening stroll around the perimeter of the walled-in yard, filled with shrubs and flower gardens. A fake paradise. He looked at the cameras above, watching his every move. As he got to the security dead spot, Charlie's voice shattered the solitude.

"Ben," Charlie whispered. "You there?"

"Yeah."

"Just kneel down and tie your shoe."

"Okay."

"We're leaving tomorrow."

"You got a way out?"

"Yeah. I'm going to trick the cameras. It'll give us enough time to get past security. I have to go into town tomorrow. This is a best chance of escaping."

"What do you need from me?"

"Just be ready to go in the morning. I'll disable the AI machines just long enough that we can exit the house. I have the override to unlock your door. I'm going to trick the cameras to show your image in the room, and all the other cameras will just show the day before. I'll be driving a pickup into town. I'll put you in the back under something. They usually check, but I've been working on one of the security guards, and the last time he just let me go without checking."

"You think it will work?"

"It has to work. They won't figure out the cameras' images until it's too late. If we get through the gate, I'm not looking back. Then I'll get you to a payphone for you to call the state police."

"What about you?"

"I'll be okay. I'll send them on a wild goose chase, and by the time they find me, it will be too late. You're in, right?"

"Yes. I'm in."

"Alright. There's no turning back, Senator. Be ready to go. We both have a lot to lose if we fail. I'll see you tomorrow morning."

Ben got up from tying his shoe and took a chair. He wanted out. And he was going to do whatever it took.

The sky was overcast as a hard rain drenched the mansion. Ben was restless, ready to go. His heart was pumping louder than normal. He hadn't slept. The last time he'd been this uneasy was waiting for the results of his last election. Now all he needed was Charlie to carry out his part.

Ben looked at the clock; it was 10:00 a.m. and no sign of Charlie. All was quiet. Then he heard the door unlock. Ben stood still, almost paralyzed, waiting to see who was on the other side of the door.

Charlie pushed the door ajar and whispered, "It's all set. Let's go."

Ben opened the door, which led to a farmer's porch, and came face-to-face with the voice from the other side of the wall. Charlie, who was a lot younger than Ben had pictured, paused at the doorway.

"Before we go out there, Senator, here's a gun. You know how to use it?"

"Yeah." Ben reluctantly took it. "But why do I need one?"

"I thought you wanted to get out of here."

"I do."

"You really think they're just going to let you walk out? There's too much at stake. If you step out on to the grounds, their orders are to shoot to kill."

"Okay."

"You have any other concerns before we step out? There's no turning back."

He shook his head. "I'm good."

"Okay, let's do it."

Ben climbed onto the bed of the truck, and Charlie covered him with a tarp. "Remember, Senator, if they check the tarp, don't hesitate to use the gun. You're only going to have one chance."

"Okay."

Charlie hopped into the truck and pressed the accelerator, the tires spewing sand into the air. He drove down a bumpy gravel road for about a half-mile, his face showing no emotion. He told himself he had done this enough times. He knew the guards. He had deliberately joked around with them every time he passed. Nothing would indicate that an escape was in progress. Their guard would be down. He slowed the truck as he came to the checkpoint.

Two well-dressed men with guns came out of the booth.

"Hey, Charlie, going into town?" one of them asked.

"Yeah, got to get some supplies. The usual shit. Hey, did you catch the Sox game the other night? What a comeback."

"Yeah," the guard said.

The second guard was walking around the truck.

"Am I all set to go?" Charlie asked, nervously noticing the second guard getting curious.

"Wait right there." A third guard appeared at the door of the booth. "What's underneath the tarp?"

"Just some old shit. Paint and stuff."

"Can we see it?"

"Knock yourself out."

Charlie had his foot close to the gas pedal. He was going to ram the gate if he had to.

As one of men started to unwrap the tarp, Ben pulled the trigger, firing two shots. He didn't hesitate. His life was on the line. The truck jolted, and the bullets missed their intended target. Charlie ducked and floored the truck, busting through the gate as a barrage of bullets shattered the rear window. He heard a loud alarm going off behind them.

"You okay, Senator?" Charlie hollered.

"Yeah."

"Hold on. I'm going to get you out of here."

Charlie pushed the pedal to the metal.

Chapter 53

AI Senator Johnson drove a black pickup truck while Senator Brock rested in the passenger seat. Joe checked his phone as rain pelted the windshield. It was 8:45 a.m. They had been driving for over four hours and were now on I-95 near Portland, Maine. The conversation was non-existent. Empty coffee cups littered the floor by Joe's feet. It just wasn't the same with this impersonator. He pretended to snooze. It was amazing that this thing could drive. The only problem with him driving is that he stayed at the speed limit as if an override was in place.

Joe just stared ahead as deep thoughts percolated. This trip was not to kick back and do some fishing or drink some beers. It was all work, an update to the memory software that would add some zip to the AI's emotions. The group had gotten concerned that Hannah was getting closer to the truth.

He laughed to himself. Did they really think they could pull this off? Good luck trying to make an organic machine interact with the emotional instincts of a woman. Hell, that was a tough task for any real man on the planet, let alone an AI clone. As perfectly planned as this operation had been, its biggest flaw was that its main actor simply wasn't human.

"Hey, Joe, how about we stop for breakfast?"

"Good idea."

They took the next exit and found a diner in South Portland a few miles off the highway. The two senators walked into the crowded eatery as if they were regulars. They were recognized by a few patrons, who smiled and said hello. They sat in the last remaining open booth by a window, and a petite waitress dropped menus on the table.

She came back with coffees. "You two look familiar."

"We're both senators, on our way for a little vacation time up in Bridgton, Maine to do some fishing," Ben replied with a smile.

"Wow. The cook was right. He said that's who you were. I'm sorry to bother you; he just wanted me to find out."

"No problem," Joe said. "The blueberry pancakes look good."

Ben handed the waitress their menus. "I'll take the same." After she left, Ben sat back and looked at Joe. "I know why you wanted to bring me up here."

"You do?"

He nodded. "Hannah and I are having some issues. And I know she talked to you about it."

"The only thing she said to me was that she was concerned with your health."

"Since when do you get into my affairs?" he asked, his voice rising.

This is strange, Joe thought. It was almost like Ben was getting upset. Could it be a malfunction?

"What are you talking about, Ben?"

"I want you to keep out of my business, okay?"

"Sure. I didn't mean a thing by it," Joe said, trying to diffuse the situation.

"I've been meaning to talk to you about Hannah."

"What about?"

"Are you having an affair with Hannah?" Ben said loudly enough to be heard by the diners at the surrounding tables.

Joe leaned closer. "Where the hell is this coming

from?" he asked in a low voice. "I'm not having an affair." He couldn't believe he was defending himself to this cloned imposter.

"Tell me the truth," Ben demanded, his voice even louder. Patrons started openly staring at the table.

"Keep your voice down, Ben. The last thing I need is this shit on the internet."

"You're having an affair with my wife, aren't you?" he asked, his voice raging.

"No, I am not. Let's drop it," Joe pleaded, trying to diffuse the situation that was spiraling out of control.

Ben hit the table with his fist. "Admit you're having an affair with my wife!"

The owner of the diner came over, visibly uneasy. "You guys okay? It seems a little loud over here. The patrons are getting uneasy. Aren't you guys senators? I would think you'd be a little more civil."

"We're sorry," Joe said. "It's just a misunderstanding."

"No, it's not," Ben said. "Senator Brock here has been having an affair with my wife. But I will work it out. I'm sorry."

"We're okay," Joe told the manager.

"If this continues, I'm going to have to ask you two to leave."

"It's okay. really. We're best friends. I promise."

The manager walked away but kept an eye on the table. "What the hell is wrong with you, Ben?"

"I can't let this happen. You've been manipulating people all your life. You're just a fucking drunk."

"Oh, I see. This is about me? You're a frigging machine. I'm not playing this game. You guys can go to fucking hell."

Ben abruptly stood up. "Your affair with my wife is over." He pulled a Glock 17 from the back of his pants.

Joe stared at him in disbelief. "Fuck you."

Ben fired two shots, striking Joe in the chest. After a frozen moment, chaos erupted. There were screams, and parents shielded their kids. Some ran for cover while others froze in horror. Ben just walked calmly out of the diner as if nothing had happened, got into the pickup, and drove off. People rushed to Joe's aid as he hung onto the table, gasping for air. He slid to the floor, and after a few more breaths, he was gone.

Within minutes, a news flash was lighting up the internet.

Charlie drove at a fast rate of speed, then once he was sure there was nobody in hot pursuit, he pulled the truck over to the side of the road.

"Senator, you okay back there? Come get in the cab."

Ben jumped out of the truck bed and got in the passenger side. He was still shaking from firing two shots and the fear of getting caught.

"That was close."

"Yeah."

"Get me to a payphone."

"Let's get as far away from here as we can. I don't know who they have in their back pocket up here. We can't trust the local police. You need to call the State Police."

Charlie spun the tires and got back on to the main road. They drove along Route 302 for ten miles until they entered the town of Windham, Maine. Passing a strip mall, Charlie pointed.

"There's a payphone. You can call the State Police right over there."

"Okay."

Charlie pulled the truck close to the payphone, which was at the end of the strip mall.

"What do I do with the gun?" Ben said.

"I'll take it."

"Where're you going?"

"There's a tracking device on this truck. We can't take any chances. I'm going to drive it as far away from here as

I can. Then I'll abandon it. I'll touch base with you later. I just want to make sure my family is safe, okay?"

"I understand."

"Can't take any chances, Senator. These people are closing in on this location as we are speaking. Good luck. Don't worry about me."

"Thank you."

Charlie floored it out of the strip mall. Ben dialed 911.

"What's your emergency?"

"I'm Senator Ben Johnson. I need help immediately."

"Where are you?"

"I'm in a strip mall in Windham, Maine. I think it's on Route 302. I need help right away."

"The police are on their way. Just stay put, sir. They'll be there in a couple of minutes, okay?"

Minutes seem like hours. He couldn't wait to see flashing lights. He thought about Hannah and the kids. If he was out here and his duplicate was with them, what would these people do? He needed the authorities to get to his home as soon as possible. He was scared how his abductors would react to his escape. Their plan would be in disarray.

He exhaled a sigh of relief when he saw blue flashing lights heading his way. Two police cruisers flew into the strip mall, soon followed by two more. The cavalry was here; it was the best sight ever. Pedestrians stopped in their tracks. Customers rushed to the store windows to see the commotion.

The police cars stopped twenty yards in front of Ben. He smiled. Thinking his nightmare was over, he had to get immediate protection for his family.

The officers jumped out of their cars with guns drawn. "Put your hands up and lie on the ground."

Ben was stunned. He had no idea why the dramatics. The officers approached cautiously. He did what they told him.

"I'm Senator Ben Johnson. I've been kidnapped," he said, looking up from the ground.

The first officer frisked him then handcuffed him. He pulled Ben to his feet and read him his rights.

"What the hell is going on here, officer? I've been kidnapped. I can prove it. Charlie, who helped me escape, will tell you I was kidnapped. What the hell is going on? Why are you arresting me?"

"You don't remember? Did you blackout or something? Well, let's just say you probably need a good lawyer."

Ben's mind was a whirlwind. "What the hell did I supposedly do?"

"You killed Senator Joe Brock. Does that ring a bell?"

The officer maneuvered Ben into the back of a cruiser. He sat stunned, listening to the officers discussing the situation outside. He wasn't free. His nightmare was just beginning.

Charlie pulled a buzzing smartphone from underneath the seat as he drove and answered. The person on the other end thanked him for a job well done.

"Thank you, sir," he replied, then listened a moment. "Yes, the mansion has been cleaned out. Nobody will ever know he was there."

He hung up then drove as if he was a tourist sightseeing the countryside.

Chapter 54

The girls were at a sleepover. The house was quiet. Wyatt prepared a cup of coffee in the confines of his suburban home located in a neighborhood of manicured lawns. He relaxed in jeans and a sweatshirt and sipped his coffee slowly, enjoying some free time. He stared out the kitchen window as the rain rolled down the glass. He wondered about Cole and Josh. They were being harbored in a secluded area by the same men who had tracked down the players in a human trafficking ring, the same ones who were now resting peacefully in a morgue. He thought about the Adams's farm and what he had uncovered with a little detective work. He was close to something but wasn't sure exactly what it was. The mystery man, Ross, was so confident that something big was on the horizon. Then there was Senator Brock's tease of a conspiracy, yet it just told him riddles.

One thing he did know was it all centered around Round Robotics. There were just too many coincidences. There were two confirmed deaths: one by murder, Sid Martin, the other by suicide, Cal Jensen. There was the murder at the Wilbur Hotel, by a Paige Turner look-alike. Then there was the missing Charlie Nash who had worked at Round and was never seen again after a night of drinking.

What were they building in that place? After talking to Cole's father and brother, Wyatt had put together a theory, as crazy as it sounded, that just maybe they had the tech-

291

nology to build an AI human replica. The question was, were they doing something diabolical with it?

His wife joined him downstairs. "I haven't seen you this comfortable in a long time," she said, wrapping her arms around him.

"Patty, you know that every time I settle in for some downtime the phone lights up. I could use a vacation, that's for sure."

"You're always working. And the sad part is the girls are growing up without you. I understand. Somebody has to earn the money, and you are a good guy, Wyatt."

"You're just being nice. It's not fair to you. Why don't you relax? I don't know, pamper yourself today. I'll pick up the girls today and hang out with them."

"That sounds really nice, but I know the phone is going to ring any moment."

Seeing his wife's expression, he said, "Is there something I don't know?"

"I didn't want to tell you, but you're going to find out soon enough. Senator Joe Brock was shot and killed today at a diner in Maine."

"Senator Brock is dead?"

"I'm sorry, honey. Didn't you just meet with him?"

"Yeah, a few weeks ago. He told me they were going to kill him." He remembered Senator Brock's prophecy: *Whatever happens, it will be obvious yet not what it appears to be.*

"Who was going to kill him?"

"He didn't say. He thought it would look like a suicide. How did it happen?"

"This is the real kicker. He was shot and killed by Senator Ben Johnson."

"What? Did they arrest him?"

"I believe they did apprehend him."

Wyatt needed to hear it first-hand. He found the remote and clicked to a twenty-four-hour news channel. A reporter was in front of a strip mall in Windham, Maine, where Senator Ben Johnson had turned himself in, calling 911 about an hour after the shooting. They found his vehicle about a mile up the road.

"Investigators will have to figure out the motive of the shooting," the reporter said to the camera. "But according to witnesses at the scene, the two senators seemed to be arguing about an alleged affair Senator Brock was having with Senator Johnson's wife."

Wyatt turned off the TV. He didn't believe it. He remembered Senator Brock's last question: *Do you believe in cyborgs?*

His phone buzzed.

His wife sighed. "I told you."

Wyatt answered. "Sir?" He listened. "I can be there in two hours." He put the phone down. "So much for being with the girls today. I have to go to Maine. I'm the lead investigator."

"I know. Just be safe, okay?"

"Yeah. There's more than meets the eye here, Patty. You know what Senator Brock told me? His death wouldn't be the end; it would be just the beginning."

A horde of media descended upon Senator Ben Johnson's home, where a line of police officers held back the media and onlookers. A black SUV was allowed to pass through and park in the driveway. Two men in suits got out as Hannah Johnson emerged from the house, prompting a cacophony of shouted questions from the media horde.

The one she heard over and over again was: "Mrs. Johnson, were you having an affair with Senator Brock?"

Chapter 55

T he sun hung just above the mountains in the western sky. A helicopter landed on a small pad outside a ranch in Deer Lodge, Montana. Ed Ogden stepped off the helicopter and ducked beneath the blades swirling slowly above. He was escorted by a ranch hand to the main house. He felt like royalty. He entered the house and walked down a long hallway until he came to a large outside patio adjacent to a pool shaped in a figure eight and a cabana.

"Ed, how've you been?" Phil Reed greeted him with a firm handshake.

"Phil, you look lean as ever."

"Got to keep in shape, you know. I still jog a couple of miles every other day. Except my hair keeps getting whiter. You need something to drink? I think we have some of your wine around. Let's sit down."

"A beer will do."

"Okay." Phil made a call.

Ed admired the view. The manicured landscaping included waterfalls sparkling with LED lighting, and in the distance were untouched rolling hills. "It's quite beautiful out here."

Phil nodded. "Just imagine if we had to give up all this and live in a bubble on Mars in a hostile environment."

"I can't."

"Let the scientists work on Mars. Fortunately for us,

we now have an alien technology to bring us to Earth-like planets."

"You know that for a fact?"

"Well, we will know very soon. We should start getting images back anytime now from the drones. It's quite amazing when you think about it. I believe we were meant to have this technology from an alien race that knew we would eventually expire here."

"So somebody out there is looking out for us?"

"Just maybe."

A waiter came out with two beers.

"Thanks," Ed said. After the waiter left he asked, "So how does it feel being the chairman of Aerosonic now?"

"Feels like I'm retired after being CEO for thirty years."

"I know what you mean. So why did you call me out here, Phil?"

"I'll get to that. But first I want to tell you a story. As you know, I was an avid test pilot back in my day. I test flew the X-15 back in the '60s. My fastest time was more than four thousand miles an hour—Mach 5, which is about four times the speed of sound. Quite a kick. A mistake would kill you. I've always had a fascination with the stars since I was a little kid. It's in my blood. This alien technology was a gift.

"You probably don't know this, but Chip Butler broke the code on how to use this technology. As we constructed the first prototype, I told Chip I wanted to test it. To his credit, he was all for it. So we took it out for a test drive without authorization. It was frigging amazing to have so much power at the wave of your hand. You didn't feel the speed. We teased an airplane by pulling up next to it then took a 90-degree turn. I'm sure the pilots thought they had seen a UFO. As I recall, there were a lot of calls that evening about UFO sightings.

"But we weren't done. I took it through the atmosphere and orbited it around the Earth. The ship has a hyper-drive, giving it the capability to go faster than the speed of light.

It also has a halo drive. Chip explained that's like a sling-shot. It works by firing laser beams that can curve around a black hole and come back with added energy to propel a spacecraft. We didn't test any of that functionality."

"This stuff is way over my head, Phil."

"Next, we took a ride to Mars."

Ed's eyes went wide. "You took it to Mars?"

"We hit speeds that you can't even imagine, and the cockpit shields you from the G-forces and radiation. It keeps you in a comfortable, protected environment almost as if you were back on Earth sitting in your living room."

"How long did it take you?"

"That's the amazing part. We flew to Mars in one hour and took a scenic tour of the planet. The entire trip took a total of two hours. Can you believe it? Going the speed of light would have been a six-minute round trip, but we weren't ready to test the hyper-drive."

"That's amazing."

"Now back to Chip," Phil said, his eyebrows knitted. "The next time you do something without my authority, Ed, there'll be consequences. Everybody is expendable, even you."

"He and his army of gangsters killed my son. The kid had issues, but he's blood. They deserve what they got."

"The endless cycle of revenge. It makes me wonder if we will ever change. Your son wasn't coming with us, Ed. A frigging car explosion? You've been watching too many Mafia movies."

"And you had a senator kidnapped. That was your idea. Let's not see who the most despicable person is."

"Okay, let's not argue. What's done is done. But hey, I have a good heart; I let the Senator go."

Ed smirked. "And you framed him by killing another senator."

"I call that brilliant. The sad part is we had to pull the plug. We'll get it right the next time."

"When I met you eight years ago, I thought you were

just a businessman with big dreams. I sat in that meeting and thought: *What the hell do I have to lose to fund this crazy endeavor of spaceships, AI, and new worlds.* It was a great presentation. I'm wealthier now more than ever from that Round Robotics IPO. And I've made a bundle from your company's stock. I have skeletons in my closet, yes, but what I didn't know is that you are a ruthless, stone-cold businessman who will do whatever it takes. I misjudged you, Phil."

"Every successful company has a back-up plan. But mankind has no back-up plan. Amazing considering that one push of a button by some crazy dictator, or some pandemic, or a big asteroid crossing Earth's path, or the grid being fried by a solar surge and mankind is gone. Well, now with this alien technology we do have a back-up plan. As for our selected friends in Washington, as long as we tell them what we want them to know and nobody from the outside gets involved, we have a chance to colonize the universe. I realized I have the responsibility to ensure mankind will continue. If I have to make cold, calculated decisions, so be it."

"You're a little bit crazy, Phil," Ed said.

"And that coming from a guy like you," he said, and they both laughed. "Well, then you won't be surprised that I talked to Stan about taking care of our two little friends from Round that got too close for their own good. Now, let's get something to eat and talk about pleasant things."

Chapter 56

The morning after Chip's car exploded, Ross paced the cottage as if he was an expecting dad. He was anxiously waiting for Fred to show up. Cole made some coffee and stood looking out at the lake, aware he had no clear direction to his future. He couldn't stay here forever. He thought maybe it was time to face the music and blow up the evil empire. The longer they stayed missing, the more they would appear to be guilty of killing Sid.

Ross noticed a news bulletin flash on the computer screen and walked over to read about Senator Ben Johnson shooting Senator Joe Brock. Ross wondered if there was a connection between what happened to his crew and Chip and the strange turn of events in Maine. They knew that Senator Johnson had been replaced by an AI replica. Was it a malfunction, or was it planned? An exit strategy. This was where his connection with Special Agent Miller would pay dividends. Oh, yes. Special Agent Wyatt Miller was about to be dragged into a diabolical conspiracy.

"Hey Cole, come take a look at this," Ross said.

Cole walked over and watched the news coverage. "What's this mean?"

"It means that your AI replica killed Senator Brock. And more than likely the person being held for the murder is the real Senator Johnson. And if that's the case, he's screwed."

"How would they pull something like that off?"

"Good question. I don't know."

"What are we going to do?"

"I got a few ideas."

As Josh walked out of the bedroom, they heard a car pull up outside. Cole froze.

"Get down!" Ross said in a hoarse whisper, pulling out his gun. He moved to the window and peeked through the curtains. His body relaxed. "It's just Fred."

He opened the door and greeted Fred with a smile. "I'm glad to see you; come in."

"I heard what happened. I can't believe our guys got executed like that, Ross."

"It's a silent war now."

"And they killed Chip. What the hell are we going to do?"

"I don't know yet. Let me introduce you to Cole and Josh. Our next project."

Fred half-smiled and nodded.

Josh was looking at an outside surveillance monitor. He pointed to the screen.

"Hey, guys. What the hell is that?"

Ross looked over at the monitor, which showed three black SUVs approaching the cottage. He raced over to a closet and unlocked it. Against the wall was a cache of high-powered, semi-automatic rifles.

"Fred, here you go. You two, it might be better if you head to the lake."

"Where we going to go?" Josh asked.

"Just hold on for a minute," Cole said.

He zoomed the camera in on the vehicles, which had stopped fifty yards from the cottage. A man got out from the lead car and looked directly at the surveillance camera. Ross peered closer.

"I can't believe it. It's Chip."

Relief filled the room like a sigh. Ross ran out to greet him, and they shook hands as a group of men with high-power rifles sealed off the cabin's perimeter.

"Chip, I thought you were dead. Your car exploded. How are you still alive?"

"I figured I could be a target, so I sent out my AI doppelganger to start the car, and that was the end of him. I am going to miss him," he grinned, then grew somber. "I'm sorry for what happened to your crew."

As they walked to the cabin, Ross asked, "You have ideas who did all this?"

"Sure. We did kill Ed Ogden's son, so I suppose a little payback was in order. But in going after me, he would have had Phil Reed's approval. So that means I'm on the outside. But the good news is they think I'm dead, and that will work in our favor."

"I'll take care of it, Chip."

He smiled. "That won't solve our problem. Anyway, I have a better idea."

"I think we should go home and plead our case," Cole said.

"There's the door," Ross snapped. "You can leave any time. But you aren't safe out there."

"Well, now, wait a minute," Chip said. "Maybe that's a good idea. We'll draw them out by using you guys as bait."

"What do you mean by bait?" Josh asked.

"They're not going to take any chances that you might know too much."

"That seems a little bleak, Chip," Cole said. "You've been playing with me. I'm the inside guy. What bullshit."

"I'm sorry about that. I know the players. But I just wasn't sure of what lengths they would go. You were a big help. And the news of yesterday tells us exactly just what lengths they will go to. Ross and Fred will be your guardian angels."

"Come on, Chip," Ross said. "We have to watch these guys."

"Unless you got a better idea. And then you'll have your chance to get revenge."

"He's got a point," Fred said.

"It sounds like you're just using us again," Cole said.

Chip smiled. "Well, we are."

The landline phone rang.

Ross stared at it. "Who could be calling? We're all here." He answered the phone then handed it to Cole. "It's for you."

Cole frowned. "Who is it?"

"I don't know."

Cole took the receiver. "Hello?"

"Hello, it's Robby. I hope you are doing okay."

"How did you know where I am, and how did you get this number?"

"This world is pretty easy to me. I don't have time to explain. I saw Paige in San Antonio."

"Did you help her?"

"Yes. I owed you. I'm very persuasive when I need to be. You wouldn't believe where I am."

"Where's that?"

"I'm in Area 51. I'm working on spaceship prototypes. I'm going home, Cole."

"How did you get in there?"

"I've got special skills. Anyway, say hello to Chip. I'm not the only one here. I'm sure we will cross paths down the road."

"What do you mean, I'm not the only one here?"

The phone went dead.

"Who was that?" Chip asked.

"Robby, the AI I found in the lake. He said he's in Area 51 and to say hello to you. He also said he's going home."

"Really?" Chip rubbed his beard. "So what are his true intentions?"

"He also said he wasn't the only one there."

"That's what happens when you open Pandora's box. There's a price to pay when you tap alien technology. We have a dead senator, and my guess more to come. Ross, you and Fred take these guys back."

"So that's it?" Cole asked.

"What do you want from me?" Chip asked. "To erase

the past? You have buyer's remorse. I never promised you anything but to find Paige. She's home. You opened Pandora's box."

"It wasn't you who got Paige home. It was my alien friend."

"True. But he couldn't have found her if he wasn't monitoring us, which is why he knows all about me. So before you get on your high horse, you put yourself in harm's way the moment you started working with alien AI. Don't blame me."

Chip walked over to Cole and stuck out his hand. "We've all been under stress the last few months. We'll get through this. But none of this changes the future. The planet is eventually going to die, and those ships in Area 51 are our way to extend the human race."

Cole and Josh got in the back seat of Fred's black sedan. Fred slid in behind the wheel with Ross in the passenger seat. The car maneuvered by a group of men carrying AR-15s. It felt like they were leaving a military installation. As they got on the road, Cole didn't want to think anymore about what his future might bring. Instead he let his thoughts turn to Paige.

Chapter 57

Senator Johnson made himself at home in a small interrogation room, leaning back in a wooden chair in front of a small, square table. He stared at the large, two-way window facing him. He knew the State Police were on the other side watching him and discussing his despicable act. He looked the part of a criminal. His clothes were soiled, and his appearance was disheveled. Of course, just a little while ago he was running for his life, going from one nightmare to another.

The door squeaked open, and a broad-shouldered gentleman in a suit walked into the room with a laptop in his hand. He placed it on the table. He smiled as he greeted the Senator and took a seat opposite him.

"I'm Detective Cleaver of the Maine State Police. I wish these were better circumstances to be meeting a senator. Is there anything I can get you while I'm here?" he asked in a soft voice.

Ben knew the game: butter-up the suspect and get as much information out of him as possible. He gestured toward the water bottle on the table in front of him.

"I'm good, Detective Cleaver."

"Okay. Just to let you know, you probably won't be able to make bail until at least Monday when court is in session."

"That's okay. This is a step-up from where I've been, believe me."

"Okay."

"Before I start, my lawyer is on his way. But I will say a few things against the advice of counsel."

The detective smirked. "Okay. This will be videotaped. You understand?"

"I know the game, Detective. How many people are in the room behind the window?"

He glanced back and shrugged. "Quite a few."

"I must be the big catch of the day."

"Well, you certainly are. There's a large contingent of media already outside."

"Well, why don't you start. I'm sure you don't want my lawyer around because he'll tell me to shut up. But I have nothing to hide."

"Okay, I'll get right to the point. Did you shoot Senator Brock at Casper's Diner in South Portland this morning?"

"That one is easy. No, I did not."

"So that wasn't you who pulled the trigger?"

"No, that wasn't me. You know, Detective, we were friends since childhood. So this has been a really bad day all around, okay?"

"So you are saying that you weren't with Senator Brock today."

"That's absolutely what I'm saying."

"We have eyewitnesses and video that say you were there, Senator."

"Detective, it's the truth. I didn't do it. I was kidnapped two months ago. Jot that one down. Find Charlie; he broke me out this morning."

"Bad timing, huh? Where were you then?"

"I don't frigging know. It was maybe twelve or fifteen miles up the road."

"Does Charlie have a last name?"

"I never got it."

"Senator, I really want to work with you. But the shooting points to you. Maybe you should just come clean."

"I'm telling you it wasn't me."

"Who was it then."

"Somebody who looks like me."

"You said you were kidnapped two months ago."

"Yes."

"Think about this; that would mean this individual would have to fool your entire family, friends, and fellow senators. The list is endless."

"I know it sounds crazy, but I'm telling you that wasn't me who shot Senator Brock. It was some genetically engineered AI thing."

The detective rolled his eyes. He knew the Senator was in denial.

"I think I've heard enough. First, I will bet that the bullets recovered from the deceased will match the gun found in your pickup. You also have gunshot residue on your clothing."

"That's because I used a gun to escape from where I was being held captive."

"The pickup truck you were seen driving was a mile from where you made the phone call."

"It's a coincidence." Ben starting sweating. He didn't want to believe that he had been set up. It was impossible.

"Senator, look at my laptop." He turned it toward him.

Ben saw the whole horrible thing go down. It hit him hard. He didn't want to look at it anymore.

"Do you have a twin, Senator?"

"No."

"That's you, sir. Your mind doesn't want to believe what you did. I've seen it before. I'm just doing my job. Take a good look at the man you say isn't you. Take a real hard look."

Ben peered at the screen, and it hit him like a thunderbolt. His shoulders slumped.

"You see what I'm seeing, Senator? The man in the video who shot Senator Brock had the same clothes that you were found wearing when we picked you up."

"I know how it looks. But I didn't do it," he muttered, trying to hold back tears. "I was set up."

The police officials observing the Senator from the room behind the window couldn't believe the shit that the Senator was slinging. He was guilty without a doubt. Special Agent Wyatt Miller took notes while intently watching the proceedings. He wasn't smirking like the rest of them in the room. He was confident the Senator was telling the truth, as far-fetched as it might appear. Wyatt was witnessing a broken man trying to come to grips with a reality that wasn't his.

Tucker received a call about his next assignment. The location of his targets had been established. He studied the images that popped up on his smartphone and the instructions for his next hit. He packed a bag and loaded the trunk of his GTO with a cache of guns and ammo. He got in the car, pushed in his eight-track, and cranked up the volume. The car squealed onto a dirt road, leaving his farmhouse in the rearview mirror.

A local network crew were busy interviewing a group of alien hunters on the outskirts of Area 51, a closely monitored, highly classified Air Force Base in Groom Lake, Nevada.

"I'm Heidi Chambers with CBTK. This is the closest we can get to Area 51 without sensors going off and private security teams turning you back or actually using deadly force if you ignore the warnings. We are interviewing Owen Green, one of the alien hunters here tonight. How long have you been doing this, Mr. Green?"

"Ten years. We've been out here for a while. A lot of boring nights, but on occasion we have seen UFOs."

"So you believe you've seen an actual UFO?"

"No question. That's why it's such a high-security area. They're hiding something over there."

"You really believe that?"

"Absolutely. In fact, we believe they've dug up alien technology and are now using it as their own."

"That's quite a theory you have there, Mr. Green."

"Not a theory. A true fact. We've seen boomerang-shaped objects hovering and then taking sharp turns at incredible speeds."

"You think it's coming from Area 51?"

"No question."

"I wish your group luck, Mr. Green. Maybe if you capture some images, we'll have your group back. This is Heidi Chambers reporting from the outskirts of Area 51 surrounded by alien hunters."

Little did they know Mr. Green's prophecy reflected the truth and a harbinger of events to come.

Rose's eyes fluttered open; she rested in a dark room. It was lonely. She didn't know where she was or for that matter who she was. She had probes attached to her head as if someone was trying to reprogram her inner thoughts. She tried to reset her mind and block out the bad thoughts that raged inside her. She thought of Cole and Josh. They were nice humans who cared about her. The people who now watched her had evil intentions. They were the thorns that Cole had talked about.

A voice rattled around inside her head, "I'm Robby, a friend of Cole's, I'm going to get you out of there."

And then it was quiet. She wiped the tears away and smiled.

ABOUT THE AUTHOR

Best known for the riveting *Slip of the Hand* trilogy and *The Common Cure*, novelist J.P. Farrell lives outside of Boston, Massachusetts, with his family.

BURIED CODE
J. P. FARRELL

Publisher: SDP Publishing
Also available in ebook format

Also by J. P. Farrell
The Common Cure
Slip of the Hand
Slip of the Hand II
Slip of the Hand III

 **SDP Publishing**

www.SDPPublishing.com
Contact us at: info@SDPPublishing.com

www.ingramcontent.com/pod-product-compliance
Lightning Source LLC
Chambersburg PA
CBHW020409260626

47156CB00007B/2306